SEBASTIAN

A MYSTERY ROMANCE

GIULIA LAGOMARSINO

For Cheryl, my first real fan. Your message made me do a happy dance and fired me up. This book is for you.

CHAPTER 1

MAGGIE

"We need to get this taken care of right away. No one can ever know. We've already had a leak from someone in this building. Some reporter has been calling, trying to get information on budget spending."

I listened intently as Mayor Richard Johnson spoke to someone in his office. Was I supposed to be here? Hell no, but now that I knew he was hiding something, I had to find out what it was. It was clear our mayor wasn't nearly as squeaky clean as he led everyone to believe.

"People always want to know about the budget. That's nothing new, Richard. You need to relax."

"Relax? *Relax?* Are you fucking kidding me?" Richard boomed. "If they keep digging, you know what they'll eventually find. We need to make sure our bases are covered. Make sure it's buried."

I cursed myself for not having some kind of camera that I could slip through the supply closet to spy on him and his cohort. My phone wouldn't work, and it would only draw attention. I'd done my digging. He was supposed to be gone by six. It was either really good luck that he showed up in time for me to hear this conversation, or really shitty luck on my part. I'd only gotten to snoop for five minutes before I heard his voice booming down the hallway outside his office. There was nowhere else to go, so I slipped into the closet where I sat scrunched up and really needed to pee.

The worst part was, they talked about everything, but never really gave any useful information. Maybe the room was bugged and that's why they were talking in riddles. I'd have to find a way to sneak back in and look for any devices. At least I knew I was on the right track. He was definitely hiding something. Now I just had to find out what. But how the hell was I supposed to get ahold of the budget? Even I knew that things could be hidden under the guise of another area of the budget. It would take forever to find out anything.

"I'll make sure no one knows. I've been talking with someone I think we can use. He's got a lot of gambling debt I think he'll want taken care of."

"Do it. I want this taken care of by the end of the week."

There were a few more minutes of conversation about meetings that would be occurring over the next few days and then the footsteps clicked across the floor to the door. A soft snick led to silence. I waited a few more minutes in the darkness of the closet before slowly opening the door and peeking out. The only light came from the soft glow of some lights they kept on at night in the cubicle area of the office.

Quickly tiptoeing over to the door, I checked the hallway, seeing it was clear. I crept over to the desk and searched for anything that would hint at what the mayor was trying to cover up. Obviously, he wouldn't keep it laying around on the desk, but I searched anyway. The bottom drawer of his desk was locked and after searching the others, I pulled out my lock pick set and quickly opened the drawer. Dozens of files were stacked neatly, none of them labeled.

About halfway through the drawer I found one file that had a list of properties and their market value. The list was odd because none of these properties were in a particularly good part of town. I couldn't tell exactly what was at these locations, but I knew they weren't where any of the public offices or public services were located. I pulled out my phone and quickly snapped photos of everything in the folder.

A noise from somewhere out in the main office drew my attention. I quickly shoved the files back in the drawer and decided not to outstay my welcome. Irritated that I didn't get through the whole drawer, I quickly shut and locked it up. I pulled out a rag from my back pocket and quickly wiped down everywhere I had touched.

After assuring myself that I'd left no trace behind, I walked to the door and peeked into the hallway. When no one appeared, I softly shut the door and was turning to head down the hall when I heard the dreaded voice.

"Hey, what are you doing in my office? Stop right there!"

I took off at a dead run for the stairs. I had to get down five flights of stairs and across the lobby to reach freedom. Until then, someone could easily snatch me without anyone knowing. There were now two voices behind me yelling after me. They both belonged to the men that had been in the mayor's office earlier.

I was just opening the door when a gun fired and I felt pain slice through my arm. I fell through the stairwell door, landing hard against the cement floor. I quickly got to my feet, ignoring the pain for now. It wouldn't do me any good to dwell on how bad it was. If I stopped, I would be caught and no doubt end up with my feet chained to a cement block at the bottom of the Allegheny River.

Pushing myself harder, I burst through the first floor door and bolted across the lobby. I'd just made it to the front door when more bullets pinged around me. Luckily, none hit their target and I was able to escape into the night. The streets were still fairly busy, so I was able to blend in with the semi-crowded sidewalk. I had parked about a block away, so I quickly made my way back, resisting the urge to look behind me. I didn't want to draw any more attention than necessary.

Unlocking my car was a little tricky since my hands were shaking. Normally my job didn't scare me, but then again, getting shot at wasn't a daily occurrence either. When the lock finally turned, I slid into the seat of my twenty-year-old car and quickly pulled into traffic. My eyes kept flicking to the rearview mirror, but when it didn't appear that anyone was following me, I made my way back to the office. I worked at *The Pittsburgh Press* and my boss Mr. Hughes was usually at the office until well past ten. The paper was his life and he took everything about the entire operation very seriously. In fact, his wife had left him years ago because she knew she would always come in second. He had never remarried, deciding that no woman could ever come close to his baby.

My vision was getting a little blurry and I thanked my lucky stars when I pulled into the parking lot of the paper. More sluggish than before, I made my way into the building, trying to stay as inconspicuous as possible. If the man that shot me looked for people that were brought in with gunshot wounds at the hospital, they would find out real fast who was in the office building. My only option was to attend to my wounds alone.

By the time I reached my boss's office, I was sweating and stumbling everywhere. My legs barely held me up anymore and I faintly heard my boss asking if I was okay before passing out on the ground. I didn't stay out for long, though, as I felt a sharp slap across my face. I came back to reality grudgingly and lifted up as gently as I could on my good arm. Wincing as I stood, Darren Hughes helped me to my feet and over to a chair where I plopped down.

"You want to tell me what the hell happened? Is that blood on your arm?" He pulled my jacket sleeve down none too gently and examined the wound. "Jesus Christ, Maggie. You're not supposed to get yourself shot! You're a damn reporter, not an enforcer for the mafia."

"This story is big, Darren. I'm onto something here."

"First, we need to get you to the hospital and have you looked at."

"No. Absolutely not. Anyone looking for GSWs would find out it was me and I'd be as good as dead."

He rolled his eyes at me. "Only you, Maggie. Why is it that you're my only reporter that's always causing trouble?"

"Because I'm good at my job."

"Yeah, well, one of these days, being good at your job is gonna get you killed."

"Do you want to hear about the story or not?"

Sighing, he pulled me to my feet. "Let's go to my bathroom and I'll get that cleaned up while you tell me about this story that's worth getting shot over."

"You know it wouldn't be that good if they weren't shooting at me."

"Yeah, yeah. Let's go."

He started cleaning the wound with soap and water before finding some peroxide and gauze. Believe it or not, this was not my first injury on the job and not the first time Darren had done this. This was, however, my first gunshot wound. Not that I hadn't been shot at before, this was just the only one that connected.

"So, tell me what you found."

"Well, I broke into the mayor's office after a source told me she found some documents that pointed to public funds being sent into offshore accounts. She said there's been a bunch of strain on the city recently because emergency services keep having their budgets cut. The mayor assigned a special budget oversight committee over a year ago, but so far, nothing has come from it.

He put some gauze over the wound and taped it in place. "Sometimes politics gets in the way. It's unfortunate, but it happens. I haven't heard a smoking gun yet, and I'd love to hear the part where you broke laws by breaking and entering."

I gave him a pointed look. This wasn't the first time I had gone to extreme lengths to get my story. Unethical? Maybe, but the people I helped take down were corrupt.

We walked back out to his desk where I sat in a chair, and he leaned against the front of his desk.

"They were talking about the budget and said if someone dug enough, they would find something. They also mentioned that a reporter was calling and digging around, so I'll have to be a little more inventive about getting my information."

Darren rubbed a hand over his face. "Maggie, you are by far the most challenging employee I have."

"But I always bring you a good story."

"Yeah, you do. Did you get anything else?"

"They talked about paying off someone with gambling debt to take care of their problem. Maybe an accountant? Anyway, after they left, I found some files that were locked away—"

"Of course they were."

"—And one of the files had property listings and values, but none of those properties were anywhere near any public buildings. I snapped photos of everything in the file to look over later. I didn't really get to go through all the files, but this is a start."

Darren sighed heavily before standing up and walking back around his desk to sit in his worn leather chair. He leaned back and tapped his finger against his lips for a minute. I could see the wheels in his head turning. He was trying to decide if he wanted me to pursue this story or not. Whether he liked it or not, this story had the potential to be explosive. He wouldn't be able to pass on it, which he confirmed a minute later.

"Fine. Run with the story and see where it takes you, but watch your goddamned back."

I stood a little too fast and the blood rushed to my head, but I recovered quickly. "I'll probably work from home tomorrow while I do some research on the property listings."

"That's fine. Do you need an assistant on this?"

"Not yet. I don't know exactly what I'm looking for yet. Besides, you know I work better alone."

I smiled at him as I walked out the door and headed for my car. In the six years since I had graduated with my degree in journalism, I had gone after every hard hitting story I could find. At first, I was just the newbie around the office and was given shitty assignments, but I quickly learned that researching other stories in my own time got me noticed a lot faster than just hanging around the office paying my dues.

I headed back to my house in a small subdivision that was probably better suited to grannies, but was exactly what I needed. I did a lot of research after work and didn't want to be kept awake by loud neighbors that partied until all hours of the night. My neighbor to the left was an old woman that had lost her husband twenty years ago. She had stayed single and that was surprising to me. She was really feisty and was constantly giving me advice on my love life, and not the kind you want to hear from an older woman either. I'm talking about really dirty advice. The kind I didn't even talk about with my friends.

My neighbor to the right was an older man, Harry, that had been single his whole life. He had never wanted to be tied down to one woman, sure that the good life was sleeping with as many women as he could. When I first moved here, I doubted that he was still living that lifestyle, but then I met Aggie, my neighbor to the left. I saw the looks that Harry shot her and the way Aggie flirted with him. If you've never seen two people in their seventies flirting, it's definitely something for your bucket list.

When I pulled into the driveway of my two bedroom, nine hundred square foot house, the neighborhood was already silent. It was September now and the leaves were starting to change color. Soon I would be raking leaves and getting ready to shovel snow, which really depressed me. There was nothing I hated more than having to take care of snow first thing in the morning. I liked to grab my coffee and head out to the office right away.

My left arm throbbed as I shifted my bag from my right hand to my left so I could open my front door. I was definitely going to need some painkillers to take the edge off. Still, it wasn't the worst I'd ever been injured. Somehow, I always got lucky and escaped relatively unscathed.

I pushed the door open and was just stepping inside when the front window broke and something fell to the floor in my living room.

Time stood still as I stared at the object laying on my floor. I thought vaguely of running, but didn't have time to fully process that thought before light exploded around the room accompanied by a loud bang that disoriented me.

I dropped to the floor, covering my head and praying that when they found my body, I wouldn't be in little bloody pieces. My grandparents didn't deserve to bury me like that. The longer I laid there, the more I realized that I wasn't actually going to die. I uncovered my head and looked around the room, my head still spinning from the loud sound that had occurred so close to my ears. I was still partially blinded from the bright light that filled the room moments before.

"Maggie! You alright, girlie?"

Harry came ambling up the steps of my porch and barged into my house wielding a shotgun.

"Harry! Please, put some pants on! I don't need to see that."

Harry was standing in front of me in a pair of tighty whities and nothing else. I shielded my eyes from the view as he walked further into my house and checked it for anyone that might be lurking. Thank God I couldn't see very well.

"Maggie, dear. Is everything okay? I heard a loud bang and thought I saw Harry run over...oh dear Lord. Would you look at that." Her hand was laying against her chest and her mouth was hanging open. She started adjusting her old robe and fixing the tight curls on her head. It was then I realized Harry had walked back into the room and Aggie was preening for him.

Harry stepped forward, still holding his shotgun at the ready, not at all ashamed of his rather exposed body. In fact, as Aggie checked him out, he stood up straighter and puffed out his chest. By the way these two were acting you would never guess there had just been an explosion at my house.

Sirens sounded in the distance and soon cops were pulling up to my driveway and running toward the door.

"What the fuck?" One officer asked as he walked into the house and saw me on the floor with an almost completely naked

Harry and Aggie in her ratty bathrobe. "Sir, you need to put down your weapon now." Harry did as the officer asked and another officer entered, going to retrieve the weapon that was now on the floor. "We got a call for shots fired. Who lives at this residence?"

"That would be me," I said as I stood. The officer came toward me, his gaze assessing. "I'm Officer Redding." He turned to Harry, eyeing the man that didn't seem at all ashamed at his almost naked state of undress. "Was this man threatening you in any way?"

"You mean other than threatening to blind me further?" I asked sarcastically. Harry obviously wasn't a threat to anyone at this moment. He could look pretty mean when he was fully clothed, but right now all I wanted to do was run from the underwear that were slipping from his wrinkly body.

"Can you tell me what happened here?"

"I got home and walked inside when the window broke and something landed in the room. Then this bright flash and explosion happened. I thought it was a grenade or something, but nothing happened."

Officer Redding walked over to the burnt mark on my carpet and examined the spot. "Flash bang." He stood and looked at me questioningly. "Do you have any idea who would do this? Make any enemies lately?"

"I'm a journalist for *The Pittsburgh Press*. There's rarely a day when I don't piss someone off."

There was no way I was going to tell the officer what had happened tonight. I was definitely onto something if someone tried to kill me twice in one day.

"So, why didn't it go off? I mean, I was expecting the house to explode or something."

"Flash bangs are used to disorient. Most likely, it was to scare you, make you think that you were about to die. So, I'm gonna need a list of names from you, anyone you feel would come after you."

"Most of the people that would come after me are already in jail.

The list is long, and I'm guessing they have bigger problems than coming after a reporter."

"Revenge is an awfully good motivator."

I pursed my lips. There was no way he was going to get me to talk. Time to put my theater skills to work. I stumbled slightly and sank down into the chair I had been standing next to.

"Are you alright, miss?"

"Yes, I think...I think it's just a little too much right now. I think I just need to rest for a little bit."

The officer eyed me skeptically, but relented. "Alright, well I'm going to need your name and contact information. I'll talk to the officer outside and we'll get a crime scene unit in here right away to find out what we can. In the meantime, you need someplace safe to stay for the night. Are you alright to go on your own, or would you like an escort?"

"I'll be fine on my own. I think I just need to sleep."

"Right." He didn't sound too convinced, but he let it go. "We'll just get your information and you can be on your way. I'll expect you down at the station tomorrow to give a statement."

"Of course."

He walked closer to me and leaned down, his mouth next to my ear. "Next time, try acting a little more shaken up *earlier*. No officer would buy the bull you just pulled."

He pulled back and gave me a smile. I gave the officer my information, then grabbed my bag from the floor. While the officers were outside talking, I quickly grabbed my pertinent files and laptop, shoving them into my purse and heading back out to my car.

With a quick wave, I headed to the office, figuring that might be the safest place to stay tonight. Darren was still at the office, big surprise, so I headed over to fill him in on the latest.

His eyes went big when I walked through his door for the second time in just a few hours. "Maggie, what are you doing back here? Don't tell me that you broke into someone else's office tonight."

"No, but someone knows that I'm investigating the mayor."

"Oh, shit. Alright, lay it on me."

"I got home and someone threw a flash bang through my front window. The crime scene unit is working there now, so I can't stay there. I thought I'd just hang out here tonight. I can sleep on the couch out there."

"You can stay on my couch in here. It's more comfortable." I nodded. "Other than that, you're okay?"

"Yeah, it just threw me off balance for a little bit. I think I'm just going to look over some documents for a while. Don't mind me."

I walked over to his couch and pulled out the information I had been going over earlier in the day. As much as I wanted to start researching the new documents I found at the mayor's office, I needed to finish what I had already started.

Before I knew it, hours had passed, and at some point Darren had gone home. Looking at my watch, I saw it was well past midnight, so I turned out the light and spread out on the couch. It was comfortable, but I rarely slept well anyplace other than my own bed. I used my sweatshirt as a blanket and finally dozed off closer to sunrise than I would have liked.

CHAPTER 2

SEBASTIAN

I was running late getting into the office this morning. I hated not being the first in at Reed Security, but it couldn't be helped this morning. I had to stop at Sarah's house. She was nervous about some things going on with WitSec and needed someone to talk to. After testifying against Giuseppe Cordano, she was placed in WitSec, but that didn't stop the Cordano crime family from taking out a hit on her. It would be overwhelming for anyone, but she also had twins she needed to protect, and only a handful of people that knew her situation. If WitSec ever found out we knew who she really was, she would be forced to either move or give up WitSec.

I took the elevator up to my office, thinking of all the things I had to do today. Sometimes I wished I could go back to not being the leader. Things were easier. There would be no hard decisions to make, no employees to look after. But when I was in the military, I was too close when an explosion went off and I lost some of the vision in my left eye. I could still work just fine, but out in the field, I couldn't risk others' lives with only part of my vision.

I hated giving up my career in the military, but had decided that if I was going to be put on desk duty, I was going to be the one making all the calls. I had two silent partners that worked for me, Derek "Irish" Cortell and Sam "Cazzo" Galmacci. Neither of them wanted anyone else to know they were shareholders in the company. Things became more difficult once others knew you had a say in the company. They just wanted to go out on jobs and take it easy. Well, as easy as you can take it when you're risking your life.

I walked into my office and sat down, barely getting my computer turned on when Derek walked in and took a seat. He was the team leader for Team 1 and had been with me the longest. I had been wanting to bring him in to take on more responsibilities for a while now, but he had yet to show interest.

"Hey, Cap. We got a call from *The Pittsburgh Press*. They want you at their office ASAP. Something about a protection detail for a reporter."

"Shit. I haven't even started the day yet."

"I would go in your place, but the editor, Darren Hughes, specifically requested you."

"Can you handle things around here? That's probably going to be an all day trip."

"I can handle one day. Give me a rundown of what needs to be done and I'll take care of it."

"You could handle more than one day."

"I could, but you don't need me to."

"Have you seen this mountain of paperwork? I'll never get through all this."

"Have you seen the hot chick I'm dating? I'll never get inside that if I stay here to work on paperwork."

I rolled my eyes and started filling him in on everything going on at the moment, along with calls that needed to be returned. We finished up and I was preparing to leave, but as he stood to walk out, I decided to try one last time. This shit needed to stop. I couldn't keep running this business solo—not at the rate we were expanding.

"You know, if you would consider taking on a little more at the company, it wouldn't be so difficult when I need to go for meetings," I told him in frustration.

"You know I don't like dealing with people. Security I can deal with. Fielding calls every day, all day and dealing with administrative bullshit is not my thing."

"Then consider taking over the logistical side of the company. I know that planning ops was in your wheelhouse in the military, so it's definitely something you could do here. There's also organizing the training sessions and recruiting. At the rate we're going, I'm going to need to hire at least two people to help me with all of that. I would rather it be someone I already trust than someone I just hired."

"Cap, you know why I don't want that responsibility."

Irish suffered guilt from his days in the military. He was in the army, serving as an Infantry Team Leader. His team went on a mission and he was the only one to come out alive. The intel had been bad, and despite having a bad feeling about the situation from the start, he followed orders and proceeded.

His team was ambushed and two of his teammates were killed instantly. He and two others survived three days evading insurgents, but his two teammates were killed on the fourth day on their way to the extraction point. Derek had walked away with a bullet to the shoulder. His teammates were recovered later, and though the higher ups admitted they'd gotten poor intel, it weighed heavily on Derek that he hadn't trusted his instincts.

"I would never put you in that situation if I didn't trust you," I said, trying to make him understand that I had full faith in his abilities.

"Yeah? Look what happened to Hunter and Lola."

"That wasn't your fault and you know it. If anything, that responsibility lies with me, but you and I both know there was no way we could have predicted that one of our own would turn on us."

"And he's still here," Irish bit out.

I hadn't yet decided what to do with Cal. His wife and kids had been taken hostage by the serial killer that was after Alex, my friend Cole's wife. He hadn't come to us and had worked behind our backs to get his wife and kids home safely. They died anyway and Cal lost everything, but I didn't have it in me to get rid of him yet. He was on administrative leave for six months and was now working strictly on desk duty. He had no access to records or important documents. He was basically a glorified secretary until I could figure out what to do with him.

Sighing, I rubbed a hand over my face. "I wish I could cut him loose so easily, but I feel partially to blame for what happened. What would you have done if that psycho had your family?"

"I would have come to you."

"Easier said than done. Look, I don't know what his role will be in the company in the future, but right now he's hurting and he's lost everything. He was a good man and still is. He just made a really bad judgement call."

"One that severely hurt members of our team."

"And if you chose to take on a larger role with the company, you would have some say in what happens with him. Until then, he remains part of this company in whatever capacity I choose for him. I won't cut him loose when he needs us most."

Derek scowled at me but said no more. I stood and grabbed my bag that had all my office materials for this meeting.

"I have to head out to Pittsburgh. I'll have my phone on me if anything comes up." I headed for the door, but turned back to him one last time. "Think about what I said. You have a lot more to offer the company than you realize."

Walking past the lobby where Cal sat, I nodded to him before stepping on the elevator. The man was miserable and didn't feel he had a place here, but I had bullied him into staying. I told him he didn't have a choice, that he owed it to his teammates to stick around and help where he could. Granted, he wasn't offering much at the moment and the man was in such a state of depression that I wasn't sure he was even working most days, but I just couldn't turn my back on a brother. He hadn't willfully turned against us, and that was the heart of the issue.

The hour drive to Pittsburg grated on me as I thought of all the work I still had piled up waiting for me at the office. A call from *The Pittsburgh Press* probably meant a reporter had stuck his nose somewhere it didn't belong, and now I was going to have to send someone to babysit. Derek could have easily handled this assignment, but since they requested a meeting with me, I had no choice but to go.

I spent twenty minutes sitting in the waiting area because the editor was in a meeting. It pissed me off that I was forced to sit and wait after I had been summoned here so quickly. I must not have hid my irritation well because the secretary kept peering over her computer at me in what looked like fear. I was a tall guy at 6' 4" and had quite a bit of muscle. It was a requirement at Reed Security that everyone work out regularly. If my staff wasn't in shape, they couldn't properly do their jobs. Even though I didn't go into the field much, I had to lead by example and be sure if the occasion ever arose, I was capable of keeping up with my team.

Finally, the editor's door opened and a tired looking man walked out. He was skinny and about average height, but what really showed his age was his graying hair and lines that framed his eyes. Probably from late nights and reporters that drove him nuts.

"Mr. Reed. I'm sorry about keeping you. Please step into my office."

He walked back in and around his desk. I followed and sat in one of the chairs across from him, wincing at the uncomfortable seat. Springs dug into my ass, making me want to stand instead, but he spoke before I had the chance to move.

"That will be all, Stacy. Hold my calls."

Peering over my shoulder, I saw the secretary pull the door shut with a nod.

"Mr. Reed, I have a somewhat unfortunate situation going on that requires security for one of my reporters. A story is forming that seems to be pointing to some rather serious allegations about the mayor of Pittsburgh. Two attempts have been made already to put a stop to our digging, but the story cannot be stopped now that certain information has come to light."

"I can have one of my men here in a few hours—"

He waved his hand, cutting me off. "No. That won't work for us. We would like you to be the security detail. I've read up on you and I'm very impressed with your resume."

"Mr. Hughes, all of my team members are impressive. I run the administrative side of Reed Security. I very rarely go into the field anymore."

"Still, I wouldn't want anyone else protecting—"

"Darren, you have got to see what I found. I was looking over..."

I looked at the woman who came barreling into the office, not even bothering to knock first. She was beautiful in that wild sort of way, with strawberry blonde hair and green eyes that shined bright. But she was a mess. Her outfit was wrinkled and her hair looked like it had just been thrown up to keep it out of her face. There were pieces sticking out everywhere. In fact, she looked like she'd just rolled out of bed.

"Oh, sorry, I didn't know you were with anyone."

The woman didn't immediately retreat, though, which had me curious. She was holding a stack full of papers, all crumpled just like she was. She had dark smudges of some kind on her face as well as her clothes, and she was favoring one arm.

"Good, Maggie. I'm glad you're here. This is perfect timing."

"Perfect timing for what?" she asked warily.

"This is Sebastian Reed from Reed Security. He's going to be on protection detail for you until you finish the story."

"Wait a minute, Darren—"

"I never agreed—"

We both started talking at the same time, both of us obviously on the same page.

"Mr. Reed, I'm sure you're very good at your job, but I don't need a mall cop to watch over me."

I narrowed my eyes at the judgmental little minx. "I'm a far cry from a mall cop and if you don't feel you need protection, I'll gladly head back to my firm. I have other clients to attend to. Good day, Mr. Hughes."

"Now hold on just a minute, Mr. Reed." He turned to the woman with a stern look. "Maggie, if you don't take this threat seriously, I will pull you from this story so fast and hand it over to Daniel."

"Daniel? You can't be serious! Darren, he couldn't shit in the toilet without proper instruction. If you hand this over, the story will go nowhere."

"Then I suggest you let this 'mall cop' protect you. I can't afford to have you end up dead because you're too busy chasing a story to watch your back."

"I've stayed alive this long, haven't I?"

"How about we tell Mr. Reed what has happened so far and let him be the judge of whether or not you need protection? If he says no, I will gladly send him on his way."

"Fine." She sat down in the chair next to me and crossed her arms in a childish pout.

"Okay, lay it on me. What's happened so far?"

"Maggie went searching for some information last night in a rather...unorthodox way. When she was seen, gunshots were fired and she was grazed."

"Did they recognize you?"

"No."

"That's what she says, but then she went home and someone threw a flash bang through her front window."

"It's a scare tactic," I said. "Obviously, someone wants to keep you from investigating."

"And yet here I stand today, still able to do my job." Her voice was condescending, leaving me dreading having anything to do with this job. I didn't want anything to do with her, but if I turned down the job and she didn't get protection elsewhere, she'd end up dead.

Whatever she was investigating, it was clear they would escalate the threats if she didn't stop digging.

"So, Mr. Reed, what do you think of our little predicament here?"

"Well, as much as I can see, this little ray of sunshine is able to take care of herself, but if she's working on a story, she's not going to be watching out for herself. That's a one way ticket to the graveyard."

"I've dealt with dozens of stories that could have gotten me killed and nothing's ever happened to me."

"Sure, if that's what you call a broken arm, bruises, cuts, almost being run over by a train..."

"Alright, fine. There may have been one or two incidents."

He raised an eyebrow at her, as if to prove that she was being ridiculous.

"How long do you expect this story to take?" I asked.

"Well, considering I just got the information a day ago, it could take a few weeks. It all depends on how fast I can connect the dots."

"Mr. Hughes, I can send someone here to take care of her, but—"

"Take care of me? I hardly need a babysitter."

I shook my head, frustrated the old man couldn't see that I wasn't equipped to deal with her situation. I would have to call someone in. "I run a security firm and I'm needed there to run the day to day operations."

"Mr. Reed, may I call you Sebastian?" I nodded. "I run a very popular newspaper here in Pittsburgh. As I understand it, you're from a small town, correct?"

"Our base of operations is out of a small town. That doesn't mean that we only operate there."

"Of course, of course," he said, waving a hand in front of his face dismissively. "I'm simply saying the paper is in the position to send a lot of business your way. All I ask is that you personally see to the safety of my employee."

He leaned back in his seat and steepled his fingers. Damn, I didn't want to take this job, but advertising was expensive, and I could get a lot of it for free if I took this job. I didn't know how the hell I was going to convince anyone else in the company to take over. My conversation with Derek this morning didn't show a lot of promise, and Sam was no better than him. However, if I took this job and forced them to take over, it might help push them into taking a bigger role in the company.

"Look, I can check and see if I can shuffle some things around, but I make no promises. There are commitments I need to keep and if this case takes too long, I'll be forced to have someone else take over."

"I completely understand. Why don't you make the necessary calls and we'll talk again in a few hours after you've sorted everything. There's a conference room down the hall to the right that's available. Once we have all the details sorted, all I ask is that you call and update me daily so that I'm assured my employee is still safe."

I stood and made my way to his office door, barely there when this Maggie lady started in on him. I slowed my steps in hopes of gaining some more insight into the situation.

"Darren, I don't need a babysitter. He's only going to get in my way. I need to be stealthy and he sticks out like a sore thumb. No source will ever come close to me if he's always on my tail."

"You will accept his protection or I will take you off this case. You are too valuable to go up against the mayor unprotected."

The conversation continued as I walked down the hall. I couldn't walk any slower without it being noticed, so I went to the conference room and dialed Sam, leader of Team 2.

"Yo, Cap. What's up?"

"It looks like I'm gonna need to take this case in Pittsburgh myself. Can you take over admin duty for a while?"

"How long is a while?" he asked warily.

I grinned to myself as I heard the dread in his voice. "Shit. I don't know. Maybe two to three weeks. I'm hoping this case will be over faster, but from what I understand, the reporter is just getting started and is already in trouble. Apparently, this has something to do with the mayor. It could be messy."

"Are you thinking of getting a team together?"

"Not yet. I need some more information before I take it any further."

"I can go there and do it myself if you need to get back here," he offered. I could practically hear him grabbing his stuff, ready to drive here and take over, just to get out of paperwork.

"I would gladly take you up on that, but he's insisting it be me. What I need is for you to step up and take over. Irish is taking over for today, so talk with him and get it all straightened out. My cell will be on if you need me."

Sam blew out a harsh breath before speaking. "Cap, you know I hate this shit."

"I know, but for now, this is what we need to do. Work it out with Irish. You're both shareholders, so start taking a little more responsibility in the company. If you don't want it on a permanent basis, that's fine, but for now, this is your job."

"Yeah, yeah," he grumbled. "I gotcha Cap. We'll take care of it. What are you gonna need while you're there?"

"I don't know yet. I need to have a talk with the reporter and find out just how bad the situation is. So far, she hasn't been very forthcoming. I think I have what I need for now in the back of the SUV. I'll call if I need more."

"Sounds good."

I hung up the phone, not bothering with goodbyes. Polite? Yes. A waste of time? Most definitely. Why waste time with unnecessary words?

I walked over to Mr. Hughes' office and saw the reporter was no longer there. Darren saw me and pointed across the cubicles outside his office. It wasn't hard to spot her strawberry blonde hair in the sea of blondes and brunettes. No wonder she was spotted so easily last night. She was a walking target.

"We need to have a talk now."

She turned to me with a glare. "I don't have time. I'm in the middle of something and the sooner I get to the bottom of this, the sooner I can get you out of my hair."

"That sounds good to me, but in the meantime, you won't get to the bottom of anything if you're dead, so let's go to the conference room and you can fill me in on what's going on."

She narrowed her eyes at me. "Instead, how about you drive and I talk. I have a property I want to check out and you can take me there."

It wasn't the smartest idea to leave the office with her before I had all the facts, but she was right about one thing. The sooner we got the investigation done, the sooner I would be rid of her.

CHAPTER 3

SEBASTIAN

I was driving Maggie to a property in Wilkinsburg that she wanted to check out. I wanted to sit down in the conference room with her and get a better idea about what was going on with her story, but she insisted that she would fill me in on the way. It was stupid as hell. I had no idea what I was walking into with this woman, and I had a feeling she was a live wire, ready to go off at any moment.

"I investigated the list of properties, and from what I can see, none of these properties are government related. They weren't ever food shelves or homeless shelters. There is nothing that would indicate these properties would be of government interest."

We drove through Wilkinsburg and it was devastating. Most of the homes had boarded up windows and the streets were littered. This part of town was obviously in need of some intervention, but it didn't seem that anyone cared about cleaning it up.

"Most of the locations on my list are in terrible parts of Pittsburgh. They all look similar to this. So you tell me, why would the mayor be interested in these properties?"

"Maybe he's starting a program to clean up the city."

"And that would warrant me being shot at?"

She had a point. Even breaking into a government office, she wouldn't have been shot at. She would have been arrested and taken in for breaking and entering.

"So, what exactly do you think is going on here?"

"I'm not sure. All I know is that my source told me that she saw documents showing funds going into offshore accounts."

"Okay, are you sure they were government funds?"

"Pretty sure. Here's the gist of it. There are communities all across Pittsburgh, much like Wilkinsburg, where we're headed, that are sorely lacking funding. Emergency services have been cut all across Pittsburgh, but these communities are really suffering because they weren't getting enough help to begin with. Now all the sudden, the mayor has documents on these communities, but nothing has ever been said about rehabbing these communities. In fact, he hired a special oversight committee to look into where funding was going."

"That sounds like a good thing to me."

"Well, normally it would be, but they've had the committee set up for over a year and so far, nothing has come of it."

"Still, I don't understand why you think there's a story here."

"Intuition. Something just screams dirty to me— And the fact that I was shot at last night and someone came to my home to scare me."

"Well, there is that, but you don't exactly come off as the most amiable person."

Her head whipped to look at me. "Excuse me, but I am plenty amiable. I can do amiable as good as Bingley."

My brows knitted in confusion as I glanced over at her. "What?"

"Bingley. You know, Jane Austen?"

"Who the fuck is Jane Austen?"

"What?" She screeched so loud that I swerved and almost hit a car.

"Next time you fucking do that, I'm throwing you out of the SUV and you can walk."

"How can you not know who Jane Austen is? Were you raised in a barn?"

I nodded my head side to side as if considering. "Pretty much."

"Men." She grumbled on about something, but I couldn't tell what because she was muttering under her breath. I found it highly irritating. If you want to fucking say something, then say it.

We pulled up outside the first address moments later and stared at the dilapidated building in front of us. There were boards over some of the windows, but those without boards had no glass left in them at all. This was probably a prime location for squatters.

"According to records, this building has been sitting empty for fifteen years. The whole building would probably have to be torn down and reconstructed to put anything here."

She opened the door and hopped out, walking over to the chain link fence. I got out and slammed the door. "Hey, next time you get out, you let me know the plan first. I can't protect you if you go off and do your own thing without informing me."

She ignored me and started climbing the fence. "What the fuck are you doing?"

"Has anyone ever told you that you have a potty mouth?"

"Get the fuck down. Now."

Still, she ignored me and was over the fence before I could drag her back. Sighing, I climbed the fence and hopped over, clicking the remote lock for the car. Not that it would make much difference in this neighborhood. If someone wanted to steal it, they would get away before police got here.

I caught up to her quickly and walked slightly in front and to the left of her, hoping to protect her from any threats. However, I was only one man and she was still unprotected on her other side and from behind. My eyes scanned the area for potential threats, not detecting any, though. We made it to the side of the building where a door was slightly ajar. Maggie reached for the handle, but I batted her hand away and took up my position in front of her.

"Stay here while I check it out," I said as I pulled my gun from my lower back. I briefly thought of giving her my gun in my ankle holster, but not knowing if she could shoot, I thought better of it.

She rolled her eyes at me, but did as I asked. Weapon in hand, I entered the building and scanned the darkness for any movement. This was a nightmare to clear since the interior of the building had little light and multiple places for squatters to hide, or anyone looking to take you out where no one would likely find you for weeks.

The slamming of the door had me swinging my gun around to where I entered. The nearby broken window allowed in a little bit of light, allowing me to see Maggie standing in the doorway.

Turning around, I cleared the rest of the first floor as best I could, unable to see where the stairs were that led to the upper floors. Most likely, they were in the corner with the unlabeled door, but this building was so old and neglected, there was no clear picture of where the stairwell was. Usually, you could tell by the outside of the building.

A flashlight clicked by the door I entered and I shook my head in annoyance. I made my way back to Maggie, who was still standing by the door.

"I told you to stay outside."

"Well, I thought I would come help."

"And how's that? I was going for the whole not getting shot thing and you drew attention to yourself when you let the door slam. I was on the other side of the building and wouldn't have been able to protect you."

"Oh, would you relax? This building is old and decrepit. Nobody's here but us."

"How do you know there aren't squatters here?"

"It's not like I have a food truck outside they can rob."

I lowered my voice and got right up in her face, bending down to whisper in her ear. "You think that's all they would be after? A gorgeous woman like yourself...You don't think they might want to search you for...other things?" I ran my hand softly down her side, just enough to make her shiver. "There are plenty of things a woman like you could offer to a lonely man."

Her breathing hitched, telling me I made my point as she stepped back from me. The glow from her flashlight barely illuminated the slight fear on her face. She swallowed thickly as her eyes flicked around the dark space.

"So, what are you hoping to find here?" I said as I took a step back, my voice returning to normal.

"I...um... I don't know. I was hoping that something would stand out to me. You know, give me some clue as to why the mayor would be looking into this property."

"Well, let's take a look around quickly and get back to the SUV before someone decides to steal it."

We walked around for a few minutes, her flashlight flicking over the space. Nothing seemed to stand out until we were closer to the far wall. She knelt down and ran her fingers over the floor.

"What is it?"

"Why would there be no cement here?"

I got down on my haunches and ran my hands over the floor, feeling thick dirt under the pads of my fingers. I started digging, searching for the edge.

"What are you looking for?"

"I'm wondering how big the patch is. Maybe it's just where the concrete cracked and was filled in with dirt."

My fingers found the edge of the concrete and I ran my hand along the jagged edge for about seven feet. The edge took a ninety degree turn and continued for another three feet before taking another ninety degree turn.

"Well, it's roughly seven feet long by three feet wide and it wasn't done by a professional. The edges are jagged."

"What would be the reason for having a hole in the floor that size?"

"What was the building used for?"

"It was a manufacturing plant. Plastics, I think, but they went out of business."

I started digging the dirt out, wondering if I dug long enough, what I would find. I had a sneaking suspicion, but wasn't sure I wanted to know.

"What are you digging for?"

"What do you think would fit in a hole this size?"

I stopped digging and looked at her. She looked confused for a second before she put the end of the flashlight in her mouth and started digging. We were probably about three feet down when I heard it. I put my hand on hers to still her movement and strained to listen.

We were in the center of the building and the voices were right outside, but moving toward the side of the building. I grabbed the flashlight from her mouth and quickly turned it off.

"Someone's here. There's a truck right outside the gate. You two take the far door and we'll take this door."

My head whipped in her direction as her breathing increased and she started panting. I placed my hand on her shoulder and squeezed slightly.

"Calm down. We have to get out of here."

She started scooping the dirt back in the hole, but I pulled her to her feet and started dragging her to the window. I could see two men with guns drawn moving toward the door we had entered on the other end of the building. There was a bang against the door off to our right, but it didn't budge. Our quickest escape was through the windows, which thankfully didn't have any panes.

"I'm gonna hoist you up through the window. When you're through, you run like hell to the truck and don't look back. Here are the keys. If I'm not right behind you, you leave. The SUV is bullet-resistant, so you should have a good chance of getting away."

"Are you serious? There is no way I'm leaving you," she whisper-hissed.

"If you don't, we're both as good as dead."

"How do you know they're here to kill us?"

"The guns they were carrying would suggest that." I locked my fingers together and made a holder for her to boost herself up with. "Get your ass moving before they walk through that door and shoot us."

She glared at me and hoisted herself up, glancing out the window in both directions before swinging herself over the window ledge and dropping down to the ground. I'd just gotten up on the window ledge when the door to the left swung open and two men appeared in the doorway.

"Hey! Stop!"

Maggie was running across the gravel to the fence, and luckily no one was giving chase yet. I leapt to the ground just as a bullet ricocheted off the wall where my head was. Landing in a squat, I jumped up and took off running for the fence. Bullets started raining down on me, so I spun and dropped to one knee, placing a well aimed bullet in the first shooter who obviously didn't have any real training with guns. Quickly shifting my focus to the second shooter, I popped off a shot and got back up, running for the SUV.

Maggie had already started the SUV and was quickly driving away. I was still a good fifty feet from the fence when more bullets were fired in my direction. I had no choice, but to return fire, as these gunmen obviously had better aim. I took a few shots, but they hid around the corner of the building. I ran backward, trying to get closer to the fence, but keeping my gaze on the corner of the building.

A large, metal crash sounded behind me and my gaze swiveled to the fence where Maggie had just crashed through the gate. The SUV swerved wildly in front of me, acting as a barrier for the incoming bullets.

"Get in!" Maggie yelled from the driver's side. I pulled the back door open and climbed in, slamming the door moments after Maggie spun the tires, kicking up gravel and dust in our wake. The bullets pinged off the SUV as she drove through the gate and headed to the highway.

"What the fuck were you thinking?" I yelled at her. "I told you to leave."

"And you'd be dead right now if I hadn't come back for you."

"You could be dead too." I snarled at her. "You need to learn to listen if I'm going to protect you."

"Relax. You said the SUV was bulletproof."

"Bullet-resistant, not bulletproof."

"What's the difference?"

"The difference is that a bullet could still get through the window. Bulletproof is a highly misconstrued term."

"Then why did you say it?"

"I didn't say it!" I shouted. "I said bullet-resistant and that's why you were supposed to leave. Goddamn it!" I punched the seat to release some of my anger before pulling out my phone and dialing the office.

"Yo, Cap."

"Cazzo, I need you to run plates for me. 2015 Dodge Challenger, dark blue. Plate number XZ15371. Get me everything you can ASAP."

A large jolt pushed me forward into the back of the driver's seat as Maggie struggled to regain control of the SUV. She yanked the wheel and stepped on the gas, sending me back into the seat.

"Fuck! Maggie, head out of the city."

"Are you crazy? We can't lose them outside the city!" she shouted at me as she swerved around cars.

"Do you know how many casualties we'll have if we stay on this road? We're about to hit the highway and we're closing in on rush hour. Get off this fucking road and head out of the city."

"Cap! Cap! What the fuck is going on?"

I heard Cazzo yelling at me from where the phone dropped on the floor. I quickly grabbed it and started yelling into the phone at Cazzo. "Get me the information on that car, now! They're fucking shooting at us and chasing us through Pittsburgh."

Another jolt sent me flying, but I was better prepared this time and caught myself before hitting the seat. Staying on the phone was a distraction, so I quickly hung up and climbed into the front seat.

"Move the seat back and then get as close to the wheel as possible. I'm driving."

"Are you crazy? We'll crash and then we'll definitely be dead."

"Trust me and do this."

She moved the seat back as far as it would go and I climbed in behind her. It wasn't as easy as it sounded, but I managed to do it without making her crash. Patting her left hip, I gripped the wheel and started to push her over to the other seat. She stood up and climbed over to the passenger seat, giving me a spectacular view of her tight ass. Now was not the time to be ogling her, but when in Rome.

I quickly adjusted the seat and pressed down the gas, swerving around anyone that was going too slow.

"It would be really fucking nice if the cops would show up right now."

"Budget cuts. There aren't enough police officers to patrol as much as they should."

We were both looking in the mirrors, watching the Challenger gain on us again. I continued heading south out of the city, along the river.

"How are we going to lose them?"

"I'm working on it. The most important thing right now is getting away from civilians."

"I'm a civilian!"

"Sweetheart, you're the reason we're in this mess, so suck it up and hang on."

The Challenger pulled up alongside me and smashed the back left side of the SUV. Up ahead there was a bridge over the river that didn't have any traffic on it. Pulling onto the older bridge, the Challenger once again rammed into us, sending us into the guardrail.

"Enough of this shit."

I lowered the driver's side window and slammed on the brakes, letting the Challenger pull ahead of us. Once it was in front of me and out of range, I pulled my gun and shot at the tires, unloading the rest of my magazine until the tires blew and the Challenger swerved across the bridge, hitting first the left side and then over in front of me. I stomped on the gas, hitting the front end of the Challenger and speeding past it.

The Challenger eventually lost speed and was stopped on the bridge as we sped off and out of sight.

"Holy shit."

I grinned at her apparent admiration of my skills.

"What the fuck took you so long? You fired like seven shots. I thought you were some badass security guy."

Okay. That was not what I thought she was going to say.

"I was shooting with my left hand at a moving vehicle while in a moving vehicle and driving said vehicle. Should I let you shoot next time?"

She huffed and crossed her arms over her chest. "Where are we going now?"

"We're heading back to my office."

"What? No. I have a story to follow."

"I need to get a new vehicle. This one looks like it was in a war zone, which it kind of was. If we drive back through the city looking like this, we'll be dead in six hours."

"And then we're heading back to the city."

"Then we'll use my resources to see if we can find out more about this case before we head back. Do you have the stuff you need?"

She lifted a messenger bag from the floorboards. "I have everything in here. As long as your bad driving didn't destroy my laptop."

I rolled my eyes and prayed for a different case. This woman was going to drive me insane. A half hour later my phone rang.

"Cazzo, what d'ya have?"

"The car belongs to a Juan Cruz. He's part of the Diablos gang. As far as I can tell, they run heavy with Mexican drug cartels. They've become a real problem in the city, but so far there haven't been any attempts to flush them out. Very rarely do any of them get picked up for anything. The cops don't even get called out to the area of the city where they're usually seen. There have been a lot of murders in their territory, but they never seem to be investigated."

"Alright. We're on our way to you. We're about thirty minutes out."

"The reporter's with you?"

"Yeah."

"Do you want a report on her also? I should be able to have one by the time you get here."

"That would probably be a wise decision."

"See you in thirty."

I hung up and glanced at Maggie to see her looking at me with a raised eyebrow.

"What?"

"Are you going to tell me what that was about?"

"It was business."

"Business that involves me."

"Look, can we wait until we get back to my office and we can lay this all out and go over everything at once?"

She narrowed her eyes at me and crossed her arms over her chest, pushing her breasts up in the process. Much as I tried to pay attention to the road and only the road, her perfect breasts forced me to take a second look. Discreetly, of course. I was still a professional.

Sighing, I filled her in briefly on what Cazzo had relayed to me.

"Who's Cazzo? Is that his last name?"

"No. His name is Sam Galmacci. The guys call him Cazzo."

"Is that like a call sign?"

I rolled my eyes at her. "That's the Air Force."

"Whatever. So how did he get the name Cazzo? What's it mean?"

I laughed at the memory of Pappy giving him the name. "One of the guys on the other team gave him the name in Italian. It means 'dick'."

"And why is that funny?"

"Because even though Cazzo is Italian, he doesn't speak a word of the language. He was pissed that they wouldn't tell him what it meant and he refused to look it up. The name stuck and he's still called Cazzo to this day."

"Why didn't someone else tell him? Wouldn't that have been the nice thing to do?"

I snorted. "Maggie, you obviously haven't been around men that much if you think we're going to share something to be nice. If the asshole wants to know what it means, he can look it up in two seconds."

"Men. I will never understand the way your brains work."

"That's probably a good thing, sweetheart."

"Don't call me sweetheart. I'm not your sweetheart or any other endearment."

"Maybe I should call you Gingersnap."

"I said not to call me anything. You can call me Maggie."

I continued on as if she wasn't speaking. "Of course, you don't really have a ginger color. Maybe 'Red' would be better."

"No."

"No, you're right. You're not really a redhead either."

"How about you stick with Maggie?"

"I could call you Freckles..."

"I don't have freckles."

"Yes, you do. Now that your makeup has worn off a little, I can see those cute freckles poking through."

"What?" She threw down the visor and looked at herself in the mirror. "Oh my God! Why didn't you tell me I looked like this?" She started running her fingers through her hair and wiping the dirt from her face, which only cleaned her makeup off more, revealing that beautiful, creamy skin.

"Actually, you look about the same as you did this morning. Didn't you take a shower last night?"

"I was busy trying not to be blown up."

"Maybe I should call you Strawberry. You are a strawberry blonde, after all."

"Can't you just let this go?"

"The guys will be naming you if I don't. Better to let me name you, otherwise you'll end up with something like 'Fire Crotch'. I glanced over at her and then down toward her pussy. "How do I know for sure that you're really a redhead? Maybe you want to give me a sneak peek? See if the carpet matches the drapes?"

"Ugh." She said infuriated. "You are so irritating. My name is Maggie. Not Red. Not Ginger. Not Strawberry or Fire Crotch. Maggie. Get it right or I'll be giving you my own nickname."

"It'll never stick. I already have one. Besides, the guys would never side with a woman over a brother."

"Then I'll tell them I had to save your ass today!"

I shrugged. "When I tell them what a pain in the ass you are, they'll take my side."

"Then I'll tell them you have a small cock!"

Now she was just grasping at straws. I laughed at her. "Honey, most of the guys have seen my cock at one time or another. Good luck with that one."

She huffed in annoyance and glared out the side window.

"I think I'll go with Freckles. It was a toss up between that and Strawberry, but Freckles rolls off the tongue nicer."

"Whatever."

She continued to ignore me, so I just kept talking. She had seriously pissed me off earlier, and now I was going to return the favor.

"So, Freckles. What made you want to become a reporter?"

She didn't answer.

"Was it your inquisitive nature?"

No reply.

"Penchant for getting into trouble?"

Still nothing.

"Sleeping with the boss?"

"Excuse me? I am not sleeping with my boss! He's old enough to be my father!"

I shrugged. "Well, you never know nowadays. Look at Hugh Hefner. He was pretty old and wrinkly and the ladies still went after him."

"He was also rich."

"Well, judging by how much your boss is paying me, I would guess your boss is pretty well off."

"The paper is paying you."

"I'm guessing not. No paper would pay that much to keep that pretty little head in tact. No, this job is most definitely funded by Mr. Darren Hughes himself."

She was silent for a minute as she thought that over. "No. He doesn't have that kind of money. There's no way he's funding you protecting me."

I just shrugged. It mattered very little to me how I was paid as long as I was.

"So, what's your name?"

"Cap."

"Cap? As in, baseball cap? Bottle cap?"

"As in Captain."

"Were you a captain of a ship?"

"No, I was a Captain in the Marine Corps."

"Wow. Impressive. What made you get out?"

"Damage to my left eye. I couldn't pass the vision test to get back in the field."

"Do you miss it?"

I looked over at her with a stony face. "Every damn day."

CHAPTER 4

MAGGIE

The look he shot me sent chills down my spine. It basically said that he could be out doing important work, but was instead forced to be here babysitting me. Well, I didn't ask for his protection, so he could just lump it. Maybe if I pissed him off enough, he would leave me alone.

The key would be getting his guys on my side. I had to make them like me, and I had a feeling that guys like this would only respond to a strong woman that could put a man in his place. If only I had time to clean up a little first. Then I could make a better impression. Of course, looking like I did said that I had seen action and survived, which I had. Three times now. Okay, so there may be something to needing protection. I wasn't sure how I would have made it out of that building alive without Sebastian. My getaway car would have gotten me killed in less than five seconds, even if I had managed to get away.

We pulled into an underground garage with an entry code. I discreetly looked over and watched him punch in the code 21573. I locked it away in my memory in case I needed that information later. The garage was filled with vehicles that looked much like the one we were in, except they weren't riddled with bullet holes and a smashed fender and front bumper.

We got out and walked over to an elevator where another code had to be entered. 65932. Inside the elevator, yet another code had to be entered. 79395. Geez. These people were paranoid.

"Preparing for war?"

"We're a security company. We wouldn't be very reputable if you could break into our facility. The codes are changed daily, by the way."

"Okay. Good to know. I'm glad you're on top of your game." Rats. That meant I was memorizing codes that would be different tomorrow.

"I was telling you so you wouldn't have to worry about remembering all three codes. They won't work if you come back here."

I scowled at him. "How did you know I was watching?"

"Well, I wasn't exactly blocking the numbers. If I was worried about you seeing the codes, you wouldn't have seen them."

"Well, it looks like you entered the wrong code because the elevator isn't moving."

He placed his hand on a glass window on the wall. There were some lines that appeared to be scanning his palm and then a green light surrounded it. The elevator started moving with a jolt and he smirked down at me. Bastard.

When the doors opened, a surly looking man was sitting at the entry desk looking more like a warrior than a secretary. Though, he was looking a little haggard at the moment. He looked skinnier than Sebastian and his face looked like it could use a good shave.

"Cal. This is Maggie. She's a reporter from Pittsburgh. We're on protection detail until her story is finished."

The man gave a jerk of his head and continued to stare off into space.

"He doesn't look too friendly."

"He's...going through something right now."

There was definitely more to the story, but that wasn't my

concern right now. Looking around, the office was very clean and organized. There was a series of doors that probably held offices, and one right across from the secretary's desk, which was where we were headed. When Sebastian opened the door, I gasped in surprise. There were computer monitors along three of the walls in the room and some kind of large glass screen that was on the fourth wall. There was a ledge along the bottom that held markers and an eraser.

"Welcome to our war room."

"War room?" I asked as I stared around the room in amazement.

"This is where we strategize."

"Hey, Cap. I see you made it back in one piece. This must be the little reporter you were sent to protect. I'm Derek, but people call me Irish."

I raised an eyebrow at him. "I'm guessing you're Irish."

"Right you are, ma'am. I was unfortunate enough to get some unimaginative brothers when I served. The name stuck and here we are today."

"So, does everyone call you Irish?"

"No, ma'am. Only half the time."

"Please stop calling me ma'am. I'm not an old lady."

"Would you be willing to prove that?"

Flirting. That was the name of the game today. I sauntered up to him and wrapped one arm around his neck while I leaned in close, whispering in his ear. "Anytime, Irish." I leaned back slightly and lifted my driver's license in front of his face with my pointer and middle finger.

He looked confused for two point five seconds before pulling back and laughing a huge belly laugh. "Damn. You are one sassy little lady."

I did my best curtsy and placed my driver's license back in my pocket. "It's Maggie."

"Shit, Cap. You didn't tell us you brought a little hellion back with you."

"Just wait. You haven't seen anything yet," Sebastian muttered. "Get Cazzo in here so we can go over what Freckles got herself into."

"Freckles. I like it." Irish turned and walked out of the room, returning moments later with seven large men ambling to get in the room all at once followed by a kickass woman who looked like she'd rather be anywhere than here.

"Freckles, meet the other members of the team. This is Hunter, Sam, Blake, Mark, John, Julius, Chris, and Lola," Sebastian said as he pointed to each team member.

"And do you all have nicknames as well?"

"Hunter Papacosta, but they call me Pappy for short." He extended his hand and gave a firm handshake. He was about six feet with olive toned skin. He either had no hair or shaved his head, but it only made him look sexier, more lethal. He wasn't overly large, but his muscles strained against his t-shirt and his arms were covered in tattoos that made him look even more lethal. His brown eyes seemed almost wary as he looked me over.

"It's a pleasure to meet you." My voice came out almost as a croak and I had to clear my throat.

"I'm Blake Reasenberg, but they call me Burg."

"Burg? Is that because of your last name or because you're the size of an iceberg?"

A round of laughs filtered through the room and I found myself blushing slightly. I glanced at Lola, who just rolled her eyes. She probably thought I was flirting, when in actuality, I was a little nervous surrounded by all these badasses, and words tended to fly out of my mouth unfiltered when I got nervous.

"It's because of my last name," Burg said with a charming smile. No doubt, with a name like Blake and a hulking body like his, women flocked to his side for a chance to get one night with him. His ocean blue eyes were disarming enough without his dastardly good looks. He was blonde with a large portion of his face covered in stubble. His shirt also appeared to be either child sized or they didn't make anything bigger at the big and tall store.

A panty melting man stepped forward, holding out his hand to me. "I'm Sinner."

"I bet you are," I said with a grin. This man was by far one of the most gorgeous men I had ever seen. He had jet black hair that was shorn in a military cut. He had the most gorgeous dimples that were barely noticeable through the trimmed beard he was sporting. He was the perfect size all around, not overly muscled, but enough to make me want to run my hands all over his body and feel them ripple under my fingers. His piercing blue eyes held me captive as I gulped and then licked my lips as if I could taste him already.

"Geez, Freckles. Pull yourself together. These are my men, not slabs of beef. We aren't shopping today." Sebastian's irritated voice cut through my lust filled haze, making me flush in embarrassment at his observation of my perusal.

"Freckles. That's cute. Give me a call if you ever want to trade up from the Cap here."

His smirk told me that he was trying to get a rise out of Sebastian, so I wisely kept my mouth shut. I had already been embarrassed enough for one day. I managed to keep my libido under control for the rest of the introductions.

John "Ice" Peters was named for his ridiculous resemblance to Val Kilmer in *Top Gun*. I mean, down to a T. This man was also the epitome of gorgeous. Of course, who was I kidding? They could make a security calendar out of these guys.

Julius "Jules" Siegrist was nicknamed to shorten a name that he obviously hated, and insisted I call him Jules. He was probably around six foot two, and again, built just like all the others. Insanely ripped and gorgeous. He had a very sharp nose that only added to his rugged good looks. In fact, his whole face was sharp angles. I imagined a caricature of him and almost started laughing, but held back.

Chris "Jack" McKay, Jack because he liked his Jack Daniels and was from Tennessee, was wearing a cowboy hat and looked slightly out of place compared to the rest. He had a leaner body that was still heavily muscled, but he wasn't nearly as scary. That is, until he looked at me from under the rim of his cowboy hat and I saw his menacing eyes. They were almost black and his brown hair and brown stubble only made him appear even more evil. Evil wasn't the right word. He was just really scary. Not someone I would want to meet in a dark alley.

"And this is Lola 'Brave' Pruitt. She's our only female operator," Sebastian said.

"And why's that? Are the standards that high or you just don't like working with women?"

"Whoa, Freckles. Pull back before I put you on a leash."

"Excuse me? I am not a dog!"

"I just meant, rein in your temper. She's our only female operator because, yes, the standards are that high and Lola is top notch."

I glared at him for another moment before turning to Lola and extending my hand. "Maggie. It's nice to meet you."

She reluctantly held out her hand and gave me a look that said she clearly wasn't impressed with me. She was a beautiful woman, slender, but muscular with dark, long brown hair pulled up in a ponytail. She looked like she could be on the cover of a Victoria's Secret catalogue. Her face was beautiful with perfect lines, except for one. She had a scar that ran from one temple to the other along her hairline. I would like to say it wasn't that noticeable, but it was one of the first things I saw when she entered the room.

"Now that introductions are done, let's get all the information into the system and get a plan in place."

"Um, excuse me, Sebastian. What do you mean 'all the information'?"

"I mean all the information from the properties and any other details that will be helpful in this investigation."

"No. I work alone. I don't want you sticking your nose in my story."

"Your story almost got us killed this morning, so unless you want to end up dead the next time we go out, you're going to give me the information we need so we can be sure to secure each location before we approach."

"You think checking out these properties with a bunch of meat-heads is going to be inconspicuous? No offense." I threw that in, not wanting to offend anyone.

"None taken. We're only taking one person with us. The rest of these 'meatheads' have other assignments more important than keeping your ass alive."

I looked around the room and noticed that most of the guys had already left and the only one in here still was Cazzo. "Fine." I walked over and sat down at the table, grabbing my messenger bag and pulling out my laptop. After starting the laptop, I opened my notes I had put together on the story so far. It wasn't much, but it was all I had to go on. I also pulled up the snapshot I had taken on my phone of the list of properties.

Sebastian took my phone and uploaded the properties into his system. On the glass screen, a map of Pittsburgh appeared with a dot locating each of the different properties.

"Okay, Maggie. Tell us what you know about these properties."

"There's really not much to tell. They're all in run down neigh-borhoods, have no connection to anything with the government, and they're all abandoned."

"Tell us specifically about each property. What was the function of the buildings before they shut down and when did that happen?"

"Okay, Wilkinsburg was a plastics manufacturing plant. They went out of business fifteen years ago. The owner died and there was no one to take over operations. It shut down about a year after his death."

"Who owns the property now?"

"Um...I didn't get that far in my research. You know, people trying to kill me and all."

"That's okay. Sam, have Becky start digging into this company. What else do you have?"

I looked over to see Sam on the phone already. Man, these people worked fast. "Okay, well the other properties are much of the same. A lot of the communities went downhill because of a project to rebuild the communities in the 1950's. A lot of the buildings at the time didn't have indoor plumbing and the buildings were subpar. In an attempt to revitalize the city, the Civic Arena was built with the thinking that it would benefit The Hill District. But when they demolished buildings that were thought to be beyond repair, they displaced eight thousand residents, which pushed them into other neighborhoods, like Homewood.

"Homewood used to be an upper class neighborhood where Andrew Carnegie lived, but after all the lower income families were pushed into the area, housing values dropped and there were a lot of racial tensions. Middle class families moved out and so did many businesses. One of the properties was a brewing company that left the area when crime skyrocketed.

"Another property is in The Hill District, not too far from the Civic Arena. It was a grocery store. Again, it went out of business when families were forced out due to the rebuilding efforts."

I looked through my notes and looked at the last two properties. "The next property is in Beltzhoover. It has a very high crime rate and a lot of the community has shut down. This property looks to be bare except for an old warehouse.

"The last property is in The Strip District. In the mid to late nineties, shipping became a huge form of transportation for goods and one shipping company on the river was small and couldn't keep up with demands. They didn't have the funds to expand and were eventually forced to close their doors. The building has been rented several times, but always available again within a year. That one seems the most fishy to me."

"Why's that?" Sebastian asked.

"Well, less than a year for all the businesses? That's not really giving your business a chance to grow. Either there's something wrong with the building or there was something else going on."

"Could it have been the location?"

"No. The location was great. It was right in the middle of The Strip District."

"I thought you said that you didn't have a chance to look up anything?"

"No. I said I didn't have a chance to look up anything on Wilkinsburg. I still haven't thoroughly checked out these other locations. Someone came in and interrupted the meeting I was going to have with my boss."

I narrowed my eyes at him and scowled. He sighed heavily as he stood. "Okay, well, Becky can look into who owns these properties now and see if anyone has been making any bids on the land."

"The other thing I need to start working on is the list of offshore accounts."

"You have the actual list?"

"Yes."

He sighed in exasperation. "Why didn't you mention that sooner?"

"You didn't ask. Besides, this is still my investigation."

"Freckles, we're not planning on swooping in and taking credit here, but the sooner this investigation is over, the sooner you can get your ass out of here."

"Then why don't you give me your internet access and I can get to work."

"If you work with Becky on this, she can help you get what you're looking for a lot faster."

I crossed my arms over my chest. This man just didn't get it. It was my investigation and I didn't work with others. In fact, I had a reputation at the office for being one of the most stubborn reporters when it came to accepting help and I was okay with that. It meant that I could never be taken advantage of. I'd seen others in the office that worked in a collaborative effort and someone always ended up getting screwed over.

"Thanks, but I work alone."

"Fine. Cazzo, can you get Freckles set up?"

"Sure thing, Cap. Come over here, Freckles. I'll set you up at a work station."

"I just need the wifi password and I'll work off my laptop."

"What? Are you afraid we're going to steal your intel?" I gave him a pointed look. "Jesus. Fine. I'll give you the password."

After getting the password from Cazzo, I spent the next four hours working on researching the offshore accounts. I wasn't an accountant so following the money was a little difficult. I ended up printing off page after page of documents and sorting them into separate categories. Since I didn't have access to bank records, I was having to work backward.

I was able to trace the money back to different accounts, but it branched off into smaller amounts that I then had to add up to match the final amount. Then I hit a brick wall when I couldn't access the next set of bank records. I was going to need someone to hack into the bank to get the account information. As much as I didn't want to ask for help, I was probably going to have to.

The ringing of my phone brought me out of my work haze. Looking at the clock, I realized I had been working for most of the evening on this and it was all starting to look like random numbers. I was going to have to take a break so I didn't lose my mind.

"Hello?"

"Maggie?"

"Yes."

There was a pause at the other end. "It's Danielle. I need to meet you tonight."

Danielle was my source in the mayor's office. She was the one that originally suspected something was off with the Budget Oversight Committee and then found the paperwork for the offshore accounts. The mayor had been scheduled to be out of the office for a few days, so she took the opportunity to copy all the offshore documents she could. When she met with me, she handed it all over and asked me to look into it.

"What's going on? Did you find out something else?"

"Not on the phone. Meet me under Panther Hollow Bridge on the lake side."

She was speaking quickly, as if she only had a minute to get this out.

"What time? I'm not in Pittsburgh. I'll need an hour to get there."

"Meet me at eleven. Maggie, please don't be late. I think...I think someone knows what I did."

"Listen, I have a security company protecting me. They can protect you, too. Why don't you come back with me and we can keep you safe."

"Are you sure they're not working for the mayor?"

"I'm positive. You know I wouldn't be with them if they were."

I heard her take a deep breath. "Okay. But I think they might be following me. I'm gonna try to lose them in the park."

"I'll find you."

Danielle hung up the phone before I could say anything more reassuring to her. I wished there was something I could say, but I had already been on the receiving end of the mayor's disapproval. I gathered up the documents that I had spread all over the war room and put them in neat stacks, then put them back in my bag, along with my laptop. I was working fast because I only had an hour before I had to leave and I still had to convince Sebastian that I had to get back to Pittsburgh, which he would no doubt nix.

"Going somewhere?"

I shrieked at the voice in my ear. Putting my hand to my chest to calm my racing heart, I took a deep breath before spinning around and was pushed right up against the hard body of Sebastian. I hadn't really given him a second look before. He was my bodyguard and nothing more. I was too obsessed with finding out the story that was currently causing my brain to go haywire.

Now that I took a moment to look at the man in front of me, I saw that his chest was perfectly sculpted through his shirt. His pectoral muscles were strong and made his nipples stand out against the fabric. The muscles in his arms rippled as he caged me in against the table. My breathing quickened as I did my best not to run my hands down his perfect arms.

I finally tore my gaze from his perfect body and looked up into the most gorgeous pair of chocolate brown eyes I had ever seen. They seemed to be assessing me in much the way I was him. The dark stubble along his jaw had me reaching up to run my fingers over the course hair. I felt his jaw clench as I ran my hand along his chin to the cleft that was hidden underneath his stubble.

As I traced the hairline back to his short sideburns, I felt desire build inside. I had never wanted a man more than I did right now. I was so lost in him that I didn't even notice that he had pushed me back against the table and his now sizable erection was pushing against me. My eyes flicked back to his as he released a ragged breath and then pushed back from me. He closed his eyes for a moment and when he opened them, he was back to the man I met earlier in the day. Indifferent. He was here to do a job and so was I.

"I have to get back to Pittsburgh to meet a source."

"No. That's not gonna happen until we know more about what's going on."

"Listen, buddy, my source said she thinks they caught on to her. I have to meet her and bring her back here, otherwise she's as good as dead."

"You want to bring her back here? This isn't a puppy shelter. We don't take in any stray you think needs protection."

"If you don't protect her, she'll be killed. Are you that heartless?"

"My job is to protect you. If she got involved in something she shouldn't have, that's her problem."

"If she's dead, she can't give me the information I need."

"And if you meet her and someone's after her, it will lead them right to you."

"Fine. You don't want to help? I'll go alone."

"Not gonna happen. You don't go anywhere without me and or one of my guys."

"God, you're an asshole."

"That may be true, but I'm the asshole that's going to keep you alive."

I started pulling out my stuff and setting it back on the table. Methodically, I set each stack where it previously had been and then took my laptop out and started it up.

"What are you doing?"

"Well, if you're not going to let me go meet my source, then I'm getting back to work."

"No. My guys are leaving for the night. There's only a bare bones staff that stays here at night."

"That's fine since I won't be going anywhere."

He left the room in a huff. When I was sure he was gone, I pulled out my phone and called a cab. It would be here in ten minutes, so I was going to have to hustle. Walking out of the war room, I looked in both directions and headed for the lobby.

"Where are you going?" I cringed at Sebastian's voice behind me. I turned around and put on my best bitch face.

"To the bathroom. Is that alright? Or do you need to follow me in and protect me there, too?"

"Down the hall to the left."

He turned and walked away and I scurried down the hall. When I looked back, he was gone, so I headed for the elevators and pressed the button, but nothing happened.

"Shit."

"You need a code to leave. Going somewhere?" Sinner, the really hot guy that I had fawned over, stepped up to my side.

"Oh, I left one of my bags in Sebastian's SUV. He said that I could get it. He gave me the other codes, but I guess he forgot this one."

"No problem. I can take care of it for you."

He entered the number and took a step back.

"Thanks. I appreciate your help."

I stepped into the elevator and was surprised when he stepped onto the elevator with me. "Um...I got it from here. Thanks."

"Yeah, I don't buy it. Sebastian knows that you need a hand print scan to move the elevator, so I call bullshit on your story, but I'll still take you down to retrieve your 'bag'." He actually did the little air quotes when he said bag. Bastard. Sweet talking might be the only way out of this. What was his name?

"Sinner, right?"

He gave me a panty melting smile as he turned to me. "Yeah. That's me. You wanna know how I got the name?"

He leaned against the elevator wall right in front of me. His chest would brush mine with a deep breath. God, I really wanted to find out how he got that name, but I was on a mission and I couldn't fail. I was just about to try something seductive when the elevator doors opened and broke the spell between us. He straightened and headed to the elevator door with his hand on his gun. Lord, these men were paranoid.

Walking out behind Sinner, I looked around the garage and followed behind him as he led me to the banged up SUV we arrived in. Shit. This was about to get bad for me. I needed to figure out a way out of here. An idea came to mind and I wasn't overly happy with what I was about to do, but I had to get back to Pittsburgh.

He had his hand on the door when I dropped my wallet on the ground. Being the gentleman that I took him for, he held out his hand for me to stop and then bent over to retrieve it. I grabbed onto the door handle and pulled it open as hard as I could, slamming the door into his head. He dropped to the ground and appeared to be out cold, but I wasn't taking any chances. I ran to the garage door and was pleased to see a side door. I pushed it open and ignored the alarm that blared as I ran out into the night.

I almost wept in relief when I saw the taxi waiting for me at the curb. I barely heard someone yelling as I slammed the door and yelled at the driver to go. He peeled away from the curb, only asking me where we were headed after we were well away from the security firm. I didn't see anyone tailing us, so at least I had that on my side.

With any luck, I could get to my meeting without anyone knowing where I was headed.

Of course, there would no doubt be hell to pay later when Sebastian caught up with me, but I couldn't think about that now. My phone dinged and I was afraid to look at it, in case it was Sebastian calling to chew me out. I looked and saw I had a text message from an unknown number.

Hi, Grandma. I don't know if I'll make it to dinner tonight. Some friends wanted to get together at The Steel Bar. Don't worry. My friend, Tom the bartender, is looking after me and making sure no one steals my stuff.

Obviously, this was sent to the wrong person, so I quickly sent a message back that it was the wrong number. I sat back in my seat and tried not to think about all the trouble I was going to be in when Sebastian finally caught up with me and how angry he would be. Those thoughts led to images of him pushing me up against the wall in a fit of rage and then ravishing my body. I shook off those thoughts and closed my eyes for the rest of the ride, trying my best to blank my mind.

CHAPTER 5

SEBASTIAN

That woman was infuriating. She wanted to traipse back into the city just hours after someone tried to kill her. She had no regard for her own life, or the fact that she was putting others in danger. It wasn't just me that she almost got killed. Any number of people on the road today could have been severely injured if we had caused a car accident.

I found myself pacing around the office, trying desperately to get myself under control. I couldn't figure out if I wanted to slap the shit out of her or kiss her until she saw things my way. Not that I condone violence against women, but I could really wring her neck right now.

"Boss, alarms are going off downstairs!" Irish was still here finishing up with the day's paperwork since he'd taken over office duty for the day.

I ran over to the door and followed him down the hall to the war room where Becky already had the video footage pulled up on the screens.

"What do we have?"

She was typing furiously on the computer and shifting different footage around. What I saw made my blood boil.

"Looks like your girl pulled a Houdini."

"Goddamn it!" I punched the wall, putting a decent hole in the drywall before turning back to Becky. "Pull up all the footage. I need to know how she got out of here."

"Already on it, Cap." She pulled up a few more feeds before pressing play. We watched as Sinner took her downstairs in the elevator and then walked over to the SUV where she smashed the door into his head. I ignored the fact that they had some kind of moment in the elevator, and the fact that Sinner had allowed her to pull a fast one on him.

"Becky, get the taxi information and see if the company will give us the tracking information."

"Cap, she got away," Sinner said, staggering into the room holding his head. "She said she forgot her bag in the SUV. I took her down there because I didn't believe her, but—"

"Yeah, we saw the rest."

My voice was sharp and cutting. I didn't allow my guys to get away with this kind of shit. We were the best because we were always aware of potential threats and paid attention to our surroundings. Even a client couldn't be trusted to be honest and follow the rules. She had already proven to us that she wouldn't listen when told, so Sinner should have damn well known that she would try to pull some shit on us.

"Cap, I swear, I was trying to find out what she was up to. I didn't think she would attack me. I just thought she was hiding something from us."

"She is. She wanted to meet with a source tonight, and I told her no because we don't know enough about what the hell is going on. That's where she's headed, only we don't know where that is at the moment. You'd better pray that we get to her before she gets herself killed, or you won't have a job anymore."

Sinner didn't argue or even try to defend himself further. He knew he had fucked up, so he just nodded his head. Since the mess with Cal, I had to have a tighter rein on my employees. I wouldn't tolerate people going rogue and doing their own shit. We had protocols for a reason. Of course, that was a little hypocritical considering Cal was still here with us.

"Is Pappy still here?"

"Yeah," Sinner replied. He pulled his hand away from his head and looked at his hand that was now covered in blood.

"Go get checked out and then come check in with me."

He nodded and then staggered out the door and down the hall. "Becky, I want you to call in Rob. The two of you need to go over all Maggie's stuff. Go through her computer and get anything related to this case and find out what else she's hiding from us. Also, look over the offshore accounts. I'm sure she got stuck when she couldn't access the bank records. See if you can follow the money."

"She's gonna be pissed."

"Yes, she will be, but we operate as a team here and if we don't know what she's after, she's gonna get one of us killed. I won't allow that to happen, so we'll work around her."

Becky nodded and then picked up the phone, calling Rob in. When she was hanging up, a ping came over the computer and Becky opened the document. It was the tracking data sent over by the taxi company. She had been gone for about ten minutes now and had quite a head start on us.

"Alright, I'm going after her. Send me updates as I get closer."

"I'll send you a link to the data so you can see her movements from your phone."

"Thanks, Becky."

On my way down to the SUV, I realized I had told Sinner to stay behind. I placed a call to Pappy to check in on him.

"Yo, Cap."

"What's the status on Sinner?"

"Concussion. Pretty nasty one, too."

"Alright, get him taken care of. I'm going after our escapee."

"Sinner's gonna have to stay here tonight. I need to keep an eye on him."

I remembered how just a year ago Pappy had been in a much worse situation. When Alex's attacker went after her, our teams had been there to protect her, but Cal had betrayed us, causing several team members to be injured in the process. Pappy was one of them. He had been outside keeping watch when he was attacked from behind and hit with a large rock. He just recently came back to work after much time off from being in a coma. There had been a lot of swelling and the doctors weren't sure if he would recover. Luckily, he had recovered and took some time off to rest and get his head on straight. When I insisted that he take more time, he told me that if he had to sit on his ass for one more day, he was going to find a job somewhere else. I didn't believe him, but he had since proven he was ready to be back.

"Take care of him and check in with me in four hours."

"Will do, Cap."

We hung up and I took off from Reed Security to find the woman who had recently become the biggest pain in the ass I had ever known.

"Talk to me, Becky."

"Bossman, she isn't answering the phone."

"Fuck! I need to know where she's headed."

"I'll keep trying her."

"Do that, and if she answers, I need you to convince her that I can only protect her and her source if I know where she is."

"Anything else?"

"Yeah, remind her that if someone is following her source, and she's caught with her, she's expendable."

"Will do, Bossman. I'll call you back as soon as I get her."

I hung up and punched the steering wheel. This was ridiculous. I had an employee with a concussion, a reporter running wild that I couldn't protect, and employees that had no desire to help take control of the company.

The phone rang again and I quickly picked it up. "Yeah?"

"She's headed to Panther Hollow Bridge."

I frowned. "Isn't that in the middle of Schenley Park?"

"I'm sending you her destination now. It's pretty secluded, boss. Do you want me to send backup?"

"There's no way anyone would catch up in time. I'll put a tracker on just in case."

"Send me a text when you have it on and I'll activate it."

"Will do."

I hung up and opened the link Becky just sent me with the location. It took me another fifteen minutes to get there, which meant that I could already be too late. As I pulled up to the bridge on Panther Hollow Road, I knew we were screwed.

"Fuck. This has to be a joke."

I'd been driving without my lights on for the last mile so I didn't draw attention to myself out here. The place was secluded and if Maggie already found trouble, absolutely no one would hear her scream. What the hell was she thinking coming here?

Climbing out of the SUV, I quietly closed the door and headed for the lake side of the bridge. The embankment was quite steep and it took me a few minutes to get to the bottom safely. I swore again, thinking about Maggie doing this without regard for her own safety. When I reached the bottom, I pulled out my gun and scanned the area for anyone that might be lurking, but didn't see anyone. I walked steadily toward the sandy beach under the bridge looking for Maggie.

I clenched my jaw when I found her. Her hair was a dead giveaway even in the dark. The light from the moon was enough to highlight her red locks, making her stand out when she thought she was hidden. She hadn't spotted me yet, so I thought I would set a little example for her. I crept as close to the trees as possible, keeping watch for any branches that may give away my location. When I got behind her, I placed my hand over her mouth and pulled her back against my body. She stiffened immediately, but then relaxed into me as if she knew it was me.

"You ever pull that shit again, I'll kill you myself."

She spun out of my grip and glared at me. "You already told me I couldn't come, so what was the point in listening to you? I needed to meet my source."

"And when are you supposed to meet her?"

She huffed and crossed her arms over her chest. "She was supposed to be here fifteen minutes ago, but I was a few minutes late. Still, I don't think she would have left just because I was a few minutes late. I told her I was an hour away, and it took me longer to escape your goons than I thought it would."

I took a menacing step toward her, towering over her smaller frame. "One of those *goons* has a pretty good concussion, because he was trying to look out for you. You're lucky I don't just hand you over to the mayor myself."

"Why don't you? You obviously don't like me, so what's holding you back?"

"Freckles, I'm getting paid to do a job. I intend to finish that job. I don't get paid if you end up dead."

"Well, it's good to know that you genuinely care about keeping your clients safe," she said sarcastically.

"My job isn't to hold your hand and make sure you feel cared for. My job is to make sure that at the end of your story, you're still in one piece."

"And I never asked for that. In fact, I don't recall asking for your help at all, so why don't you just leave me alone so I can do my job?" she snapped.

This woman was such a pain in the ass. I rolled my eyes as I looked at the sky and prayed that this assignment would be over quickly. I didn't know how much more of her attitude I could take. On the one hand, her inability to follow instructions infuriated me, but on the other hand, her spitfire personality got me hard and left me unfulfilled. I had barely known her eighteen hours and already I wanted to bend her over my desk and fuck her.

"Can we just meet your source and get out of here? We can debate what my responsibilities are later."

We both shut our mouths and waited for about five more minutes in complete silence. I was just about to tell her we should head out when I heard movement coming from down the shoreline. I pushed Maggie back slightly with my arm and raised my gun in the direction of the snapping twigs. At first I didn't see anything, but then a figure that was most definitely not a woman emerged from the trees carrying a rifle. I couldn't make out what kind in the dark, but a rifle was still a weapon that could kill, no matter what kind it was.

"Shit. That is not a woman."

"It could be her. How can you even see in the dark?"

"Unless your source carries a rifle around with her, she was most likely followed here to get to you. Since we haven't seen her yet, I'm assuming that she's already dead."

"We can't just leave and assume she's dead. We need to be sure before we leave."

Maggie was leaning in by my ear so I could hear without anyone else hearing. Her hot breath on my neck was sending all my blood rushing south, leaving me very uncomfortable considering what I was supposed to be doing. Shaking my head, I brought myself back to the mission and the current unfortunate events that were currently taking place.

"We don't have time to sit around and wait. We need to get out now while we can. If we wait any longer, that guy will be too close and we won't have a chance at getting away. Follow me and step where I step."

I started making my way up the embankment with Maggie close on my heels. We were about half way up when Maggie stumbled and made so much noise there was no way it went unnoticed.

"Jesus, Freckles. I said to be quiet."

"No, you didn't, asshole. You said to step where you step, and I did, but your gigantic feet took too big of steps and I couldn't follow in your steps anymore without breaking my neck!"

I pulled her to her stomach when bullets started flying around us. Swearing under my breath, I returned fire a few times before getting up and pulling her with me. We ran up the rest of the embankment, no longer caring if we made noise or not. By the time we reached the top, Maggie was out of breath and panting hard, but she didn't show any signs of stopping. We ran in the direction of my SUV, but bright lights headed our way, cutting off our escape.

"Come on. This way."

I pulled her along behind me as we headed across the bridge. There was no way we could outrun the SUV barreling down on us, but between the SUV and the man that chased us up the embankment, we didn't really have a choice. God, I hated when clients didn't listen.

Panting hard and running harder, we made it about halfway across the bridge when another set of headlights appeared in the direction we were running. Glancing behind me, I saw that the other SUV was almost on top of us and there was a guy leaning out the window, pulling a weapon out to shoot.

"Fuck!"

I pulled Maggie to the side of the bridge and helped her over the side. "Jump with your ankles crossed!" I swung back around and shot at the SUV just as it was screeching to a stop. I heard Maggie drop into the water with a loud splash and a scream. Not allowing any more time for them to catch me, I swung my legs over and immediately dropped to the water below, just barely crossing my legs in time.

When I came up, I saw that Maggie hadn't surfaced yet. I dove under water to find her a few feet away, struggling to swim to the surface. I swam over to her and pulled her up.

"Deep breath." Then I pulled her back under and swam for the other side of the bridge. I didn't want to head back in the direction of my SUV because that's where they would expect us to go. I had to stop several times and pull us back to the surface so she could breathe. I was a very good swimmer, but it was obvious that she wasn't and possibly didn't know how to swim at all. Yet, she still jumped.

When we reached the shore, I pulled her up next to me and held on to her. We stayed somewhat in the water so we were hidden from view. She was shivering from the cold water, and I knew that we couldn't stay in the river too much longer if we hoped to survive. She snuggled into me as if she could gather some warmth from my freezing body.

"If I didn't know better, I would say you were trying to get in my pants right now," I whispered.

"As t-tempting as that s-s-sounds, I don't think even you c-could get it up in this fr-freezing water."

I chuckled at her humor. "I didn't think you were interested."

"Oh c-come on. Any w-woman would be interested...you k-know that."

"You sure seemed interested in the meatheads on my team," I said as I rubbed my hands over her shivering body.

"Jealous?" She looked up at me and then her eyes dropped to my lips. Her tongue darted out of her cute, little mouth and ran over her top lip. I wanted to lean down and kiss her, but I held back, not wanting to get involved with a client.

"Yes. I don't want any of them touching you. It pisses me off that you flirted with them."

"I don't re-recall any of them caging me in against the t-table."

"What can I say? You're a pain in the ass, but my cock doesn't know the difference. In fact, I think it excites me even more."

She giggled before burrowing in closer to me. "Then I'll be s-sure to cause lots of trouble f-from now on."

I kept rubbing her arms as best I could to keep her warm, all the while listening for any sign of movement from above. They must have assumed we drowned because after a while, the SUV's started up and drove off.

I half dragged Maggie out of the water and then back up the

embankment. She was losing energy fast and I had to get us out of here. When we reached the top, I set Maggie down on the ground and squatted in front of her.

"I'm going to get the SUV. You stay here and I'll be back in a flash."

"Uh-uh. No way. You'll leave me here to fr-freeze."

"I wouldn't do that."

"R-Right. Like I'm gonna believe y-you."

Sighing, I helped her up and wrapped my arm around her back to help her across the bridge. Realistically, I could have gotten to the truck and back to her by the time we were halfway across the bridge, but then it occurred to me that maybe she was scared to be left alone at the other end of the bridge. We made it back to the SUV and climbed inside, cranking up the heat.

"We need to get to a safe house. There's no way I'm driving back to Reed Security in wet clothes."

Maggie didn't bother to answer. She sighed and leaned her head back against the headrest and closed her eyes. I headed to the nearest safe house, which was located just outside of Pittsburgh. This had been the original safe house where Alex and Cole had stayed, and was way too big for what Maggie and I needed, but it was close by and would keep us safe until we could figure things out.

I pulled into the driveway ten minutes later and entered all the necessary codes and scans. When I stopped the SUV, Maggie leaned forward to get a better look at our dwellings.

"Are we staying in a mansion?"

"This is a safe house. We'll have access to the team back at Reed Security and we're close to Pittsburgh. It should help give us a chance to figure things out."

She started to open the door, but I stopped her. "For once, will you just wait for me to secure things?"

"I thought this was your safe house. Why would you need to secure it?"

"You can never be too sure."

"With the level of security I saw back at your office, I'm sure your safe houses are secure also."

I wasn't about to get into how a member of my own team had betrayed me. It wouldn't instill trust in me, and it would probably give her all the more reason to resist my instructions. As much as I wanted to just call the team and have them check all the sensors on the safe house and the video feed, I found myself second guessing that decision. At some point, I was going to have to put complete faith in my team again. In the year since Cal had betrayed us, I found myself micromanaging the team more often than not, and I could see on their faces how much that distrust affected them.

"Just wait here while I check things out. It'll take me ten minutes to clear the property on my own, so I want you to wait in the driver's seat and leave if I'm even a minute late. You head back to Reed Security and tell them what happened."

"Geez, you're paranoid."

"I would say the events of tonight would suggest that I'm being perfectly reasonable. Stay here and do what I say. I'll be back in ten minutes."

I got out of the SUV with my gun raised and proceeded to the house. After clearing the entire house, I walked back to the SUV, seeing I still had thirty seconds to spare. To my surprise, Maggie was still sitting in the driver's seat, just as I had asked. I half wanted to pat her on the head and tell her she had been a good girl, but patronizing her right now was probably not a good idea.

"It's all clear. Let's get inside and get cleaned up. Then we can go over all the shit you haven't been telling me."

To my relief, she walked in behind me and didn't say a word, though I could feel that she was dying to. I led her up to the bathroom and showed her where the shower was. Heading down to the secure house phone, I put in a call to Derek at Reed Security. Either he or Cazzo would be there since we had several clients at the moment and I was out in the field.

"Cap, is everything okay? We've been trying to get ahold of you for the past two hours."

"Yeah, we got ambushed by whoever was after her source. The source never showed, so I can only assume she's dead. It was a helluva getaway."

"Who do you want me to send? Everyone is on assignment right now or about to go on assignment."

Shit. I had been meaning to hire another team, but hadn't found the right candidates yet. I couldn't put Cal on a team with any of the guys yet. No one trusted him, and I couldn't leave a team down a man, which left me no choice.

"Send me Cal."

"Boss, you sure about that?"

I could hear it in his tone. He didn't trust Cal and didn't think he should be out in the field, but Cal had been a good field operative. As much as I didn't want to trust him, I knew his record proved that he had been loyal up until his family was taken from him. With them out of the picture, that threat was no longer an issue.

"I'm sure. I need someone else here with me. I had to clear the house and left her by herself in the SUV. That's not the ideal situation. I'm gonna have to put my trust in him at some point. Better with me than someone else on the team."

Sighing, Cazzo blew out a harsh breath. "I don't like it, Cap, but I'll send him your way. Just keep an eye out. It's not just that I don't trust him because of what happened. He's different since his family died. He's got no reason to live and that makes him dangerous."

"I know. Believe me, I know. Did Becky get anything?"

"She's taking a nap right now. Do you want me to wake her?"

"No. We need to get some sleep too. Just have her call first thing in the morning. How's Sinner?"

"He's doing alright. He's got a bitch of a headache, but otherwise, still in one piece."

"I'll be sure to let Freckles know," I said with a laugh. "Alright, check-in at 0600."

"Ten-four, Cap."

I hung up and sat down for all of two point five seconds before I realized that I hadn't given Maggie anything to change into after her shower. Dragging my tired ass upstairs, I went to the closet and pulled out a t-shirt that would be way too big on her. I briefly considered checking out the clothes that were here from when Alex and Cole were here, but that required too much effort at the moment.

I had let myself slack off too much being the boss. I rarely did field work anymore, and working out and training just wasn't the same as doing the grunt work. I made a mental note to take on a few more assignments to stay on top of my game.

Walking over to the bathroom door, I could still hear the shower running, so I gently knocked. When I didn't hear anything, I opened the door and peered inside. My jaw dropped and I stood frozen at the gorgeous sight before me. Maggie was standing in the shower running her hands over her body as she washed herself. Her willowy body could barely be seen through the fog that covered the glass of the shower, but I could see the outline of her beautiful body and it was enough for my cock to stand at attention. When she raised her arms to run her fingers through her hair, her breasts pushed up and out, begging me to touch them.

I imagined going over to the shower and stepping in behind her, running my hands over her luscious curves. I could almost taste the salt of her skin as I ran my tongue along her neck. My pants were painfully tight around my straining erection. The damp fabric did nothing to tame the beast that was threatening to break free.

Before I could think better of staring at her, Maggie turned and wiped the fog from the glass. I could see her staring at my body, her eyes running down my chest. I saw the moment her gaze landed on my cock. Her eyes widened slightly, and then she totally shocked me by running her own fingers down her body until they were sliding along the folds of her pussy.

Fuck. I had to have her. I stepped forward until I was in front of the door and slid it open. Not wasting a second, I stepped into the shower and pushed her up against the wall as I devoured her mouth. God, she tasted just as good as I thought she would. My erection dug into her belly as I rocked against her. I needed her. I needed to touch her and feel how wet she was for me.

Sliding my fingers down her soft curves, I groaned when I touched the soft curls on her mound. A slight gasp followed by a soft moan let me know that she wanted this as much as I did. My fingers touched her wet heat and I almost came in my pants. She was soaked and it had nothing to do with her standing in the shower. I strummed her clit as I sucked on her neck and nipped at her collarbone. She spread her legs wider when I slid one finger into her tight pussy. Adding another finger, I fucked her, imagining it was my cock inside her.

"Oh, God. Sebastian, more. I need more."

Her eyes were closed as she kept calling for me and telling me how much she needed me. I imagined taking her in bed and fucking her all night long, hearing her tell me how much she needed me.

I ran my thumb over her clit as my fingers continued to thrust up into her tight body. Bending down, I drew one of her nipples into my mouth and sucked it into my mouth, gently biting down on the taut peak. Her walls tightened around my fingers as she came all over my fingers. Still, I didn't stop pumping into her until she stopped screaming my name.

Breathing harshly, she finally opened her eyes and looked at me. Lust filled her eyes and she licked her lips as she looked down at my straining erection. She slowly lowered herself to her knees and pulled the zipper down. My heartbeat increased as I felt her fingers brush over me. When she pulled my pants down, my erection bobbed in front of her gorgeous face. She looked up at me through her lashes as she took me in her mouth.

Goddamn. Her mouth was hot and wet, reminding me of what her pussy felt like just moments before. She licked and sucked on my shaft as my hips started jerking from the feel of her around me. Running my fingers through her wet strands, I thrust my hips forward, forcing myself deeper in her throat. Her eyes widened, but she got the hint and took me deeper and deeper.

"God, yes. Maggie, you're killing me."

That seemed to spur her on further as she picked up the pace and sucked me until I exploded in her mouth with a roar. I tried pulling myself from her, but she continued to suck me until every last drop was in her mouth. Fuck, that was hot. I had never had a woman so willingly suck me off like that. She wanted me like no other woman had, and there was nothing sexier than a woman who liked to give head.

Never in my life did I imagine I would find a woman like Maggie, let alone someone that I was protecting. Shit. Someone that I was protecting. Pulling back from her, I pulled up my pants and quickly tucked myself back inside. Maggie stood with a confused expression.

"Is something wrong? Should I have not done that?"

I ran my hand over my short hair and then wiped the water from my face. "Freckles, I shouldn't have done that. I'm supposed to be protecting you."

"What's the big deal? It's not like I'm asking you to date me. We just...performed a service for one another."

I groaned at the thought of her servicing me because it brought up fantasies that practically every guy has about being served by a delectable woman.

"Listen, it can't happen again. If I start looking at you as someone I want to fuck, my focus won't be on you the way it should be. This can't happen again. Just forget everything we just did."

She raised an eyebrow at me. "Yeah, I don't think that's going to happen. There's no forgetting what you just did to my body."

Clenching my teeth, I turned and walked out of the room, shutting the door behind me. I couldn't believe I had just done that. I was supposed to be protecting her and I was in there ready to fuck her instead. If someone had broken into the house in the last fifteen minutes, would I have even noticed? It was bad enough that I wasn't as fresh as the other guys on my teams. I was the boss. I was supposed to be doing it better than them, and instead I was breaking all the rules of protection. Do not get involved with a client.

As I berated myself for another fifteen minutes, I shucked my clothes and put on some sweatpants and a t-shirt. I really needed to get some sleep if I was going to be on top of things. I couldn't share a room with Maggie, though. I'd end up fucking her, and I needed to avoid that if I was going to keep any perspective on this job.

After making the rounds downstairs and checking all the monitors, I headed in the direction of the stairs. I was about halfway up when the front gate alarm sounded. I quickly ran to the bank of monitors, cursing myself for not bringing my gun with. God, I was getting sloppy. I saw from the video feed that it was Cal pulling up. Checking the clock on the wall, I saw that he must have left as soon as I talked to Cazzo.

I headed for the front door and pulled the gun that was in the table next to it. Checking the gun quickly, I waited by the inside of the door for Cal to approach. Before a year ago, I might not have been such a suspicious bastard, but now, I just couldn't shake the feeling that I had to be extra cautious.

After Cal knocked, I peered out the window next to the door and saw no one else with him. Blowing out a breath and berating myself for not trusting members of my own teams, I opened the door and let him in. He looked at me like he knew what I had been doing and what I had been thinking. I just shrugged and walked into the living room.

"I didn't think you would be here so fast," I said with only a hint of suspicion.

"Cazzo told me you needed backup. I wasn't about to wait until morning to come out here."

"No, I didn't think you would. You just seemed to get here awfully fast."

"Cap, I know I screwed up big time and you have no reason to trust me. No one does. If you don't want me here, then I'll leave, but not until someone else can get their ass over here. From what Cazzo told me, there is no one else. So, what do you want me to do? You either have to trust that I'm on your side or fire me. I'm no use to you if you don't trust me to do my job."

"It's not that simple."

"No, it's not, but I've got no one left to be used against me," he admitted defeatedly.

He was right. I asked him to be sent out here, yet I wasn't trusting him to do his job. If I was always looking over his shoulder, I would put us all in more danger because I wouldn't be focusing on my job, which was keeping Maggie safe.

"I need some shut eye. Becky is supposed to be calling around six. I'll be up by then. Wake me if there are any developments."

I headed upstairs to the rooms on the other side of the stairs and let myself into one. Setting the alarm on the clock, I laid down and drifted off in minutes.

CHAPTER 6

MAGGIE

I listened from the door of the bedroom as Sebastian spoke with someone downstairs. It looked like the guy that sat in reception when I entered Reed Security, but I couldn't be sure. It sounded like Sebastian didn't trust this guy, and I had to wonder why he would call him to come if he didn't trust him. Was Sebastian going to leave because of what happened between us? And was he replacing himself with this guy? Great. I didn't want to be protected in the first place, but definitely not by someone that no one wanted on the team. What was it Sebastian said when we passed him at Reed Security? He's got problems? Something along those lines. That didn't bode well for me.

When Sebastian started up the stairs, I scurried back to the bed and jumped in, waiting for him to open the door. When he didn't after five minutes, I rolled over and shut off the light. I hadn't really slept well in the last few days, so it was easy enough for me to drift off to sleep, but just as I was entering the land of Nod, my eyes popped open. I scrambled from the bed and pulled my phone out of my soaking wet jeans. I tried powering it on, but had no such luck. The thing was dead.

Making a split second decision, I went over to the closet and found some sweats to pull on. They were way too big and I had to roll them several times to get them to stay up. Then I pulled a sweatshirt over my head to cover my perky breasts. I laid my bra out after my shower, hoping it would be dry by morning. I could wear someone else's clothes, but I still needed a bra.

I headed for the stairs and saw the man sitting at the table by the bank of monitors with a gun on the table next to him.

"Shouldn't you be sleeping?" He asked in a bored tone.

"I couldn't sleep because I thought of something and I need to see if it pans out."

He turned to me finally with an inquisitive expression. "Alright, what is it?"

I took a seat next to him at the table and pulled my knees up under me. "I got a text on my way back to Pittsburgh last night. It was someone texting their grandma about not making it to dinner."

"And you think that's newsworthy?"

"Well, this person made a point of saying that the bartender, and she gave a name, was watching over her and making sure no one stole her stuff."

"Ooh. Sounds like you cracked the case on that one."

I huffed in annoyance. "You don't understand. It was the language of it. It sounded like she was trying to convey a message, but at the time I thought it was a wrong number."

"And now you think it was meant for you?"

"Well, considering that I was supposed to meet my source last night and she didn't show, I'm willing to bet that it could have been her sending me a message, but making it look like it was from someone else. That way if anyone looked at my phone records, it would just look like a wrong number."

"Okay, so let's see your phone and see the message."

"Well, that's the thing. It's kind of water logged at the moment."

"How did that happen?"

"Well..." I cleared my throat before continuing. "We sort of had to jump off a bridge last night because people were chasing us."

"I see."

"That's all you have to say?"

"Sebastian has filled us in on your...precocious talent for getting into trouble."

"I don't...I..."

He held up his hand to stop me. "Please. Let's not pretend that you didn't run off when you were supposed to be at Reed Security. Let's also not pretend that you didn't give one of my teammates a concussion while escaping."

I turned red with embarrassment when he reminded me of injuring one of the people that was supposed to be protecting me. Well, technically he wasn't protecting me. Sebastian was. Not that it made it okay, but it was my own little sort of justification. I would never have done that to Sebastian.

He held out his hand to me and I gently placed mine in his large one. He rolled his eyes and pulled his hand back. "The phone. I don't want to hold your hand. I want to see your phone."

"Oh." I pulled it out and handed it over, watching as he got up and pulled out a Ziplock bag and some rice. After he took apart the phone, he poured the rice in, dropped the phone into the bag, and sealed it.

"Now we wait. Why don't you go get some sleep."

"I don't think I can now. I'm awake."

"I'll make you some tea. Maybe that'll help."

He pulled out a kettle that I hadn't expected to be in a safe house and filled it with water, before placing it on the stove. Then he grabbed a mug and plopped a tea bag in it. He looked like he had done this before many times, and I couldn't help but wonder what he meant when he told Sebastian that he didn't have anyone left to be used against him. Before I could stop myself, I opened my mouth and did the unspeakable.

"I heard you talking to Sebastian. What did you mean by 'you don't have anyone left that could be used against you'?"

He stared at the counter for a minute before turning to me. "Are you asking on the record or off?"

"Off, of course. I would never write anything about you guys. That is, unless you wanted me to."

"Definitely off." He brought my tea over and came to sit down. "About a year ago, we were protecting a woman, Alex, that was being hunted by a serial killer. The serial killer took my wife and kids and used them against me. Said that if I didn't help him, he would kill my family. I'd seen what he did to his victims, so I went behind my teams' back and fed him information."

I gasped in shock. I couldn't imagine anyone working with a serial killer, but then again, I had no idea what I would do if I was in that situation.

"Couldn't you go to Sebastian for help?"

"This guy, he was psychotic. I didn't want to take the chance that he would find out and kill them." He sighed heavily as he stared at the table. His fingers drew patterns in the grain of the wood. "In the end, he tied them up in the basement of his cabin and then blew the cabin when the police found it. At least they died quickly."

"That's horrible," I said with tears in my eyes. My hand covered my mouth as a lump caught in my throat. I had never been much of a crier, but when you heard stories like that in-person, it was hard to not be affected. "Did the police catch him?"

"Cole, Alex's boyfriend, killed him, but not before he hurt several members of the team." He shook his head as he stared off into space. He seemed to be lost in his head. "He was going to scalp Lola. That's where that pretty, little scar across her forehead is from. Hunter was in a coma for a while after having his head bashed in with a rock. Derek was shot in the leg."

I could hear the pain in his voice over the choices he had made and how it affected the rest of his team. He hadn't wanted to make those choices. He had only been trying to keep his family safe. I reached across the table and grabbed his hand, squeezing it tightly. He looked startled as his head swiveled to our joined hands on the table. Then he looked at me questioningly.

"Sebastian didn't fire you?"

He swallowed hard. "He should have. I tried to quit, but he guilted me into staying. He said I owed it to my team to make up for what I had done. He's right. I do owe them, but they'd all be better off if I walked away."

"Obviously, Sebastian doesn't think so. If he didn't think you were worth having around, he would have told you to leave."

"He pities me, but he doesn't trust me, and rightly so. I betrayed my whole goddamned team. There's not a single person on that team who would want to work with me."

"Yet he called you in."

"Because there was no one else."

"You have to start somewhere," I said gently.

He looked at me for a minute like he was trying to figure me out. "I don't understand. Why are you defending me?"

"I'm not defending you, but...as a reporter, I see stories from all different angles. I've learned to look beyond what a story appears to be and see it for what it really is. Your story isn't about betrayal. It's about making difficult decisions. I don't know what the right decision would have been. Hell, I don't know anything about security, but it seems like you were between a rock and a hard place. I don't think anyone, even your teammates could put themselves in your shoes and guarantee they would have done things differently."

He nodded, but I didn't think that he looked convinced. "Well, it's over now. I just want to move on with my life. Find something new for myself."

"Why don't you?"

"Because Sebastian's right. I do owe it to my team."

I couldn't argue with that. I knew what it felt like.

"I once met with a source that had proof his company was guilty of wrongdoing. He wanted someone to dig into it and he came to me for help. I was so eager for the story that I pushed him to obtain documents however he could. He got caught after he handed over the documents to me. He lost his job and was blackballed from every reputable company. He had to move his family in with his parents in Oklahoma until they could get back on their feet."

He leaned forward with his hands on his knees. "What was the company guilty of?"

"They were selling drugs that were killing people. The company didn't want to do a recall because of what would happen with their FDA approval, so they decided to change the drug and not tell anyone. Meanwhile, there was still a ton of medication on the market."

"So you saved people."

I nodded. "I did, but I cost one man his livelihood. The last I heard, he was working at a smaller company, just scraping by. It doesn't matter that I helped save all those other people by exposing the truth. I made one major error by letting my drive and ambition dictate my morals."

"Still, you didn't get anyone killed. What you did may have been wrong, but it wasn't deadly."

"My point is that we all make decisions in life that will change us forever. There's no going back once it's done. We just have to move forward and make sure we don't make the same mistake twice."

"And how's that working for you so far?"

"Well, I no longer ask my sources to do anything they aren't willing to do. Like this woman that I was supposed to meet? She gave me the information she had and I took it from there. She wasn't supposed to do any more than she already had. Yet, she was supposed to meet me last night and she didn't. That doesn't look so good for her, especially considering that some goons showed up to kill me."

"And that's who you think messaged you last night."

"Yeah. When she called me earlier to ask me to meet her, she told me that she thought she was being followed. She said she was pretty sure they found out what she had done, and if I'm correct about it being something very bad, they don't want that information floating around."

"Well, hopefully we'll get some answers off your phone when it dries out."

AT SOME POINT during my talk with Cal, I fell asleep. We had stayed up for at least another two hours talking about our lives. We steered clear of any more talks of our failures, but instead talked about good times. He was actually quite funny and had a ton of good stories from his time in the military. He had been in the Army and loved it, but left after he realized that he was missing out on his kids growing up. He hadn't wanted to miss out on any more, and even though the risk was still there with the security firm, he was still home most nights.

Cal was very easy to talk to, and I found myself opening up to him about my life and how I got where I am today. He paid close attention to everything I was saying, but he was also watching the monitors closely. He took his job very seriously. He also got up twice and did a perimeter check, making me promise to stay exactly where I was. I wasn't sure why, but I had no problem listening to Cal. Maybe it was because he already felt so much guilt over what had happened and I didn't want to add to that by doing something that would get me into further trouble. That being said, I really needed to consider what it would do to Sebastian if I ran off and did something that got me into trouble. All of these guys took their jobs to the extreme and I found myself feeling very bad for what I did to Sinner last night.

Somehow, I ended up on the couch during the early morning hours. I think I fell asleep at the table, so Cal must have brought me over to the couch. Sitting up, I stretched and let out a loud yawn when the aroma of coffee hit me. Oh, God. I needed coffee so bad. I walked into the kitchen and saw it was barely seven a.m. I needed some more sleep if my brain was going to process the details of the last few days. At least I had finally gotten a shower last night. Two days of being smelly was not something I was shooting for.

As I walked over to the coffee pot, I saw Cal out of the corner of my eye. After I poured, I turned to see him staring at me, trying to hold in laughter.

"What?"

"Nothing." He snorted a laugh and held his belly as he tried not to burst into laughter.

"What's going on?" I said as I stomped my foot. When he didn't answer, I stomped off to the bathroom and flipped on the light. Looking in the mirror, I let out a loud shriek. Booming laughter came from the other room as I turned on the water and scrubbed furiously at my face. Cal had drawn all over my face with what appeared to be marker. He made me look like the joker. My lips looked like they were extended to be wider. When scrubbing with soap and water didn't work, I dug around and found a washcloth to scrub with.

"What's going on? I heard screaming."

Sebastian opened the door and took one look at me before he pulled his lips between his teeth. His nostrils flared as he held in his laughter and his chest shook. Finally, he just turned away and went into the other room. I resumed my scrubbing, finding myself unsuccessful. Throwing down the washcloth, I let out a growl before stomping back into the kitchen. At this rate, Cal would be lucky if I didn't stomp a hole in the floor.

"I need an internet connection."

"I'm sorry. Clients aren't allowed access to the internet. It's a security thing," Sebastian said.

"If you don't give me access right now, I will pull a Lorena Bobbitt on you!"

Both men took a step back as their faces paled and Sebastian motioned for me to take a seat at the computer. He quickly pulled up the internet and asked me to limit my searches, not entering anything that could identify myself.

I quickly looked up solutions for getting marker off of skin and then went in search of rubbing alcohol. Ten minutes later, I was successful in my search and marched back to the bathroom where I vigorously scrubbed my face raw. It took a long time and my face was stinging by the time I was done, but I was finally free of all the marker several hours later.

In that time, I missed a call from Becky at Reed Security where they had been discussing my case. I was just about to ask what she found out when she called back. Sebastian put her on speakerphone so we could all hear.

"What did you find out, Becky?"

"Well, I traced the five properties back to Mayor Johnson. They were all bought up years after they went out of business and he never did anything to develop the properties. I can't see what he would have possibly used them for."

"Okay, did you find anything on the account numbers?" Sebastian asked.

"What account numbers?" I interjected.

"I went through her whole computer and got all the account numbers that she had been tracing. I also went through the paperwork. She actually got a good head start on figuring out where the accounts broke the money up. The problem was that she didn't have access to where the money was before that."

"Excuse me? You went through my things? Who do you think you are? Who gave you permission to do that?"

"I did."

I spun on my heel and glared at Sebastian, then I walked up to him and poked him in the chest. "What were you thinking? Those were confidential documents and you had no right to go through my stuff."

"Technically, it's on my property, and since you weren't exactly being the most forthcoming with the details, and then you took off on your own, leaving us in the lurch. I decided to take matters into my own hands so that you didn't get one of us killed."

"Going through that stuff is not going to prevent someone from getting killed. It does, however, compromise my investigation to have so many fingers on it."

"Don't you think that if we could figure out who's after you, we could close this case? If I don't know, how am I supposed to fully protect you from potential threats? I don't even know who to look for other than large men that feel perfectly comfortable walking around with semi-automatics and shooting at us on public land."

His voice rose with every word he spoke. Feeling the fight go out of me, I looked at Cal for help. He shrugged and shook his head, as if to tell me that I didn't stand a snowball's chance in hell of winning this one.

"Fine, what did you find?"

"We're still working on tracing the money. It's gonna take some time because of how often the money seems to have been broken up. Whoever did this knew what they were doing."

"Well, obviously it was the mayor."

"That may be true, but until we have evidence of that, you don't have a leg to stand on."

She was right and I hated that. Becky was obviously very smart and knew what she was doing. I should be grateful for her help, but there was still a part of me that was upset that I wasn't getting to solve this on my own.

"What I need to do is get back in the mayor's office and search for more evidence."

"You want to walk into the lion's den after they've made several attempts on your life? Are you insane? Besides, after the last time you broke in, I highly doubt he's keeping anything in there," Sebastian said. He had a point and as much as I didn't want to admit it, I was running out of things to do on this story.

"Okay, well we still have that text to retrieve from my phone. Maybe that will give us something to go off of."

"We still have to wait another twelve hours before we can retrieve anything. Looks like you're going to have to wait it out here for a while."

I didn't mind waiting with Cal. He seemed like a genuinely good man and he was easy to talk to, but I didn't want to be stuck with Sebastian after last night. Even this morning, my attraction to him was just as strong as it was last night, and I didn't know if I could resist him just sitting around the house all day. And then if I made a move, I would have to hear more about how he couldn't have sex with me because it would distract him. Personally, I thought a little distraction would go a long way to help loosen him up.

Sebastian turned to Cal after hanging up with Becky. "Go get some shut eye. I'll take over the watch."

I rolled my eyes at them. Seriously, these two acted like we were going to have people raining down on us at any minute. I watched with morbid curiosity as Sebastian took out his five weapons. Yes, five weapons, and laid them out on the table and started taking them apart. He cleaned them and then reassembled them with such precision, I could only guess that he had done this most of his life.

"So, how long were you in the Marines?"

"Why do you want to know?"

"Well, you take apart all these weapons with such precision, I bet you could do it in your sleep. It just made me wonder about you."

He stopped what he was doing and looked at me with his steely gaze as if he was assessing me. "Let's be clear on one thing. Anything that I or any of my employees tells you is strictly off the record. Are we clear?"

"Yes."

"I was in the Marines for ten years."

"Where were you stationed?"

"Mostly in Iraq and Afghanistan."

"So, how did you become an officer? Doesn't that take a lot of time?"

"I went to college and in my third year I attended OCS at Marine Corps Base Quantico."

"What's OCS?"

"Officer Candidates School."

He spent the next hour telling me about his time at the Candidate School and then some about his time in the military. It was fascinating to hear first hand about someone's experiences in the military. Most men didn't want to talk about it, because the things they saw and did were not easy to explain to people. I had yet to find one service member who wanted to tell me their experiences. Sebastian however, seemed to genuinely love his time in the Marines. He didn't hold back when he talked about things that happened, though he didn't always give me details. When he got to how he got injured, his eyes grew distant as he told me about that day.

"We were out doing a security patrol that day. There was intel that some of the villagers had joined the insurgents. So we went out to check the town for any unusual activity and make sure the town was secure from the rebels that wanted to come in and take over. A kid, maybe nine or ten, ran by me, screaming something in Pashto. I never learned the language, just a few words here and there, so I didn't understand him. He stood in the doorway of the building we used to have meetings with the leaders in the area. We were trying to build a good relationship with the people and help them resist the insurgents. Anyway, he pulled off this wrap he had on and strapped to his chest was a bomb."

Sebastian stared off into space for a minute as he relived that moment in his mind. The haunted expression on his face told me how much he wished he could have done more. "He looked so scared. I could tell it wasn't something he wanted to do, but over there, some kids grow up thinking that if they blow us up, they're honoring their cause." He shook his head and continued quickly. "Anyway, I tried talking him down and I kept taking small steps toward him, thinking that I could break through to him. When I was close enough, *boom*."

He used his hands to mimic an explosion. Then, he went back to checking over his weapons, even though he had already done it several times since we had been sitting here. I couldn't help but think about how good of a story this would be. Not just the story of the explosion, but his whole experience. People in the United States would never understand what war was like until they could experience it themselves. A story like this would help people understand and maybe not be so judgmental when soldiers came home.

"Have you ever thought about telling your story?"

He stiffened and I knew I was treading on dangerous ground. "I just did."

"No, I mean, like in a book or something."

Cold eyes snapped to mine and the menacing look on his face told me not to proceed, but I wanted him to understand that it wasn't just about sales or recognition for me. He had a story that people needed to hear and understand.

"Look, I'm not saying that you should do a tell all or anything, but don't you understand what hearing that story would do for the American people? To understand what you went through? I just think—"

"Don't think. I didn't ask you to write a book on me. I told you that in confidence and it better stay that way. It's one thing to tell you, it's another to have you go out and share my secrets and thoughts with the world."

"I would never—"

He stood suddenly and leaned over me, causing me to lean back as far as I could in my chair. I could feel his warm breath on my face as he breathed heavily. His menacing glare sent shivers down my spine, and for the first time, I saw the lethal man that stood before me. He had been deceptive in exactly how scary he could be, but I fully understood now. Swallowing hard, I nodded. He didn't need to say anything. I perfectly understood what he was not saying and I didn't want to end up at the bottom of a river by the mayor or by Sebastian.

Shoving away from the table, he walked outside, presumably to do another perimeter check. When the front door slammed, I finally took my first deep breath and realized that my hands were shaking. Yeah, I shouldn't have pushed the man.

Figuring that it was best to just stay out of his way for the rest of the day, I headed into the living room when my stomach let out a loud growl of protest. I had been so caught up in the phone call and then Sebastian's story that I had completely forgotten about breakfast. Not knowing if Sebastian had eaten yet, I made a huge plate of scrambled eggs and fried up all the bacon I could find. Then I popped some toast in the toaster and slathered on some butter. When I was done, I did up the dishes and covered the leftovers for Sebastian.

Sighing, I walked to the living room and snuggled up on the couch. I had really pissed him off, and since he hadn't come back inside since he walked out close to forty-five minutes ago, I'd say he was still pissed and trying to get out his frustrations so he didn't kill me. After all, he wouldn't get paid if I was dead.

I HAD FALLEN asleep while I was thinking about how badly I had pissed off Sebastian, and when I woke, it was one in the afternoon. It wasn't surprising that I had slept again. I had barely slept the night before, and the night before that hadn't been much better. This story was starting to wear on me and it had only been a few days. I needed to get to the bottom of this before I got myself killed or died of exhaustion. There was nothing to do until I could recover that text though.

A lot of people assumed that reporters found some incriminating piece of information and followed it to something else equally incriminating and voila, a story was born. So not true. It was a lot of work and usually took weeks to put together the whole story. Sure, if I wanted to get a few small runs on the story, I could break bits and pieces of the information I had gathered, but one of two things would happen. One, it wouldn't be enough to catch any wind and the story would die. Or two, other reporters would start sniffing around and I would miss out on being the reporter to break the story. No, being the first to report was not the most important. That would be having all the correct facts. Still, it always looked better if you were the first.

As I was ruminating over how I was going to get everything I needed to finish this story, Sebastian walked into the living room with a tray of sandwiches and some bottles of water. I also spied a bag of baked potato chips, which happened to be my favorite.

"Peace offering?"

He held up the tray a little before stepping toward me and setting the tray on the table in front of us. I gave him a small smile before picking up the bag of chips and tearing it open. I devoured about half the bag before I realized that he was staring at me.

"What?" I said around a mouthful of chips.

He shook his head with wide eyes. "I've just never seen a woman put away so many chips in such a short amount of time. Well, if you don't count eating contests."

"I like my chips and these happen to be my favorite."

"Well, you can thank Cal for them. He ran out this morning while you were sleeping and loaded up on food."

"Ah. I was wondering about that. I didn't think you would store groceries here all the time. Unless, of course, you use this place on a regular basis?"

"Nice try."

"What?"

"Fishing. You think I don't know that you're trying to get information out of me?"

"I don't see what the big deal is. You already told me a bunch of stuff about you earlier."

"That was about me and my time in the military. This is about this safe house and if I started telling you about how we use it and how we operate, it would compromise the safety of future clients."

"Only if I were to tell someone about it, which I wouldn't."

"Can you be sure about that? What if you were being tortured?"

"Fine. I see your point. I don't think I would stand up well under torture. I can't stand to be tickled. I would cave in less than five seconds."

He stopped eating and looked at me. "Then how does that work for you to have sources? I looked into you. You've spent some time in jail protecting their identities."

"Torture is not the same thing as jail, and I never did much time. My editor must have some pretty good friends, because I've never spent more than a few days in jail."

"That's a little unheard of, isn't it?"

I shrugged. "It depends on what kind of case is being presented. One of mine was a pretty high profile case, and I was shocked that he was able to get me released so quickly, so he must have some friends in high places."

"So, what inspired you to become a reporter?"

"My parents died in a car accident when I was a teenager. The cops said that it was reckless driving on their part, but they didn't know my parents. My mom was driving my dad home from a doctor's appointment and she was a really slow driver."

"People drive faster than they mean to all the time and don't realize it. It's not impossible to consider."

"Yes it is. My mother watched the speedometer like a hawk when she drove. She never went over the speed limit and actually usually drove a few miles under. People used to tell her she was going to cause an accident because she accelerated so slowly."

"Okay, well I still think it's a possibility."

"I have proof for you."

"Okay, let's hear this so-called proof."

"This one time, she came home from the store and was in tears. She said a cop pulled her over for going seventy in a fifty-five. We all thought someone had died with how hard she was crying. Anyway, she told the cop that she never drove over the speed limit and the cop insisted she had. She started crying and the cop finally let her off with a warning. She cried the whole way home and then sobbed to us for a good ten minutes about how she wasn't speeding and how dare they accuse her of doing so. I heard that story until the day she died. She couldn't let it go that a cop would accuse her of something so horrible."

Sebastian looked at me skeptically for a minute, sure that I was pulling his leg, but when I stared him down with a pointed look, he finally conceded that I was right.

"Okay, so she never sped or drove recklessly. What happened after that?"

"I insisted they look into other causes for their accident, but the police insisted it was an open and shut case. I tried for a year to get someone on the police department to look into it, but I never had any luck. I didn't even know where to start with an investigation, but I decided that I wouldn't let that stop me. I went to school for journalism and took some criminal investigation classes, then started at the paper after I graduated. I never got the chance to look into my parents' case, but I didn't want that to happen to another family. So, I investigate stories that I think get overlooked. Not all of them are big conspiracies. Some are small and really only affect one or two people, but I feel better knowing that people got the answers they needed."

"So, after your parents died, who did you live with?"

"I went to stay with my grandparents. They live back in Kansas, but I knew that Kansas wouldn't give me what I wanted, so I moved here when I got the job offer."

"And what do your grandparents think of your job? Do they know how much trouble you get into?"

"Trouble? I don't get into trouble."

He smirked at me and then finished eating his sandwich. After I polished off the bag of chips, I ate my own sandwich.

"Do you think I could borrow a laptop?"

"For what?"

"Something about the mayor owning those properties isn't sitting right with me. It doesn't make sense that he would buy old, dilapidated properties and sit on them for years. I need to do some digging and find out why he bought them. There have to be some city records that would shed some light on why those properties are of importance."

"If I let you have a computer, you don't go on social media, e-mail, the paper's website, anything that could potentially lead someone to you. Do you understand that? Nothing that's connected to you."

"I swear. I'm just going to search through city records and try to find anything I can on those properties."

"Alright. Follow me and I'll get you set up."

CHAPTER 7

SEBASTIAN

Maggie had been sitting in the other room for most of the afternoon working on the company laptop. I heard her sigh every once in a while, her frustration building with every moment she didn't find something. If she didn't get a break on this story soon, she would go off and do something crazy again. I didn't think I could take too much more of her brand of crazy, so we were going to have to wrap this case quickly.

Cal and I had been working in the kitchen for the last few hours. He was keeping an eye on the monitors and doing the perimeter checks, while I worked on stuff from the office. Luckily, this house was set up so that we had a direct link to the office, and as long as Becky was there to patch me in, I could work from here. Some of the other safe houses were completely off the grid with no connection to Reed Security. Those were only used if we needed to be one hundred percent off the radar. Since I didn't think anyone had linked me to Maggie yet, it was safe to say we were well protected here.

"Sebastian, you've got to hear this!"

Maggie came running into the room with the laptop in hand, looking like she had just gotten her hands on the Hope diamond. She plopped the laptop down on the table in front of me and pointed at the screen. "Look at that!"

I scanned the screen, but I didn't have the first clue what she was showing me. Show me military plans, weapons specs, security software, or any number of other things and I could tell you all about them, but this government mumbo jumbo? I had no clue.

"Freckles, you're gonna have to tell me what I'm looking at here."

"Ugh. You were supposed to look at it and then look up at me in surprise and say, 'Wow, Maggie. You're a genius. Great find'."

"Well, why don't you just tell me and I'll wow you when you're done explaining it."

"Fine. Take all the fun out of it. Okay, so I told you I thought it was strange that he bought up those properties and then didn't do anything with them for the past ten to twenty years."

"Right."

"Well, the city is required to disclose all developmental projects so that when the city needs to vote, the citizens are aware of how those projects affect them and make objections if they don't approve."

"Okay, I'm following you so far."

"Well, it turns out that lately, Cassidy Redevelopment Agency has been sniffing around a few of the mayor's properties as well as some he doesn't own. They've put forth plans to the city to take over some of those properties through eminent domain. Up until now, the mayor has thwarted their attempts and held them off, but the city council likes the plans that Cassidy has put forth."

"Has he given any reason for not approving the redevelopment? I mean, are the plans bad for the city?"

"No. In fact, Cassidy wants to turn the properties into community centers, soup kitchens, and job training centers. See all the buildings are in poorer communities. The community centers would help with families that can't afford extra activities for kids, and would help keep them off the streets. The soup kitchens are self explanatory. The job training centers wouldn't just be for job training. They would also be used for GED classes and testing. It would really help these poorer communities out, yet the mayor has found a way to keep them at bay for now. However, with eminent domain, Cassidy just needs the city's approval that the redevelopment would help the community. The mayor doesn't really have a leg to stand on."

"Doesn't eminent domain require the redeveloper to pay the owner for the land they take over."

"It does. So he would get most of his money and since he hasn't done anything with the properties so far, he wouldn't be losing out. Which begs the question, what is it about these properties that has the mayor fighting this?"

"You said that the city likes the plans, though. Is he starting to lose favor because he's against this?"

She snorted and rolled her eyes. "The mayor hasn't been in favor for a while now, but he keeps getting voted in because he has a long reach. I think that this may be the tipping point, though. By blocking this from happening, he's hurting the city. Cassidy isn't talking about displacing families or closing down businesses. They're only planning on using dilapidated properties, tearing them down and rebuilding, and providing for the community."

"How does this affect the city financially? Could he be blocking it because the costs are too high?"

"The city doesn't have the funds for a project like this. Remember I told you there's a budget oversight committee? This is part of what they're supposed to be looking into. There's not enough funding for emergency services to expand, let alone fixing up the community. From what I can see, Cassidy got several wealthy Pittsburgh business owners to donate to the project. It's a huge tax write off and they get a lot of free press."

"Okay, so what do you want to do from here?"

"I want to get back on those properties and check them out. There has to be something about them that makes the mayor not want to let them go."

"I really hate that idea. You do remember what happened when we went to the property in Wilkinsburg, right?"

"You remember what we found, right?" she countered.

There was no denying there was something hidden at that first property, and if I was a betting man, I would guess it was a body. Whether it was there when the mayor bought the property or appeared after was unknown and would remain that way until we could prove there actually was one. Still, if there was a body there, there was no guarantee the mayor put it there, but if he did, that made this case all the more dangerous.

Cal who had been quietly taking it all in finally spoke up. "If you take her to one of these properties, you're gonna want to go at night. Hopefully, no one will notice our vehicle then. We could park down the road and walk the rest of the way."

"First of all, parking down the road isn't any safer than parking in front. In these areas, the SUV would get stolen faster on the side of the road than in front of an abandoned building. Second, I never said you were coming with us."

As much as having backup would be nice, I still didn't trust him to watch my back. God, I was torn. I wanted so badly to trust him again. I knew he was a good man and I wanted to believe that what he did was a one time thing, but my gut was still churning over what happened.

"He's coming with." Maggie spoke up so fast that my head whipped in her direction.

"I don't believe I asked for your input."

"You may not have, but I trust him. And let's face it, we could have used the help last time. Well, the last few times. I say that he comes with."

Fuck, she was right. I needed him there as backup. "Fine. He comes with. Freckles, go get some sleep. We'll leave at twenty-three hundred. I need to work out some details with Cal."

Thankfully, Maggie didn't argue. She must have sensed that she got her victory and should leave it at that. After she headed upstairs, I turned to Cal and glared hard.

"I swear to God, you fuck me over on this and no one will find your body." He gave a curt nod, knowing that I would make good on my threat if he double crossed me.

"I need to try and retrieve some data from Maggie's phone before we leave. She said that it was something about a bar. Maybe we can find the bar and figure out if her source sent the text."

"I sent Becky all the information on her source. Maybe something will ping and we'll find her."

"You really believe she's still alive?"

"No, but for Maggie's sake, I hope she is."

Cal and I set about loading up all the gear in the SUV for tonight. We had to be prepared for anything, and right now, we had an arsenal in the back of the SUV. We also loaded up with some shovels, flashlights, and some cameras. We were going to need evidence of what was there, especially considering that the mayor had some nasty people working for him. Any evidence we found tonight could very well be gone in the morning, along with us if we weren't careful.

I had just come in from loading the last of the equipment when I saw Maggie in the kitchen with Cal. She was laughing with him about something and I felt anger build in my chest. The way she lightly touched his shoulder and threw that strawberry blonde hair over her shoulder brought the green eyed monster out to fight.

"Freckles." I didn't shout, but the bite I inflected in my tone caused her head to whip around. She looked confused by my tone, as if she didn't realize that I might be pissed at her flirting with my employee hours after I had my hand buried in her pussy. I motioned her over to me with a finger and then grabbed on to her bicep, leading her into the other room.

"Ouch. Do you want to tell me why you're dragging me around like I was naughty? I literally just came downstairs. I've been in the kitchen for all of two minutes. There's nothing I could have done to piss you off in that time."

After we were far enough away from Cal's ears, I shoved her up against the wall and caged her in with my hands on either side of her head.

"Were my fingers not enough for you last night?" I said as I leaned in close to whisper in her ear.

"What are you talking about?" She tried to push against my chest, but it was useless. I wasn't going anywhere.

"I mean that less than twenty-four hours ago, I had my fingers all over your pussy and now you're in there flirting and touching Cal. Do I need to give you a reminder?" I whispered as I lightly trailed my fingers down the front of her shirt and down over her crotch. I could feel her heat through her jeans and I latched on to her, causing her to moan.

"I...I don't...why would you think I.. .have a thing for Cal?"

I massaged my fingers around her pussy, holding back a groan as she twitched beneath my hand. "You were touching him and flicking your hair around. You were flirting with him."

"I was...shoving my hair...oh God...out of my face. I touched him in a...fr...friendly way."

"That better be all it was. You are mine. This pussy is mine. Do you get that?"

"I thought you didn't...want to t-touch me?"

"When this case is over..." I leaned forward and captured her mouth in mine as I worked my hand faster over her pussy. Moments later, her legs were squeezing my hand tight as she came. I swallowed her moans as I plunged my tongue deeper into her delicious mouth. When I pulled back, her cheeks were flushed and she was breathing hard.

"Maggie, I got your phone... Oh shit. Sorry. Uh— Never mind."

Cal walked back into the kitchen and Maggie turned about ten shades redder. She looked down as she nervously laughed, but I continued to watch her face, memorizing every detail for my dreams. This woman was a walking fantasy in every way. She had a great body and beautiful, long hair that I wanted to wrap around my fist as I pounded into her from behind. If I didn't walk away now, I was going to have to run upstairs for a few minutes and we had more important things to do right now. I gave her one last kiss before I pulled back again.

"Mine."

I turned and walked back into the kitchen where Cal was going over the information he was able to retrieve from Maggie's cell phone.

"What did you find?"

"Well, she won't be able to get all her information back, but I was able to retrieve her text messages. I got the number it was sent from and the message itself."

Maggie walked back into the kitchen looking more composed than she had a few minutes ago. "Were you able to get the message?"

"Yep. The Steel Bar and the bartender's name is Tom. I think we should head over there first and check it out. If anyone was looking at your phone records, it's possible they found this number and already talked to the owner of the phone. Who's your carrier?"

"Verizon."

"Verizon keeps text message content for three to five days. If they were able to get into your records, they could already have the information."

"Alright, let's load up and get over to the bar. Cal, you grab directions. Freckles, back seat."

"I want to sit up front."

"No. I need the extra set of eyes up front and you aren't trained."

She let out a huff, but did as I said and got into the backseat. When we arrived at the bar, it was just around ten and the place was packed enough that we shouldn't stand out too much. Maggie and I made our way over to the bar, as Cal watched the door. While the crowd helped us blend, it could also be more difficult to get out with all the people around. It was a crapshoot. The crowd would either aid in our escape by allowing us to sneak out, or we could get caught in the crowd and potentially put more people in danger. Either way, we needed to find out what Tom the bartender had, if anything.

"Hey, I'm looking for Tom," I asked the bartender that was currently pouring drinks.

"Who wants to know?"

"Maggie." Freckles just jumped right in, again. No thought that giving her name could put her in danger or give a heads up to anyone keeping an ear out. The bartender continued to pour drinks, flicking his eyes occasionally to us.

"Not here. Meet me in the alley in ten."

He handed us two beers and walked away without another word and went to pour more drinks for other patrons. Grabbing Maggie by the arms, I pulled her away from the bar and sat down at an open table with our drinks.

"Pretend to drink your beer, but don't drink it. We need clear heads."

She nodded and pretended to sip her beer.

"Next time, let me do the talking."

"He's meeting with us, isn't he?"

"Did you stop to think that it could be a trap, or that someone could be watching and waiting for you to show? You have to think about these things instead of running full steam ahead all the time."

"Look, I'm a reporter and I go after stories. Sometimes it's dangerous, but that's part of the job."

"You still don't get it. That's why I'm here, to keep you safe. I take my job very seriously and do whatever I can to protect my clients, but if you keep going off and doing your own thing, you're going to get us killed. We do things my way for a reason."

We sat in silence for another few minutes before I grabbed her hand and pulled her to the door, walking on the left side of her. Cal took up the right side as we headed out the door.

"We're meeting in the alley. Grab the SUV and keep close in case we need a quick getaway."

"Copy that."

Cal walked away and I continued down toward the alley with Maggie. I kept her as close to the wall as possible and continued on her left side. When we reached the back of the bar, Tom was just stepping outside.

"You're Maggie, Danielle's friend?"

"Yes."

Technically not true. From what Maggie told me, she had only met Danielle when she contacted her about the story.

"Is she okay?"

"I don't know. How do you know Danielle?" Maggie asked.

"She's my best friend's daughter. He passed some years ago and I've been looking out for her ever since. She came to me and gave me something to give you. She said...she said that she got herself into something and she thought someone was after her."

He pulled a small baggie from his back pocket and fingered whatever was inside. "She said this was really important, that it was crucial I get this to you. What happened to her?"

He seemed to say that last part to himself. I wished that I could offer him some consolation, but the most I could think of was telling him that Danielle probably died quickly. That was really only a relief to people who knew all the different ways a person could be killed. Luckily, Maggie stepped in and saved me from making an ass of myself.

"Tom, I don't know what happened to Danielle. I was supposed to meet her the other night and we were going to protect her, but she never showed. I promise you, we'll continue to look for her and we won't stop."

"But you think she's dead."

Maggie tilted her head gently to the side and gave a sad look. "I do. If this is as important as she said, then she was probably killed because of it."

He nodded his head and sniffed. "Promise me you'll get the people that got to her."

"I promise."

He handed over the little baggie that I could now see held a flash drive. Maggie took it and then placed her hand over his and gave a squeeze. Tom turned and walked back into the building. I started pulling her down the alley. We were just about halfway back when someone started running up behind us. Turning quickly, I shoved Maggie against the wall with one arm while blocking the gun that our assailant was trying to raise with the other. I gave him a hard knee to the gut while I pulled the gun from his hand and pointed it at him. He had fallen to his knees to catch his breath and stayed down now that his own gun was pointed at his head.

"Who sent you?"

"Fuck off."

"I'll ask you one more time, who sent you?"

"You shoot me and they'll just send someone else to kill your pretty, little girlfriend. They'll do her just like they did the girl in the mayor's office."

While I knew enough not to let this guy bait me, Maggie apparently didn't. This guy was desperate and would do anything for a chance to live longer. If he let us believe that he had details that would extend his life, he might have a chance of escape. Of course, what really happened was he got a better opportunity when Maggie launched herself at him before I could stop her and attempted to hit him. She stepped right in front of me, effectively blocking any shot I had. As soon as I saw her move, I reached for her, but the asshole was quicker and grabbed her around the waist and pulled her in front of him.

Again, Maggie had created a huge problem, not seeing that the man was goading her into making a move. By jumping in front of me, it allowed the guy to either grab her or my gun now that she was creating a distraction. I was beginning to hate this woman.

The guy had his hand wrapped around her throat as he pulled her right up against his body, using her as a shield. Maggie's eyes were blazing with anger as she looked at me.

"Freckles, what the fuck? Do you think you can ever listen to me and do as I say?"

"I could have had him."

"Right, I can see that based on the fact that you're now being used as a shield."

"You could have warned me!"

"Warned you that he was going to use you? How would that have gone? Would you have liked me to stop beating his ass to protect you so that I could warn you first not to do anything stupid?

The guy was slowly slipping his head away from the cover of hers. I just needed him to move a little further so I could get a shot off. Maggie would hate me, but I would deal with that later.

"I wasn't being stupid! I was just about to lay down an ass whooping when I stumbled on my shoe!"

"You stumbled on your shoe? You do realize that stumbling on your shoe is about to get you killed, right?" I peered around Maggie's shoulder, looking the guy in the eye the best I could. "Do you see what I have to deal with?"

"Bitches be crazy."

"I hear ya, brother. Maybe I should just give her to you. I'm not sure she's worth the trouble anymore. I've already been paid for some of my services."

"I'm sure the mayor would pay quite a lot for you to hand her over. You could make the rest of your fee without the work."

Now that was interesting. Finally, we got some confirmation the mayor was after Maggie. I pretended to think about it for a minute.

"Twenty-five thousand."

"Hey! I'm worth more than that! You could at least have the decency to ask a little more for me."

I wasn't sure if Maggie was playing along or if she was just so pissed at me that she wasn't able to process the fact that she was being held by a killer.

"Fifteen. You're not gonna get a penny more for this bitch."

"The remainder of my contract is twenty. I'm not budging on that."

"You're seriously going to hand me over to this asshole?"

"Shut up," I yelled at the same time as her captor.

"Call him. I want confirmation before I hand her over. You're going to have him transfer the money while he's on the phone or the girl leaves with me. You get him to agree to twenty-five and I'll cut you in for a thousand."

He pulled out his phone and made the call. "Hey, Johnson, I got something you want, but if you want her, you're gonna have to pay. Twenty-five thousand. Yeah, he's right here and those are his demands."

"Tell him I'll throw in the flash drive for free."

"You asshole." Maggie was glaring daggers at me, but I kept my expression neutral and trained on the man behind her.

"You were supposed to help me! I trusted you. What was all that crap you've been spewing at me? That I was yours? You fucking bastard."

I had to stop her before she kept going or this deal wouldn't happen. "A better offer came along."

"I'm gonna destroy you. Somehow, I'm gonna get away from this asshole and I'm gonna bring you and your whole company down!"

She was struggling against the man as he gripped her tighter around the neck and continued to negotiate with whoever was on the phone. I stepped closer, needing to shut her up.

"Do you want a fucking bullet in the head right now?" I yelled in her face. Spit flew from my mouth as I put as much anger into it as possible. I gave a menacing glare and her face shuttered as realization hit, which was exactly what I needed.

"You want this deal to go through, I need a bank account."

I pulled out my phone and dialed Becky. "I need my offshore account information." I relayed the account number to the thug holding Maggie and waited for confirmation that the money had gone through. Satisfied I had gotten as much use out of this fucker as possible, I decided to end this charade.

"Give your boss a message for me."

The dumbass poked his head out from around Maggie, thinking that he was in the clear now. I didn't hesitate to pull the trigger and nail him right between the eyes. Maggie, standing right next to him, caught some spray from the explosion at the back of his head. His hand slid from her throat as he fell to the ground in a bloody mess. Without a second thought to the body now laying on the ground next to her, she whirled on me.

"I can't believe you asked so little for me. Is that really all you think I'm worth?"

I pulled her into my arms and kissed her like it was my dying breath. She tried to resist me at first, but then she was practically crawling up my body to get more of me. Cal's honk of the horn sounded from the other end of the alley and I slowly pulled away from her.

"That worked in our favor this time, but don't ever pull that crap again."

I pulled her after me before she could argue and deposited her in the back seat. I quickly dialed Becky as Cal drove toward our second location.

"Becky, trace the money. It should lead back to the mayor. We need a clean up crew at The Steel Bar in the alley." Ending the call, I turned back to Maggie. "So, if we bring you with us, do you think you can refrain from causing any more trouble?"

"I didn't cause that trouble. You were the one that wanted to sell me off to that guy."

"Yes, and I hopefully got a trace on his accounts that will help us with some other money trails. Good job keeping your cool back there, by the way."

She turned her accusing glare on Cal. "Why didn't you help out back there? You obviously saw what was going on."

Cal snorted. "What? With that pipsqueak? There's no way that Cap couldn't handle that guy. I knew he had a reason for not taking him out from the start."

"He could have had a knife to my throat for all you knew."

"He could have, but it still wouldn't have mattered. Cap would have handled him just fine."

"When you started arguing with me, it gave me the perfect

opportunity to either draw him out from behind you or prove to him that you're a pain in the ass that's not worth keeping around."

"Excuse me?"

"For his benefit, of course. You're not at all a pain in the ass."

"Sure, you say that now. What about the next time someone offers you money to hand me over."

"I'll be sure to ask for at least thirty next time."

OUR NEXT STOP was the property in the Strip District. It had once been a shipping company that was now out of business. The office building was a two story brick building that sat at the front of the property and behind were the abandoned shipping containers that sat empty. This company hadn't been used in over twenty years, and it didn't make sense because it could have been bought up and used by another shipping company, had it been bought years ago.

After Cal and I scoped out the property, we got out and led Maggie to the fence that could barely be considered locked.

"Why aren't we bringing supplies with us? I thought you guys loaded the SUV with gadgets for when we got to these properties?"

"If we find something, we'll go back for supplies. We're not going to walk around the property with shovels and cameras until we know there's something to go digging for. What we found at the other property could have been a fluke."

"Not likely."

"Should we have a repeat of what just happened in the alley? How about we try things my way for once."

"Fine."

I took up position on Maggie's left and Cal took the right after we slipped through the gate. The building had nothing to show for it. There was some office furniture and filing cabinets, but they were covered in a thick layer of dust and I highly doubted there was anything here to find. There were no dug up pieces of concrete like there were at the Wilkinsburg address, so we walked out through the shipping containers, again not finding anything. As we walked to the edge of the dock, I looked out on the water, trying to imagine what the mayor could possibly want with this property.

"I think we need to move on to another property. I'm not seeing anything here that will help us."

Maggie sighed as she stepped closer to the water. "Yeah. I think you're right. Damn. I was so sure that one of these properties would lead us to something."

"Well, we still have a few more properties to check out. Let's get back to the SUV and see what else we can find."

Cal and I took up our positions around Maggie once again and headed back to the truck. I really felt that luck was turning our way since we made it through this site with no trouble. I just hoped our luck held.

"WHAT IS THAT GOD AWFUL SMELL?" Cal asked as we stepped into the brewery.

"It smells like drain cleaner mixed with something."

I swung the flashlight around the room looking for anything that would hint at what was causing the smell. Maggie started to walk around me, but I put my arm up to block her from passing me.

"Stay behind me."

She didn't argue and stayed behind me as I walked around the large space. As we moved further into the brewery, the smell got stronger and stronger. Maggie started gagging beside me.

"I think I'm gonna be sick. That smell is horrible."

"Put your shirt over your nose and breathe through your mouth."

"How can you stand the smell?"

"In the military, you learn how to work with smelly conditions. You never know what you're going to encounter, and puking all over the place isn't really an option when you're out on a mission."

We stepped into a large room filled with beer vats. This was where the smell was coming from. It had to be. My eyes started watering the further we moved into the room. Shining the flashlight across the room, I almost missed the large mess on the floor beneath one of the vats.

"Over here."

Cal swung his flashlight over to where mine was and we slowly walked forward. On the floor was a large, congealed mess that sure as hell didn't resemble any beer I ever drank. Maggie spun and threw up all over the floor and then continued to dry heave as Cal and I moved forward to try and figure out what was there.

"Cal, head back and get the lab kit. We need samples to try and figure out what this is. I would say this is maybe a week or two old."

"On it, Cap."

"I'm going back with him. I can't stay here."

"I'll go with you. You can't just stay out there by yourself."

We all walked back out into the night air and breathed deep, cleansing breaths. Cal quickly headed back to the SUV and came back carrying a lab case with the necessary equipment.

"Make sure you get as many samples as you can. When we get back to the safe house, we'll have one of the guys come pick up the samples and take them to the lab. They can run a gas chromatograph, and hopefully tell us what this is."

"A gas chroma— what?"

Cal stepped in. He knew all about this stuff since he studied chemical science when he was in college. When he was in the military, he was the explosives expert in his squadron. That was probably why the serial killer had chosen to kill his family in an explosion. It was poetic in its own way. Cal hadn't mentioned explosives since that day a year ago, even when a team member specifically went to him for aid on a case. He just walked away. He never expected the thing he loved to be what eventually killed his family.

"Gas chromatography is used for separating and analyzing compounds that can be vaporized without decomposition."

"Homie say what?"

"Basically, you take a sample, you heat it up, and you shine the light through the smoke of the sample because every particle reflects light on a different wavelength. From the different wavelengths you can determine what particles are in the sample."

"Okay, I didn't really understand that either, but what you're saying is that we'll know what was in that congealed mess on the floor."

"Hopefully. If I'm right and that's some kind of acid, there may not be anything left to identify," Cal said.

Maggie sighed and rubbed a hand across her forehead. She looked exhausted now that I took a closer look at her. We hadn't really taken a break since I killed that guy next to her in the alley. Cal could see it too and raised an eyebrow in her direction.

"Why don't you guys head back to the SUV and I'll go collect the samples. It should only take me a few minutes."

I didn't like leaving a teammate alone, but Maggie wasn't going to go back into that building with the smell, and I had a feeling she was going to be done here in a few minutes.

"Sounds good. If you're not back in ten, I'm coming in to get you. Don't shoot me."

His face looked remorseful as I spoke those last words, and it was only after I saw his face that I realized he thought I could actually think he would shoot me. I was going to have to fix that. Trust worked both ways and the more I let him know that I didn't trust him, the more he would wonder if I really had his back. It would lead to big mistakes while on duty if I didn't solve this once and for all.

"I'll be right back."

Cal went back into the building and I kept watch on our surroundings. Maggie had slumped against the wall and looked like she could barely hold herself up. I thought about suggesting she sit down, but the ground was wet and muddy.

"Cal's a good guy, you know."

"What? Since when do you know anything about him?"

"Since I spent the last day with him. While you were sleeping I talked with him. He's a really good guy."

"And did he tell you what happened?"

"Yes, but that's not who he is. He made a bad call and it cost him everything."

"His bad call almost got his teammates killed."

She nodded, but stayed silent. The more she stayed silent, the more I felt I needed to explain myself. I really did know that Cal was a good person, and I guess agreeing with Maggie was the first step in accepting what happened.

"I know that Cal is a good man. The choice he had to make was difficult, and while I wish that he had chosen to trust us, I understand why he did what he did. Now, he's paying for those decisions every day."

"By losing the trust of his brothers."

"No, because he lost his family. Trust can be earned back, but he can never get his family back."

Cal returned a few minutes later carrying the lab case. "I got as many samples as I could."

"Good. Let's get back to the safe house, then."

"We aren't going to check out the other properties?"

"Not tonight. The test takes a long time to perform. The sooner we get it to the lab, the sooner we'll get the results."

If I told Maggie that I wanted to head back because she was exhausted, she would only argue with me. This gave her a reason to go back to the safe house. We desperately needed some answers.

"Besides, once we're back at the safe house, we can open the flash drive and see what's on there."

"That's right. Let's get going."

I should have kept my mouth shut. Maggie just got a second wind and I had a feeling none of us would be sleeping tonight.

CHAPTER 8

MAGGIE

"Can't you hurry up? I would like to see what's on the flash drive today."

"Just relax," Sebastian said as he worked on testing the flash drive. "I'm not taking the chance that this flash drive is compromised. If there's a virus on here, it could crash our hard drive or send a worm into our system. I'm not risking the security of my business for fast results."

Cal was outside doing a perimeter check and then was taking the first shift sleeping. Sebastian insisted on being the one to stay up with me while I went over the files on the flash drive. I paced behind him for another ten minutes as he ran every check he could possibly think of on the flash drive. My patience was wearing thin, and I think he realized that and was stalling on purpose.

"Alright, let's open this up and see what's on it."

He clicked on the flash drive icon and it slowly loaded.

"Come on. Come on."

"Calm down, Freckles. You'll give yourself a conniption."

"Ah!" I screamed as a spreadsheet appeared on the screen. I shoved him over so that I could see the screen better. "Move over."

The spreadsheet appeared to be a list of account numbers and names attached to those accounts. In the next column was a list of job descriptions and then dates accompanying them.

"Okay, so it looks like these are lists of people and jobs that were performed. I don't understand what the jobs are, though. Does this make sense to you?"

The jobs were listed as "cleaner" or "filler". If this was a list of maid's service or dentistry, it was useless.

"I'm guessing that cleaner means a clean up crew."

"Like, he hired someone to come clean up for an event?"

"Highly unlikely. Did you hear me on the phone with Becky when we were leaving the alley?"

I tried to remember back, but it was all a blur. I was so focused on not focusing on what happened that I blocked some things out.

"Not really. I think I was trying to think about anything but what had happened."

He gave me a sympathetic look. "Sorry about that. I should have been a little more understanding. I forget that clients aren't used to dealing with this stuff on a daily basis. This is just another day at the office for all of us."

"It's fine. I'm not gonna break down or anything, I just momentarily blocked out what was going on."

"Well, I called Becky when we were leaving and asked her to send a clean up crew. To us, that means to clean up the situation we just left behind."

"How did she know where to send them?"

"All of our phones are monitored at all times. We always need to be aware if someone on the team is in trouble."

"Oh. Okay, so if 'cleaner' is a clean up crew, what is a filler?"

"That I don't know. We don't have a filler, but I'm guessing you can figure out what 'exterminator' is."

"Yeah. I think I can guess. Can you print off this sheet for me? I'd like to do some research on the mayor's associates. I need to link the time that these people were hired with what was going on at the time."

"Sure. Hey, wait. She wrote some notes for you on the bottom."

"Let me see."

MAGGIE, I found this on the mayor's computer when I went snooping earlier. I know you said to stay out of it, but I had an opportunity and I took it. Also, I overheard a conversation he was having with Nicholas Webb, his right hand man. Apparently, they're looking at selling Mayor Johnson's properties to the city so that Cassidy Redevelopment doesn't get their hands on the properties. Webb said that they could control the contracts if they sold them to the city instead of to Cassidy Redevelopment. I'm not sure what that means, but when I stepped into the office, they were quick to hide files they were looking at. I would suggest looking into the contractors the mayor has used in the past. Webb seemed to be very interested in that.

"DAMN. That's probably what got her killed. I bet she didn't cover her tracks and the mayor found out that she was snooping."

"I told her not to look any further. I didn't want her involved. Why didn't she listen?"

"Probably the same reason you don't listen to me."

Ignoring his comment, I got into work mode and started thinking of all the things I needed to start researching.

"Okay, I'm going to need a notebook, different colored pens, and a laptop."

"Why don't you just use the laptop for your notes?"

I sighed at him. "Because I like to write things down on paper. It helps me to sort out my thoughts. Plus, I use different colored pens for different thoughts. It helps me stay organized."

"You do realize they have this thing called a toolbar that allows you to change the color you type in?"

"This is the way I do things. Are you going to get me what I need or not?"

He held up his hands and started walking away. "Fine. Fine. I'll get you the stuff you want. I'm just saying, it seems like extra work."

When he got back with all my stuff, I sat down and got to work researching. There was so much to go over that I wasn't sure where to start. I completely forgot about Sebastian as I dug in and started researching.

I decided to start by cross-referencing the names and dates with things that were going on at the time politically. There were a few dates that I could find absolutely nothing to match. It made me wonder what these people were being secretly hired and paid for that the mayor wouldn't want anyone to find out about. I continued checking dates and what I found was very interesting.

The first name that matched a major event in the city was Rudy Moore. He was a private investigator that specialized in blackmail. I knew this because he had become quite well known a few years back when he dug up dirt on a lawyer to make him throw the case he was going to trial for. All would have gone well, but the person that hired Moore got drunk one night and bragged to a bar full of prominent citizens how he had hired Moore to blackmail a lawyer to get his way. The news of how thorough Moore was spread like wildfire, and eventually, he had to move his practice since he was so well known.

Moore was listed in the ledger as a mediator. I snorted at the name because Moore was less mediator and more extortionist. I supposed if you were trying to keep a secret ledger, you wouldn't want to put exactly what that person did for you.

The first major event I came across was back in 1992 when big box stores wanted to build in the city. Many citizens were against it, not wanting a box store to drive out the small business owners. The citizens fought back on it for months until Mayor Johnson announced the city council had come to an agreement with the companies that would ensure that local construction companies would handle construction and all supplies would be bought locally. With plans for several box stores to be built, RND construction, the local construction company that was hired, announced that with all the projects they would be undertaking, they would be hiring several hundred more workers.

After that, the uproar in the city settled down and everyone except for the local businesses were happy with the new plans. City council members applauded the mayor for striking a deal that would not only create new jobs, but also give more business to local companies.

From a first glance, it appeared the deal the mayor made was a good deal for the city. So what did the mayor get out of this? If Moore was part of this deal, why was it necessary to hire him in the first place? If citizens were against the deal, perhaps city council members weren't for this deal going through. Maybe they needed some convincing.

I made a note to check into city council members at the time and try to find anyone that changed their minds suddenly on the deal. While I had no proof that Moore was connected to this deal, it seemed awfully suspicious that Mayor Johnson would hire a private investigator months before a major city deal went down.

Looking again at the ledger, I saw that Moore's name was listed several more times and I decided to look at those dates first. The next date was 1996. I set about some research and spent the next several hours looking into the dates where Moore was listed and tried to connect the dots.

When I looked up from my work, rays of sunlight were streaming in through the windows. I had worked the rest of the night and was finally feeling the effects of sleep deprivation. I got up and went over to the coffee pot, needing a pick me up if I was going to finish working on this.

"You know, sleep would be better for you than caffeine."

Sebastian's deep timber made me jump, and I spilled coffee grounds all over the counter.

"Would you quit sneaking up on me?"

"I don't think walking into the kitchen is sneaking up on you. You've been up all night. Why don't you go lie down and get some sleep. Your research can wait a few hours."

"Not if I hope to find Danielle."

"Freckles, I think we both know that Danielle is dead. Nothing you do is going to bring her back."

I turned and stared at him, crossing my arms over my chest. "I can at least catch her murderers."

"Yes, you can, but running yourself ragged isn't going to help. If you would just get some sleep, you could look at all this with fresh eyes and maybe make some headway."

"I've already found a ton of information."

"Okay." He stood there thinking for a minute. "How about we go lie down and I'll give you a back massage? You can tell me all about what you've found and then we'll get some sleep. When we get up, I'll help you with research."

Lying down sounded awfully appealing at the moment. My eyes felt like dirt was caked inside my eyelids and my hands were starting to shake from exhaustion.

"Fine. Let's go, but I want that back massage. No take backs."

"I wouldn't dream of it."

We headed up to the bedroom and sat down on the king size bed. It was nice and soft, just the way I liked it.

"Lay down on your belly."

I did as he said and felt my eyes drifting shut as he started to massage my back.

"So, tell me about what you've found."

"Mostly, I found that a private investigator was hired at the same time that some major events were taking place in the city. The first was when big box stores wanted to come into the city. The mayor brokered a deal that the citizens seemed to hate. Somehow, city council members were on board with it.

"The second event was when the city wanted to build new schools in poorer neighborhoods. Get this, one of the schools was going to be built on one of the mayor's properties. He managed to get all the bills blocked and proposed new locations for the schools. It didn't get a whole lot of media attention because the new locations were safer, so no one thought twice about the change in location."

"You know that's not really a smoking gun, right? None of that sounds too devious." Sebastian's hands worked down to the small of my back and brushed against the waistband of my pants, causing me to momentarily forget what we were talking about. His large, strong hands gripped my waist as his thumbs dug into my lower back, eliciting a moan of pleasure from me.

"Does that feel good?"

"Oh God, yes. Mmmm." I moaned as his fingers continued to trail over my skin, his touch becoming lighter as he moved his hands higher up, his fingers brushing the undersides of my breasts. Any traces of sleepiness vanished in that moment. My eyes were now wide open and my body was on fire with need. The small taste I had of him earlier was not enough to quench my thirst for him.

My moans must have had the appropriate effect on him because I felt him hardening against my ass. I pushed myself up to brush against him, hearing a low growl rumble from him.

"You're supposed to be telling me about what you found."

"You started it by touching my breasts."

I rolled underneath him so I was facing him. He could have easily stopped me if he wanted. He was a strong, powerful man, and I was scrawny next to him. I sat up slightly and pulled my t-shirt over my head. His eyes narrowed in on my breasts that were barely covered by my lacy bra. I scooted back on the bed to pull my legs out from under him and crawled back to him, straddling his lap.

"This isn't what we're supposed to be doing."

"Do you always do what you're supposed to?" I asked as I wrapped my arms around his neck. My fingers played with the hair at the nape of his neck as I leaned forward and kissed him. His arms wrapped around me as he deepened the kiss. His hands moved up my back and released the clasp of my bra. Slowly, he pulled the straps down my arms, his eyes widening as he took in my heavy breasts.

"We're supposed to be working," he said, swallowing thickly.

I thrust my breasts out as he leaned forward, capturing my taut nipple in his mouth. "I can multitask if you can."

He responded with a sharp bite to my breast. "Oh, God."

"You were saying?"

"Right. Work." He continued to kiss my breasts as I tried to regain my thoughts. "Um, so back to the schools. Uh, ahh... The city hired RND construction, the same company that did the work for the...um...uh...big box stores back in 1992."

"Keep talking."

He pushed me back on the bed and pulled my jeans down my body before standing and pulling his shirt over his head. He put his hands on the button of his jeans, but stopped to smirk at me. I stared at the well defined abs on his perfect body. He had scars, but that didn't detract from his glorious physique. My eyes trailed along the planes of his chest and followed the well defined V that led down to his hard, thick cock. I could see him straining against his jeans already.

"As much as I enjoy you ogling me, we're supposed to be working. If you stop talking, I stop undressing."

"Right. Um...Where was I?"

He popped the button on his jeans and started to lower the zipper. "You were saying, about the construction company that was hired for both jobs."

"Right." He lowered his jeans and I saw his erection jutting out from his boxers that molded to his muscled thighs. "The mayor's approval ratings started to fall when the citizens saw that the improvements were only helping people in neighborhoods that were doing well."

His boxers were off now and his hard length was bobbing up and down as he came back to the bed. I instinctively spread my legs for him and he settled between them. He took my mouth so possessively that I could barely catch my breath when he pulled away. His hot breath fanned across my face as he rocked his body against mine. His erection ran along my panties that were now drenched.

"I thought you didn't want to get involved with me? That I would be a distraction?"

"I decided I didn't fucking care. You're already a distraction, and not sleeping with you isn't going to fix that."

His hand skimmed over my stomach and down to my panties. His thick fingers brushed my clit and slowly circled over the bundle of nerves.

"Ahh!"

"You're so responsive. Tell me what you want. Do you want my fingers in your pussy?"

A shudder ran through my body at his words. I had never been with someone who talked dirty to me, and I wasn't sure how to respond.

"Yes."

"Do you want my cock in your pussy?"

"Yes."

"Tell me how much you want it."

"I...I..." My breathing was growing erratic as his fingers moved faster, pushing me toward orgasm.

"Do you want my cock pushing inside your tight pussy, pounding you until you scream my name?"

"Yes! Yes. I need it."

His fingers slipped beneath my panties and ran along my opening, only to drag the moisture back up to my clit and circle once again.

"Oh, fuck! I'm coming!"

My hips bucked and my knees pulled together as I came hard around his fingers. He continued to circle my nub as my body convulsed in pleasure. He barely gave me time to recover before he ripped my panties from my body and thrust inside me, then stilled.

"Goddamn, you're tight."

"Move. I need you to move."

"Give me a minute. I'll come if I move right now."

He took a few deep breaths, but I couldn't wait any longer. I started moving my hips, pushing and pulling as he groaned, his eyes rolling back in gratification. It didn't take long for him to start moving again. He fucked me hard and deep before flipping me over and pulling my knees up so he could fuck me from behind.

"Your ass is so sexy." He slapped one cheek as he continued to thrust inside me harder and faster. I could feel his cock deep inside me, every ram propelled me closer to ecstasy.

"Oh, shit. I'm gonna come."

"Me too. Oh, God. I'm coming!"

A few more deep thrusts and he pushed me over the edge, then pulled out and I felt his release on my back. Thank God he had enough sense to pull out since neither of us had thought to use a condom. I was on the pill, but with everything going on, I hadn't had time to go home and get my pills, and I most definitely wasn't ready for motherhood.

I laid with my head on the bed and my ass in the air as I recovered from what could only be described as the best sex I had ever had. Mind blowing, heart pounding, and completely orgasmic. I felt a warm cloth on my back wiping off the evidence of our little fuck fest and then a light brush of his lips against my back. Completely worn out, I decided now was a good time to close my eyes and go to sleep. I faintly registered him pulling me into his arms and pulling the covers over us before I drifted off to la la land.

I woke up in what must have been late afternoon because the sun was no longer shining through the window. I was laying on Sebastian's hard chest listening to the steady beat of his heart. I couldn't remember the last time I had spent the night with a man, let alone woke up in his bed wanting more. I was usually too wrapped up in stories to worry about when the next time was that I was going to get laid.

I used to think that women didn't need sex as much as men, but now I was thinking that I just hadn't been with a man that made me crave sex the way Sebastian did. Even just laying here with him, I wanted him inside me again. I wanted to feel his body moving against mine and feel his hard cock inside me. I wanted his cock in my mouth. That was something I had never really been too fond of before, but now I wanted to give it to Sebastian. I loved how he came undone when I wrapped my lips around his hard length.

"Are you thinking dirty thoughts?"

Startled out of my daydreaming, I looked up at the smirk on Sebastian's face. "Maybe. How did you know?"

"Your heart rate increased and your breathing was getting ragged. It was either that or a nightmare, but I knew you were already awake."

In a flash, he was on top of me, his face inches from mine. His dick was rubbing against my pussy. "Were you thinking of me? Of my cock inside you again?"

"Yes, but I was thinking about you in my mouth and how much I like it."

"Really? Well, I wouldn't want to deny you the pleasure of my cock."

A half hour later, Sebastian and I made our way to the shower and spent another half hour in there exploring each other's bodies. When we finally made it downstairs, I realized how hungry I was. My stomach growled at the lack of food, so I went to the fridge and started pulling out stuff for sandwiches. Cal was sitting at the bank of monitors again and was looking through my notes.

"You've got a lot of good stuff here, but I'm not seeing anything that points directly to the mayor as criminal."

"I know. I need something more. Right now, it all just looks suspicious. There has to be more to this story, though. Why would the mayor go to all the trouble of killing Danielle if she wasn't on to something?"

"We don't know for sure that she was killed."

Sebastian walked into the room and planted a kiss on my lips before moving to the fridge. I barely caught Cal's look of disbelief before he schooled his features. Apparently, either Cal had never seen Sebastian with a woman or his behavior was frowned upon. I was guessing it was the second one.

"Do you guys want me to make some sandwiches for you?"

"Two for me, please." Cal went back to looking at my notes.

"I'll help you," Sebastian said as he came up behind me. I suddenly felt uncomfortable with him being so intimate with me in front of Cal. If this was against the rules or something, I didn't want to flaunt it in his face. I sidestepped Sebastian and went back to the fridge for condiments.

"That's okay. Why don't you go sit down?"

He gave me a strange look, but nodded and sat down at the table with Cal.

"So, what else did you come up with?" He asked as he grabbed the notebook from Cal.

"Well, basically, there are several things that happened over the years and Rudy Moore was paid at the same time some of these things occurred."

"Okay, you told me about the box stores and the schools. What else?"

I started assembling the sandwiches as I told him what else I found. "Well, back in 2002, he raised taxes so the city could better fund the schools, but the citizens weren't on board after what happened with the schools being built in '96. Somehow, he got the bill passed and it came out later that the wealthiest would get all these tax breaks if they donated just a small amount to the school. Also, there has been some question over the years if all the extra money is going to the schools. The school districts don't feel they have benefited in any way from those tax increases."

"That still just sounds like dirty politics to me. Freckles, I'm sorry, but I'm not seeing a smoking gun here. You're gonna have to have something more substantial to have a real story here."

"Well, I haven't even got to the best part yet."

He waved his hand in a regal motion for me to continue. I brought the plates over to Cal and Sebastian and set them down, then went back for my own plate.

"There was one last event that I tied to Rudy Moore. In 2008, the city passed a huge infrastructure bill that allowed the city to raise taxes to repair roads and bridges. Again, the only ones that were fixed were in good neighborhoods. There is one thing that all of these events have in common. Can you guess what it is?"

"Rudy Moore."

"Not just Rudy Moore. It's who the city hires for every project. Rudy Moore was always hired by Mayor Johnson, but I can't directly link him to the projects that went on around the city. He was always listed as 'the mediator', which I can only assume means that he dug up dirt on city council members to sway them in the mayor's direction.

"The real link in all of this is who he hired to do the actual job. Despite the fact that other companies outbid and had better timetables, RND Construction was always hired for the job. RND was not the best option for the infrastructure job since they specialize in constructing buildings. There were other, more qualified companies that were cheaper to go with and would have finished the projects six months to a year earlier. Also, it was built into the contracts that RND could choose the subcontractors that they needed for other work, such as electrical and cement work."

"Concrete," Sebastian interrupted.

"What?"

"It's concrete. Cement is a binding agent in concrete. You pour concrete, not cement."

"Whatever, Mr. Know-it-all. The point is, these companies were hired for every job."

"Well, is that unusual for the city to hire to keep the jobs local?"

"Well, they may, but when they consider taxpayer dollars, they usually try to go with the lowest bid. RND has never been the lowest bid. It just seems like there's more to it. I'd like to look into it some more."

"Why do I get the feeling I'm not going to like this?"

"Okay, so I found a news article about an RND office worker that mysteriously vanished one day. Guess when that happened."

"Please, enlighten me."

"1992. The same year that the city made the agreement with the box stores. Her name was Cheryl Haynes. She was last seen at work, and no one can remember seeing her leave, but her car wasn't there. There were never any leads on her disappearance."

"So, now you think that the mayor had an office worker murdered?"

"Of course not. RND had her killed. I'm guessing she came across something she wasn't supposed to and was killed for it."

Sebastian leaned forward and rubbed his hands over his face. "Freckles, I really don't want to rain on your parade, but none of this sounds like evidence. It sounds more to me like you're seeing things you want to. People go missing all the time. That doesn't mean that Cheryl Haynes was murdered by RND."

"In 2008," Sebastian pinched the bridge of his nose as I continued. "A reporter went missing while investigating the infrastructure bill. I'm going to talk to my boss about it."

"Did the reporter work for your paper?"

"Yep, and Darren was the editor at the time. He'll know if there was anything fishy about the story or if I'm *seeing things I want to*." I made sure to use air quotes to get my point across. Cal, who had been silent for most of this conversation, spoke as he looked over my notes.

"It says here that some of the city council members were listed as council in the mayor's ledger. They were paid in 1996. Wasn't that the same year that the mayor blocked the bills for where the schools would be built?"

"Yes!" I got up and walked over to sit next to Cal. Obviously, he was catching on to the fact that there was something more here.

"It looks like the poorer neighborhoods started fighting back against the city council in 2009."

"They did. Lower income neighborhoods organized a group called Take Back The City. They went out and protested decisions being made by the city council. Two of the leaders vanished, while other members had accidents that got them killed. Eventually, the movement died down and the people stopped fighting back. Of course, the news didn't report it that way. I had to dig to find a newspaper that covered it. They're somewhat of a conspiracy paper, so no one really took the articles seriously."

Sebastian sighed, "If there was something to these stories, don't you think your editor would have covered them? Especially when the reporter from your paper died?"

"Well, that's what I plan on finding out. It could be that he wasn't aware of what the reporter was investigating. Sometimes reporters investigate, but don't say anything about a story until they have more to go on."

"Look, I'm not saying there's nothing here, I just think it's dirty politics. What's the most that would come of it? The mayor would be forced out? You already said his popularity is in the tank."

"I still have more that I have to investigate. This is just the beginning. I can feel it."

"Fine. What can we do to help?"

"I need financial records from RND Construction connected to these projects. I'm thinking they must have some deal with the mayor in order for him to continue to use them for every job."

"I can call Becky and Rob. They can look into it, but they're already working on the offshore accounts. Cal, why don't you take a couple hours off. Freckles and I will keep watch."

"Sure, Cap. Can I talk to you for a minute?"

"Freckles, can you give us a minute?"

I stood and made my way to the stairs, but I didn't go far. I had a feeling that I should hear whatever it was that Cal had to say. I tucked into a corner so that I could still hear their conversation.

"Cap, what are you doing?"

"What are you talking about?"

"Sleeping with a client?"

"What the fuck I do is my business. Last I checked, I'm still the owner of this company." His tone was low and lethal. "I also recall that you're on probation right now, so you might want to think twice about how you speak to me."

"Cap, you know I mean no disrespect, but we've always had rules about clients. This wouldn't fly with any of us. You want to fuck her? I've got no problem with that, but don't let it go any further."

"Who said it was? I haven't made her any promises or asked for more. Neither has she. She's a good lay and if we choose to burn off some excess energy between the sheets, that's our prerogative. There are no feelings involved here and my head is perfectly clear on what my job is."

I didn't stick around to hear any more. I wasn't looking for a boyfriend or anything, but I did think we at least had some chemistry. Maybe when the case was over we could see where this would take us, but any ideas of that happening were dashed with his harsh words. A good lay. That's what I was. I shook my head in disgust as I headed to my room. Sometimes I could be so naive.

CHAPTER 9

SEBASTIAN

I had been waiting for Maggie to come downstairs for the better part of an hour. After Cal's talk with me, he went to his room to get some shut eye and I went up to see Maggie. She was lying on the bed staring at the wall. I asked her what was wrong, but she told me she was fine and was just thinking about her next step in the story. She promised she would be down soon.

So, here I sat like a lovesick fool waiting for Maggie to come down so I could spend some more time with her. It was ridiculous really. I shouldn't have slept with her, because I was already crazy about her. I didn't want to admit it, but there was something about her that captivated me. For all I knew, she really did only want sex. In which case, I would end up making a fool of myself because I thought this could go somewhere. Not right now, of course, but maybe when the case was over.

I wasn't sure how we would make it work since we lived an hour apart. Sure, it wasn't that far, but we both worked crazy schedules. The more I thought about it, the more I realized that this wouldn't work between us. Whatever happened between now and when the story was finished would be fun and nothing else.

Maggie came downstairs about a half hour later. She was biting her lip and seemed to be thinking hard about something.

"What's up, Freckles?"

"I need a phone. I want to call Darren and find out what he knows about the reporter that went missing."

"Sure."

She walked over to the house phone and dialed her boss.

"Darren, it's Maggie. Do you remember that reporter, Mark Beane? Yeah. Well, I was wondering if you could tell me about what he was working on when he disappeared."

She was silent for a few minutes, her brows furrowing as he spoke. "Of course. Okay. I'll be careful. Yep. I'll let you know when I have more to go on."

She hung up the phone and sat down at the table.

"What did he say?"

"He said that he doesn't remember what Mark was working on at the time. Doesn't that seem weird to you? I mean, if you had an employee that disappeared, wouldn't you look into anything that could potentially be connected to the disappearance?"

"I would. Is there any way you can find out from someone else?"

"There's one person I could ask, but I don't want to meet him in the office."

"Why not?"

"Because I'm not sure what to think about Darren. I get the feeling he knows more than he's saying. I don't want to tip him off that I'm going to do more digging."

"Wouldn't he already suspect that you would? I mean, I barely know you and I know you wouldn't just walk away."

"He said he didn't remember and asked me to keep working on the current story so that he could use it as a headliner for the weekend. I agreed, so I'm hoping that will keep him thinking that I lost interest."

"Okay, so what's next?"

"Now I need to make another phone call."

After fifteen minutes of making calls, Maggie tracked down her colleague that still worked at the paper. She set up a time to meet him tonight at a restaurant downtown. To anyone, it would look like colleagues going out for dinner.

At six thirty, Cal, Maggie, and I headed into the city to meet Keith Breckenridge. It was about a twenty minute drive, just long enough for me to get some information out of Maggie about her colleague.

"Okay, Freckles. Tell us about Keith."

"Well, he worked in a different department than Mark. He's not a reporter, but a researcher and archiver for the paper. He makes sure that the facts check out and then makes sure all the information is archived with the proper files. He's basically in charge of all documentation on articles. Now, he normally doesn't do the actual research. He's more of a fact checker, but sometimes people go to him when they have a really big story because he's really good at making sure reporters don't look like total asses if the details are wrong. I could be totally off base here, but I think he's the only person left that I could talk to at the paper."

"What makes you think that Darren wouldn't have already gotten to him?"

"Nothing, I guess. I'm just hoping that if Mark did share something with him, he would have been smart enough to keep it to himself when Mark disappeared. It's a long shot, but I still want to check it out."

We pulled up to the restaurant and Cal let us out, then went to park. Cal would be hanging out at the front of the restaurant, watching for any potential threats. Cal and I put in ear pieces before we left so we could stay in contact and he could hear what was going on inside the restaurant.

I took up Maggie's left side and walked her into the restaurant, scanning for anything that looked suspicious. I took note of all exits and patrons that looked like they might cause trouble. Maggie let the hostess know we were meeting someone and we were soon making our way back to a corner booth where a man sat waiting. I pushed Maggie to the inside of the booth and took the outside seat.

"Keith, this is my bodyguard. You can speak freely in front of him. He's been helping me with my story."

"What exactly do you want to know about Mark?"

"I need to know what story he was working on when he disappeared. I've found something that I think links him to my story."

Keith glanced around the restaurant and then back at Maggie. "He was looking into the infrastructure bill that was set to be passed. He said he found evidence the mayor was skimming money from the city when the construction company was paid for their services. He brought me some documents and I started to check into them, but then he disappeared. I stashed it away in case they linked me to Mark."

"Can I have the information? I think that it might connect some more dots in my story."

"What story are you working on?"

"A source at the mayor's office found documents that pointed to offshore accounts. She thought the money in those accounts might be the reason that the city is short on funding for emergency services. She also mentioned the mayor and his right hand man were talking about how they would benefit from getting to choose the contractors for an upcoming project. I feel like I'm so close to figuring all this out, but I'm missing some things."

He leaned forward and lowered his voice. "If I were you, I'd quit while you're still alive."

"I can't do that. I think my source is dead. She shouldn't die for nothing."

Keith looked toward the door once again and I followed his gaze. I didn't see anything that would warrant suspicion. Still, I was paranoid.

"Cal, check in."

"All clear, boss."

Keith's gaze narrowed on me. "Who were you talking to?"

"Earpiece." I said shifting my head slightly. "I have backup to be on the safe side."

Keith nodded, then looked back at Maggie. "Look, Maggie. I'll give you what I have, but please be careful. I don't think Mark was the first person that got in the way and was never seen again."

"I promise. I have Sebastian with me at all times."

"I have a USB drive that I use for sources. It's stuck in the wall of The Downtowner, alley side. 101st and 89th. It's about halfway down the building at about chest level. You can get the information tomorrow morning, but I'll only leave it on until tomorrow night. Then, I'm wiping the drive."

"Thank you, Keith. I appreciate this so much."

"You didn't get it from me, and whatever you do, don't tell Darren about it."

She reached out and grabbed his arm as he went to stand. "Wait. Why would you say that? Is there something I should know?"

"Let's just say there are certain stories he doesn't ever seem interested in pursuing. Maybe check into his connections with the mayor."

With that last tidbit of information, he stood and walked out of the restaurant. I glanced over at Maggie to see her looking dumbstruck.

"I've always trusted Darren."

"You don't know that you can't. Let's check out everything first and we'll take it from there."

THE NEXT MORNING, the three of us went to the building where Keith said the USB was located. The drive was slightly awkward because I'd told Maggie that I had to stay up to work on stuff for Reed Security. While completely true, I would have gladly forgone all the work to go wrap myself up in Maggie.

However, I couldn't stop replaying Cal's words in my head from yesterday. If I continued to sleep with Maggie, I would want her for longer than just a few nights, and that wasn't something that would ever work between us. I needed to be logical about what was going on between us. More than that, I needed to talk to Maggie. We needed to clear the air so we could decide if we were going to enjoy the rest of our time together or if we were going to take a step back. I didn't think my cock could take a step back from her body, but I'd do whatever Maggie wanted.

"Up here on the right," I said as Cal pulled up next to The Downtowner. He parked in front of the entrance, so we didn't have a view of the alley, but parking directly in front of the alley would be suspicious. "Okay, I'll go get the information. Freckles, you stay in the car with Cal."

"What? No. It's my information to get. I'll get it."

"Christ, Freckles. Will you listen for once? I'm going because we met with your colleague last night, and if anyone followed him to the restaurant, we could be walking into a trap this morning. So please, for the love of God, sit your ass in the truck and wait for me!"

I didn't give her even a second to respond before I was out of the SUV and headed along the side of the building in the alley. Glancing around, I didn't see anything that set off alarm bells, but the hairs on the back of my neck were standing tall. Something about this whole thing was very wrong.

I glanced behind me, but didn't see anything but the street. I ran my hand along the wall so I could keep my eyes trained on the alley, only looking at the wall every few steps. When I got about halfway down the alley, my fingers brushed the end of the USB. I was just about to connect a cable to transfer the information when something cracked above my head, sending small bits of brick down around my head.

Fuck. I hated being in situations like this. There was absolutely no cover besides one dumpster on the opposite side of the alley. I ran behind it and took cover as I scanned for where the shot had come from. Whoever took the shot was either trying to scare me off or was a piss poor shot. Based on the way this case was going, I was guessing it was the latter. We were way beyond scare tactics.

Shots pinged off the dumpster and I peeked out seeing a thug taking shots from the corner of the alley. For some stupid reason, the mayor was sending gangsters to do the job that he should be sending a hitman to do. Chances were in my favor that this punk ass kid wouldn't hit me if I made a run for it, so that was my best option at this point.

Placing a few well aimed shots at the thug, I ran forward with my keys and started digging the USB drive out of the wall. My shots hadn't delayed the guy for very long before he started shooting at me again. Bullets were ricocheting off the pavement, making me more afraid that I would be hit by a stray bullet than a direct hit. I almost had it out when that was exactly what happened.

I felt a sharp pain in my thigh as a bullet lodged itself in the muscle of my leg. Pulling the USB free, I turned once more about to lay down cover fire when shots were fired from behind me. I didn't waste another minute as I turned and did a hobble run back to the SUV. Cal was standing at the end of the alley firing at the thug at the other end.

Maggie appeared next to Cal with wide eyes. She ran toward me, even with bullets flying around us.

"Damnit, Freckles. I told you to sit your ass in the SUV!"

"Put your arm around me."

We were almost to the end of the alley, so I pulled her in close and gave her the illusion that I was leaning on her, when really I was blocking her body with mine. When we got to the sidewalk, I pulled her back against the wall out front and turned, taking several shots back into the alley so Cal could cross back to the SUV. When he was clear, Maggie and I ran back to the SUV and climbed in the vehicle.

Cal took off, tires squealing as we made a clean getaway. Lucky for us, this part of town was basically a slum town and shots fired weren't abnormal. I did my usual call to Becky, asking her to send a clean up crew. I didn't think we shot anyone, but the casings needed to be taken care of.

"You're going to have to contact Keith and let him know what happened. Tell him to watch his back. I had to take the USB, so we'll get it back to him later."

I handed my phone over to Maggie and waited as she dialed Keith's number.

"He's not answering. Should I leave a message?"

"No. We can't take the chance that someone else has his phone."

I stripped off my long sleeve shirt and wrapped it around my thigh, tying it in a tight knot to stop the bleeding. I hissed in pain as I pulled it just a little too tight.

"Back to the safe house, boss?"

"Yeah. We need to see what was on that USB that was worth killing for."

"Holy shit."

"You got that right," Cal said as he sat next to me. The three of us were pouring over the documents on the flash drive, each document more incriminating than the last. The first document showed the transfer of funds to other city council members. Maggie shoved me to the side, holding her notes and pen in hand.

"Okay, look at this. These funds were transferred days before the city council approved box stores being built in the city. This transfer was in 1994, but I don't have anything that I found for that date. The next one takes place in 1996, and guess what? Also transferred days before the council voted to pass the bill on new schools. There are a few more dates in here I don't have anything to match. It looks like the last transfer that matches my dates is the infrastructure bill in 2008."

"Did the transfers stop after that?"

"It looks like there was one more, so either the council could no longer be swayed or the mayor got nervous when Mark got ahold of this information. Maybe since the mayor didn't know where this flash drive was, he decided to stop the blackmail?"

Cal flipped through to the next item on the flash drive and what we saw was something I wanted bleached from my eyes. There were various pictures of city council members in compromising situations. Not something that could be dismissed either based on the amount of nudity. There were other pictures of a few council members doing drugs.

"So, the mayor hires Rudy Moore, the private investigator, to dig up dirt on council members so that he can get his way on certain bills. He offers them cash, but they don't agree right away, so he uses the pictures as blackmail and then records all money transfers as a secondary blackmail," Maggie summarized.

"But then the money transfers stop around 2008 when the reporter, Mark Beane, went missing. The mayor figured he needed to stop until he could find what the reporter dug up on him. The mayor never knew where Mark hid the information, so he's hesitant to do anything further."

My head popped up. "Until now. You started digging into those properties, and he started sending people to kill you. What are we missing with these properties? Cal, how much longer for the analysis from the brewery?"

"At least another day or two."

"There's still one thing that's bothering me." I looked over at Maggie. She was chewing her lip and her brows were furrowed. "Who would've thought to have Keith followed? How did someone know that he should be followed?"

"Inside job," Cal said with resignation as he looked at me.

My mind immediately went to the day I found out Cal betrayed us. Judging by the look on his face, he was thinking the same thing.

"It's not the same thing, Cal. I know I've been pissed at you, but that wasn't the same situation."

"Really? Cause I'm pretty sure what I did posed just as much risk to someone being killed as whoever sent someone to follow Keith. We can't even reach him now, so who knows if he's still alive. Seems the same to me." Cal stood and walked to the back door. "I'm going out for a perimeter check."

I had to find a way to get through to him. I kept him on the team, but had done very little to get the team rallied behind him, even though they all understood why he had done what he had. I couldn't have one team member working on the outside. He either needed to be accepted back into the team or I needed to cut him loose. So far, he had proven that he was still a member of this team. It was time I made it official.

I glanced over at Maggie and saw that she appeared quite upset.

"Sorry about that."

"Huh? Oh, no, I was thinking that if it was an inside job, there was only one person I talked to about Mark. I don't understand. Why would Darren hire someone to protect me, but then turn on one of his own staff? And if he did, that means he knew about Mark and probably had something to do with his disappearance. It just doesn't make sense."

"I would guess Darren is also on the mayor's payroll, and he tries to protect his staff as much as possible. But if Mark kept digging, there was probably nothing Darren could do about it."

"But why did he hire you to protect me? It doesn't make sense. He could have asked me to get off the story. He could have given me something else to investigate. Also, remember that first day when we went to the property in Wilkinsburg? I told him I was going to start investigating there. He's probably the one that sent those guys there that day. So, it doesn't make sense that he would hire someone to protect me."

She had a point there. So why did Darren hire me?

"He asked me to call him daily for updates. He assumed that if I was protecting you, I would call him and tell him what you were up to. Do you normally check in with him when you're working a case?"

"No. I mean, I do, but if I'm really deep in a story, I check in when I get the chance, but not regularly."

"If I had called him every day and updated him on what was going on, he would have stopped us long ago. He was using me to keep track of your movements. We need to find Keith now. If Darren knows that Keith passed us information, he's as good as dead."

Cal walked in the door looking more at ease than when he left.

"All clear."

"Good. We need to track down Keith A.S.A.P. Freckles, give Cal his number so we can put a trace on his phone. I need to call the office and talk to Becky. Also, we need to find out what's so special about these properties. Let's plan on heading out again tonight."

"Do you think that's a good idea with your leg being, you know, shot?" Maggie looked so cute with that skeptical look on her face.

"Freckles, this is a scratch. Nothing that I can't handle."

"Still, maybe you should lie down for a little bit before we head out. I mean, Cal and I wouldn't want you holding us back."

"That's highly unlikely, Freckles, but if it'll make you feel better, I'll go lie down and you can come play nursemaid."

She flushed bright red when Cal groaned behind us. "Can you two take it upstairs so I don't have to hear that shit?"

"I have to make some calls and then I'll be up."

Maggie grabbed her notes and hugged them to her chest. "I'll just be sorting through all this upstairs."

She practically ran out of the kitchen and upstairs. I shook my head and was just about to make a call, when I decided instead to settle things once and for all with Cal.

"When this job is over, I'm putting you back on your team with John."

He shook his head in disgust. "When are you going to stop and just let me go? I don't belong with Reed Security anymore. I screwed over my team. Why the fuck haven't you pulled out your gun and put a bullet in my head?"

"I hate what you did, but I get why you did it. I know you never wanted to betray your team. The guys get it. Now you have to get over it and start rebuilding trust with us."

"The guys get it? Are you sure about that? Does Hunter agree after spending months in rehab for getting his skull bashed in? What about Lola? Has she recovered from all the nightmares that plague her from almost being scalped?" He let out a caustic laugh. "I don't deserve a second chance. I don't deserve to be back on the team, and I sure as hell don't deserve forgiveness."

"Cal. We all know you. Some of us served with you. None of us could ever believe you would have done that if you were in your right mind. You've already lost your family. Isn't that punishment enough?"

"It'll never be enough. There's no way you could convince me I belong anywhere near any of you."

"Then why are you here? You've proven to me every day you've been with me that you belong here. So if you're so sure, why don't you walk away?"

Cal's head dropped as he shook it back and forth. "I owe you this. So as long as you need me, I'm here, but let's not pretend I've earned the right to be here."

Cal walked out of the room before I could say any more. I was going to have to let him go. Not because I wanted to, but because it was obvious to me now that he didn't want to work with us, and I wasn't sure what else to say or do to change his mind. He didn't feel worthy. I wasn't one to abandon a brother when he was down and out, but this was a wholly different situation. He didn't feel there were any redeeming qualities left in him, and he would never feel like he belonged with us. I could understand where he was coming from because I would feel the same way if our situations were reversed.

AFTER I PLACED a call to Becky and checked in on their progress, I slowly made my way upstairs, refusing to give in to the pain in my leg. When I got to the top of the stairs, I saw my leg had started bleeding again from where Cal had patched me up earlier. He wasn't a medic, so he did the best he could. We used glue to close the wound, but apparently it had opened back up.

When I got to the bedroom, I stopped in the doorway when I saw Maggie spread out on the bed going over all her notes and typing on the laptop I gave her. She looked so sexy with her hair pulled up high on her head, all messy with small pieces coming loose. She was chewing on a pencil as she clacked away on her keyboard, her eyes squinted in concentration.

She looked up when I started making my way into the bedroom, and then ran over to me to help me to the bed. I was doing okay and didn't really need the help, but when her sexy little body sidled up to mine, I gave in to the heat that coursed through me.

When I sat down on the edge of the bed, she quickly gathered all her paperwork and stacked it on top of the dresser along with the laptop.

"Looks like you need your leg patched up again. Why don't you take off your pants and I'll get you cleaned up?"

I groaned as images of her on her knees in front of me assaulted my brain. She quirked an eyebrow at me, so I stood and undid my pants, pushing them down my legs. I watched her reaction and saw her breath catch when she realized I was already at half mast for her. She quickly turned and walked into the bathroom, coming out moments later with a wet washrag.

"What supplies do I need from Cal? Or should I just have him come up here?"

There was no way I was allowing Cal up here this close to me in this state. "No, just ask him for new gauze pads, tape, and glue."

She walked out of the room and I did my best to calm my ever-growing erection. No such luck. When she sauntered back in a few minutes later, I was rock hard for her. She stared at my groin for a minute before she came over to me.

"I think it would be best if we removed your boxers. You know, so we can properly dress the area."

"Whatever the nurse says." I laid back on the bed and put my hands behind my head, leaving her to do all the work. Her warm fingers brushed under the waistband of my boxers and ran along the top of them before she gripped the sides and slowly started pulling them down. My body burned as she slipped the material over my erection, causing it to bounce back in the air. Her hands stopped moving as she watched it moving, licking her lips and swallowing hard. The desire in her eyes had me lifting my hips toward her mouth.

I expected her to take me in that delectable mouth, but instead, she pulled my boxers down the rest of the way. I was disappointed, but tried not to let it show. She got to work cleaning the wound and gluing it shut. When she was done, I had fresh gauze taped to my leg and a screaming erection. Several times, tendrils of her hair had brushed against my cock, causing it to jump in anticipation.

She threw away the garbage and then came back to sit next to me on the bed.

"I think we need to check your temperature and make sure you aren't getting a fever. That would be a sign of infection."

"Whatever you say, nurse." I smirked and waited for her to go get the thermometer, but instead she got down on her knees and took my cock in her mouth. The tortured groan that escaped my lips made her pull back.

"If you don't sit still, I can't get an accurate temperature."

Saucy. This woman was going to drive me crazy. She put my cock back in her mouth and slowly ran her lips up and down my length. Her tongue caressed the underside of my shaft before sliding over my slit. It took all I had not to come in her wicked mouth as she licked and sucked me over and over again. When I couldn't take it anymore, I pulled her up on top of me so she was straddling my hips.

"I need to be inside you, Freckles."

She climbed off me and did a sexy strip tease, slowly peeling her jeans down her legs and pulling her shirt overhead. Her bra and panties were next, but honestly, I wasn't paying attention anymore because the prize underneath was being revealed. She walked back over to me and straddled me once again.

"All aboard that's...coming...aboard," she said with a sexy wink. Then she bit her plump lip making my cock jump against her wet pussy.

"Oh, you'll definitely be coming on this ride."

I rolled her over and thrust inside her, reveling in her warmth. God, she was going to be my undoing. There was no way I would survive this woman. If I had to leave her when this was over, it would kill me. With every thrust, I imagined what it would be like to have this every night. Fuck her when I wanted, wake up with her every morning, and see her come undone in my arms.

My hands roamed over her body, teasing her nipples, then trailing down to her clit. I had to slow down when my leg started to weaken, but I made my strokes deeper and harder. When I felt her tighten around me, I couldn't hold back. I came so hard and fast that I barely had time to pull out before my cum was splashing over the soft curls on her mound.

"Fuck, we need to get some condoms. I almost didn't pull out in time."

My breaths were harsh as I recovered from fucking her while partially standing on my bad leg. I pulled myself across the bed and laid down, deciding that I needed to rest if I was going to go out tonight. I held out my arm, waiting for Maggie to come join me and was pleased when she didn't wait very long before sliding into my arms.

"What are we doing, Sebastian?"

"I don't know, but I'm not going to be able to let you go when this is done."

She looked up at me with hope in her eyes. "What does that mean?"

I blew out a long breath. "It means we're going to have some decisions to make when this story is over. I don't know about you, but I don't want this to be over. Not just because you're a good fuck, either. I really like you and I want to see if this goes somewhere."

"How would it work, though? You live an hour from here. You've got a company to run and I'm always working on stories. When would we have time for each other?"

"We'll work it out. Let's just get through this and we'll figure the rest out afterwards."

I didn't really want to wait to figure it out, but part of me wondered if when this was over, she would move on to her next story and forget about me. I'd already had all the excitement I could ever need. I'd been to war and now ran a security firm. There would always be excitement to a degree, but now I was ready for something real.

"How old are you anyway?"

"Twenty-seven. You?"

"Thirty-six."

"Is that too big of an age gap?"

"Not to me. Is it a problem for you?"

"No. I like older men. You know what you're doing both in and out of the bedroom."

I raised an eyebrow at her. "So, older men is a regular thing with you? Exactly how old are we talking?"

She smacked my chest. "No, it's not a regular thing with me and you're the oldest man I've dated. Well, if you can call this dating."

"I wouldn't say this classifies as dating, but I wouldn't mind taking you out when this is all over."

"Have you...been with many women?"

"I've had my fair share. When you're in the military, it's not like relationships are easy, so when I came home on leave, most women were passing amusements. Then I was discharged and took some time to heal and got right into starting this business. It hasn't left much time for dating."

"So, what made you want to start this business?"

"Well, when you're in the military, you have a certain skill set. Then you come back here and it feels totally useless. I couldn't imagine having a nine to five job, and I wanted to do something I understood. Plus, you get used to the excitement. Maybe that's not a good word to use. The danger? The feeling of always being on edge. Then you come home and you feel ridiculous for always watching your back. In this job, it's still a skill you have and use regularly. I guess I just wasn't ready to let it all go."

"Well, I'm definitely glad for all the skills you possess."

"Freckles, are you coming on to me?"

"Maybe. I think I might need to put *my* skills to use and investigate your abilities a little further."

She climbed on top of me and soon we were burning up the sheets again. It was another forty-five minutes before we finally laid down and went to sleep.

CHAPTER 10

MAGGIE

It was close to dinner time and I was starving. Sebastian was still sleeping upstairs, because I forced him to take some pain pills after we had sex. I accidentally landed on his wound and I wanted to make sure he was okay. We weren't leaving the house until around ten, so he had plenty of time to sleep off the effects of the pills.

I wandered down to the kitchen and started digging through the fridge for some food when Cal walked into the room.

"So, have you decided which location we're checking out tonight?"

I grabbed my notes I brought down with me and started scanning the properties.

"There's a property in Beltzhoover that we can check out. From what I can tell, it's just an old warehouse. I can't imagine why he would have wanted the property. It's in an area with a really high crime rate and has been that way for years. They've been trying to revitalize the area, but so far they haven't had much luck. I just don't get it."

"Well, hopefully we'll find something tonight. The SUV's already packed, so we can leave as soon as Sebastian's ready."

"Yeah, he's going to be sleeping off the pills for a while."

"Is his leg bothering him?" A look of concern crossed his face and I blushed as I remembered how I hurt him.

"Um..."

"Say no more. I don't need to know whatever you were just thinking."

I went back to the fridge and pulled out ingredients to make chicken and potatoes. While it cooked, I thought about what it must be like for Cal to sit here with Sebastian and I as we played kissy face.

"Can I ask you a question?"

"Shoot."

"If you knew Sebastian could help, why didn't you go to him?"

He was quiet for a minute and I was afraid I had overstepped. He stared at the table, his eyes distant, but then he answered me. "That psycho had my family and I had no clue how he knew about them. It's like he knew the minute Reed Security stepped in and took over. We had been involved from early on, but strictly with setting up security. All of a sudden, I get a text from him with pictures of my wife and kids."

He shook his head as grief took over. "He had them for a couple weeks before he killed them. It turned out he was working with a detective, and the detective pulled up all the information about Reed Security employees. I was one of the few with family that could be used against me.

"When he took them, my initial reaction was to go to Sebastian, but then I kept seeing the pictures of them and I just knew I couldn't take the chance. If they were killed because I went for help, I would have never forgiven myself. Turns out that I might have had a better chance with my team. I just couldn't see it at the time. I was so torn up."

"What were they like?"

"My wife Jenna was...my everything. She was my best friend and my biggest supporter with anything I wanted to do. She gave me two beautiful girls that were my whole world. Callie was seven and Jenna named her for me when I was overseas. Jessica was five. Jenna had them both when I was serving and she never once complained that I wasn't there. When I came home, she just swarmed me with love and affection, made sure that being home was a happy time and not so much of an adjustment. My girls were always so happy and told all their friends that I was their hero."

He was trying so hard to hold it together. I wondered if he had allowed himself to grieve for his family yet, or if he was still too busy beating himself up.

"I was trying to buy time. I thought if I could give him just a little of what he wanted, I could find where he was hiding them. I tried so hard to track them down, but that psycho never let on to where he was hiding them. The first thing he wanted was access into our security system. I gave it to him, hoping that I could find him in our system and trace it back to where he was staying. I didn't know enough about computers to trace it, but I didn't have to wait long before Sebastian had Becky start looking for the hole in our systems.

"It took longer than expected because this guy was really good at covering his tracks. After a few days, he got tired of me stalling on more information. I was about to tell Sebastian everything when he sent me a picture of my wife with a bomb strapped to her chest. He said that if I didn't tell him where Cole and Alex were and where they would go next, he was going to blow it. He gave me thirty seconds to answer."

Cal had already told me what happened, but this was even worse hearing all the details. I tried to put myself in his shoes. I couldn't imagine being under all that pressure and needing to make split second decisions.

Cal rubbed a hand down his face as if scrubbing away the disgust of what he'd done. "Damn. Every decision I made was so wrong. Every time I thought I was making the right choice, it came back to bite me in the ass." He blew out a long breath before continuing. "By the time we found the cabin, we only had a minute inside before a police officer found the bombs under the house. I tried to get to the basement door, but John started pulling me out of the house.

"I lost it. I was struggling to get away from him and yelling about needing to get to my family. John caught on and told me that we would get them back. We just had to dismantle the bombs first. Jules and Chris came over and helped him drag me out the door. We were only a short distance from the house when it blew.

"Afterward, Sebastian grilled me about what was going on, but it was too late. I had already given the secondary safe house location. By the time word got to Derek, it was too late. Communications were cut off and we couldn't get there fast enough. Hunter ended up in a medically induced coma to allow the pressure on his brain to go down. Lola still has nightmares about what that man did to her. I don't know how she's still functioning on the team."

He slammed his hand down on the table, causing me to jump. "If I had gone down there, I would be with them now. I let them down. I wasn't the hero they needed me to be. They died alone in a dingy basement, waiting for me to come rescue them."

I reached out and touched his hand and he startled at the gesture. He didn't look like anyone had shown him any sympathy this whole time and it broke my heart. I couldn't keep my distance anymore. I moved toward him and wrapped my arms around him. I felt his body shake, so I held him tighter, offering him everything I could. After a few minutes, he pulled himself together and I felt him stiffen slightly. I sat back in my seat as I looked at the broken man in front of me.

"How long have they been gone?"

"It's been a year."

"Do you have family close by?"

"None that care to see me." He scoffed, shaking his head. "When they died, her parents blamed me for their deaths. Not because of what I did, but because my job was dangerous. They never liked that she chose me. They figured I would get killed and leave her all alone. So when the three of them died, they had a memorial for them and didn't even tell me. There was nothing left of them to bury, so I didn't really get the chance to say goodbye."

"That's so terrible. How could anyone be so spiteful?"

"They were grieving," he said quietly. "I didn't blame them for how they felt."

"Still, you were their son-in-law. That should have counted for something."

He shrugged before standing up. "I need to check the perimeter. I'll be back in a little bit."

"Okay. Dinner is...well, it's ready if you want to try it."

"When I get back."

I watched him walk out the door, his shoulders slumped in defeat. I didn't know how anyone could be around him and not see how much he was suffering. His whole world had shattered and no one was there for him. Even Sebastian keeping him at the company wasn't truly helping in any way. The man was devastated. He had lost his will to live. When we were done with this story, I would do whatever I could to help him. I just couldn't stand to see him suffering, and I hardly knew him.

"No going anywhere Cal and I don't tell you to go. You don't enter the building until we clear it, and if I tell you to stay put, you stay put. If I tell you to run, you'd better haul ass. Got it?"

I had been getting a lecture about all the rules for tonight for the whole ride to Beltzhoover. It was getting old. Honestly, they acted as if I was a loose cannon that would go off and do whatever I wanted.

It started raining as soon as we left the safe house and it gave an ominous feel to our evening. That alone made me readily agree to follow all of Sebastian's rules.

"Fine. I already agreed to all your stipulations. You don't have to keep repeating yourself."

"Uh, Cap. We have an issue. Looks like someone's already here."

Cal pulled over to the side of the road and shut off the lights. There were several vehicles parked in front of the warehouse and flashlights shining inside the building. I scooted over to the other side of the SUV so I could see more clearly. There was someone getting something out of the truck that looked like a big bag or tarp. It was hard to see through the rain.

"Looks like they're getting ready to do some work on the building."

"In the rain? Freckles, this building hasn't been used in years. There's absolutely nothing so urgent that people would come out here to work at eleven o'clock at night in a downpour. They're trying to get rid of evidence."

"How do you want to handle this, Cap?"

"We have to get in there. If they're destroying evidence, we have to stop them," I said.

"*We* don't have to do anything. You are going to sit your ass in this SUV and not move."

"No. This is my story. I'm not sitting here doing nothing while you two go check out what's going on. I'll follow all your rules to a T, but I'm not standing by and doing nothing."

"Freckles—"

"Don't you Freckles me. Either I come with you or I'll just sneak out later and then you'll have to try to find me. This is just easier."

Sebastian looked to Cal, who just shrugged. "Fine, but you follow every order I give you."

I nodded quickly, knowing that now was not the time to argue about the fact that I was not in the military and didn't have to follow orders. We quickly got out and ran up behind the now deserted vehicles. Sebastian and Cal did quick checks inside the vehicles before taking up positions on either side of me. Sebastian was on my left as usual and Cal was on my right. Both were holding guns, making me wish I had my own.

"Don't you think I should have a gun?"

"No," they both said at the same time. I rolled my eyes and grumbled for a minute about the unfairness, but had to shut my mouth when we started moving.

The outside of the building was quiet, so we quickly made our way to the side of the building to a window we could see through. Sebastian pushed me down as he and Cal peeked in through the dirty pane.

"I can't see shit through this window. We need a different view."

"I'll go check for a different angle." Cal was off before I could even ask if I could take a look first. I took up Cal's vacated spot and peered in through the window.

"They all seem to be gathered in that corner. What do you think they're doing?"

"I don't know. We'll have to wait for Cal to get back."

The wait seemed impossibly long. "Let's get closer. They could be doing anything right now. We need to move."

"We wait for Cal. There's a reason we do things this way, Freckles."

Cal came hustling around the corner in a low crouch, avoiding the windows as he came. "They're digging something up. It looks like bones. They've got a tarp down that they're putting it into. I counted four guys. I did a quick check around the rest of the building and didn't see anyone else. We need to find a way to get that evidence."

"Maybe I could—"

"No." Their voices were sharp and that made me mad.

"You didn't even hear what I was going to say."

"No," they repeated.

"I could—"

"No."

"Would you two just listen?"

"Freckles, do you really think we're going to allow you to go off and do anything? We're supposed to keep you alive, not get you shot by a bunch of thugs."

"How do you want to handle this, Cap?"

"You go to the front entrance, I'll go to the rear. You draw their fire and then I'll take out as many as I can from the rear. Freckles, you stay behind me at all times."

"Give me thirty to get into position."

"Here." Sebastian handed over an earbud to Cal, who placed it in his ear.

"Why don't I get one of those?"

"Do you have a gun?"

"No."

"Do you know how to shout out positions?"

"What? You mean like, two guys at the front entrance?"

"Freckles, in the amount of time it takes you to say that, we'll already be dead."

I huffed in annoyance. "Well, if you taught me these things, I could be more helpful."

"Remind me to give you a crash course when we get back to the safe house."

Cal took off for the front of the building, while Sebastian and I got into position at the rear. He pushed me to the side of the door.

"You stay against this wall and don't move. I don't need to worry about you getting your pretty little head shot off."

I glared at him, but stayed where he put me. Cal must have spoken because he put his hand to his ear, adjusting the piece.

"Copy. On your mark."

I wasn't prepared for the sound of gunshots and jumped, covering my mouth when they sounded inside. I kept my eyes closed as Sebastian started firing, not wanting to see the deadly look on his face that I had seen before. When I heard bullets hitting the brick, I squeaked and squatted down to get away from any potential stray bullets. All too soon, the gunfire died down and all was quiet. The whole encounter couldn't have lasted more than thirty seconds.

"You can get up now, Freckles. We're all clear."

He helped me stand and then pulled me to his side as we entered the building. His gun was still drawn and he was scanning the darkness for anyone that could pop out. When Cal walked in, we all made our way over to the corner where the thugs had been digging. Sure enough bones were laid out on the tarp from what I assumed were human remains. They hadn't gotten them all out yet and as I picked up a flashlight, I looked closer and saw a human skull staring back at me.

I stepped back quickly, dropping the flashlight as my hand flew to my mouth. I'd already thought it was a human, but I'd never seen real bones before, let alone buried in a concrete floor. I felt Sebastian's hand at my hip as he steadied me. I was grateful for the support, as I started to feel a little lightheaded. Suddenly this story was feeling a little too big for just me.

"We need to call the police and get this into evidence," Sebastian said as his hand moved to squeeze my shoulder.

"This doesn't prove the mayor is responsible for this death. The property has been abandoned for years. Anyone could have been using this as a dumping ground," Cal said.

"True, but the mayor would have been the only one aware this building was about to be undergoing renovations. No one else would have a reason to be out here moving a body."

As Sebastian and Cal debated back and forth, I stared at the grave in front of me, wondering who it was and what they had done to get themselves thrown away so casually. It was as if this person's life wasn't important. It was then that I noticed this grave was much like what we saw in Wilkinsburg. There was a slab of concrete missing just about the size of a coffin.

"Look at this." I bent down and started digging an outline with my fingers, feeling the rough edges where the concrete had been cut. "This is just like over at Wilkinsburg. You need to send the police over there."

"Chances are they already dug up anything buried over there when they realized we were already at that property."

Sebastian pulled out his phone and dialed Becky.

"Becky, get in touch with our contact on the police department here. Tell them we're over at the property in Beltzhoover. There's a body buried here and it needs to be taken care of now. We had some trouble when we got here. We've got four bodies."

"Down!"

All at once, Cal was flying in front of me at the same time that Sebastian dropped his phone and swung around firing off several shots. Cal smashed into me and we fell to the ground, my head bouncing painfully off the concrete. I laid there for a moment, not really understanding yet what happened when I realized that Cal wasn't moving.

"Cal," my voice was quiet as I could barely draw a breath with him laying on top of me.

Sebastian was moving across the room, scanning the outside for any other people lurking in the shadows. I heard Cal groan, so I gently pushed him off me, careful not to let his head hit the ground. As I sat up, my head spun a little, but then I felt something sticky on my hands and I forced my eyes to focus.

I scrambled over the floor to find the flashlight I dropped, finally finding it and turning it back on. Cal's chest was covered in blood that was quickly spreading outward.

"No. No! Cal. Can you hear me?"

"Mag...You okay?"

Tears started trailing down my face when I saw how pale he was. "Are you fucking kidding me? You're shot and you're asking me how I am?"

He lifted his hand slightly and I took it, squeezing it tightly in my own. "Tell me what to do. I don't know what to do."

"Noth...ing. Too...late."

"No. No, it's not. Just tell me what to do. You're going to be okay." Turning I shouted over to Sebastian. "Cal's shot. Tell me what to do."

It came out as a sob and I wasn't sure if he could even understand me. I felt Cal squeeze my hand again and I heard Sebastian on the phone yelling the address to someone. Seconds later, Sebastian was kneeling next to me. He ripped open Cal's shirt and stared down at the mess before us. There was so much blood that we couldn't even see the entry wound.

"Shit." His fingers felt for a hole, finally finding one and then covering it. Cal moaned in pain when Sebastian applied pressure. "I'm sorry, man. I gotta do it."

"Cap...sorry...I should...have...trusted..."

His breaths were coming harsh and with a slight bubbling sound. Blood started to leak out the sides of his mouth when he coughed.

"Save it. I don't want to hear that shit. You can tell me all about it when you're sitting on your ass in the hospital."

"Not...gonna..." He drew in a ragged breath, his eyes closing momentarily.

"Cal, please hold on for me." The tears were coming faster now as I squeezed his hand tightly, willing my strength into his body. He had been through too much already. He didn't deserve to die like this. "You have to fight."

"Nothing...left...to..."

"Bullshit." I noticed a slight croak in Sebastian's voice, the only sign that this was just as hard on him. "You have a whole team that needs you to fight. Don't you dare go to them yet. It's not time."

"Cap, best man...I ever...knew."

I felt his hand going limp in mine and heard the faint sound of sirens in the distance.

"Hold on, Cal. They're almost here. We're going to get you to the hospital and you're going to be fine."

His eyes moved to me one last time and he seemed to be smiling at me. "'S okay...Jenna..." His lips curved up slightly before his hand went totally limp in mine and he stared into nothing.

"No! No!"

The sobs came hard as the man I had come to care about over the past few days slipped away from us. I barely heard the paramedics enter or them asking me to step aside. Sebastian's arms wrapped around me as he pulled me back from Cal, whose hand I was still holding.

"No! Stop! You have to help him. Please!" I gripped his hand tighter, refusing to let go, until Sebastian pried my hand from Cal's. He pulled me into his arms and held me as I broke down. Sebastian turned my head against his chest so that I couldn't see Cal.

"He's gone," I heard one of the paramedics say.

That was the breaking point. The tears stopped and numbness settled over my body. My whole body started to shake as the adrenaline left my body. I slumped against Sebastian as my head grew fuzzy. I heard him curse before everything went black.

"Shit."

WE WERE BACK at the safe house. I could tell by the comfort and warmth of the bed. I was snuggling back in when I remembered what happened earlier tonight. Cal was gone. He had died taking a bullet that was meant for me. I was the reason that a good man was dead.

I needed to get out of bed and finish this story. I needed to find somewhere else to stay, away from Sebastian. No doubt, he wouldn't want me around after I got one of his employees killed. I went into the bathroom and took a long shower, allowing the warm water to erase the chill that had crept over my bones. I couldn't face Sebastian yet, so I sank down on the floor of the shower and wrapped my arms around my legs.

I thought about all that happened this week and how my actions led to this whole event. I constantly pushed and put Sebastian and Cal in further danger because I wouldn't listen. Sebastian had wanted me to stay in the SUV tonight because he knew it would be safer for me, but I had insisted on going. If it wasn't for me, their attention wouldn't have been split between protecting me and watching for potential threats.

Cal wouldn't have leapt in front of me when that man fired the bullet. He probably would have responded differently, maybe pulled his own weapon. But he knew he didn't have time to protect me and shoot. He chose to step in front of me and take that bullet. I should have listened. How many times had I done this?

The first time was when Sebastian and I were in Wilkinsburg, and then the chase afterward. The second time was when I snuck out to meet Danielle, and Sebastian had to chase after me. I almost got us shot, drowned, and frozen to death. Then when we met the bartender in the alley, I got myself taken hostage because I didn't listen and stay behind Sebastian. When he tried to retrieve the flash drive, he told me to stay in the SUV and I got out anyway, risking his life even further. I felt him shield me with his body. He could have easily taken a second bullet right then. And finally, there was tonight. Only this time, someone died. Cal died and it was all my fault.

I stood and quickly washed up, feeling the need to scrub a little harder than necessary to get the feel of Cal's blood off me. When I was done, I quickly dressed and dried my hair. I gathered everything I left in the room and made my way downstairs. I hoped Sebastian was doing a perimeter check and that I could leave him a note and sneak out. Unfortunately, he was sitting at the kitchen table with a drink in his hand. I hadn't seen Sebastian touch alcohol even once since he had been protecting me. I walked forward and set my bag down on a chair.

He lazily looked up and took in my appearance, then the bag sitting in the chair. "Going somewhere?"

"I'm leaving."

"What makes you think I'd let you? You're still under my protection."

"Let's face it, my boss hired you for reasons other than keeping me safe. I think we both know you could easily get out of babysitting duty."

"Your boss is a fucking asshole and I stopped working for him a long time ago. This has nothing to do with him."

"Still, I doubt you want me around after tonight. I can find somewhere else to go until I figure out what to do. Maybe move to a new city."

"So that's it? You're just gonna cut and run. Let them rule your life?"

His voice was so nonchalant, you would think we were talking about the weather.

"I'm not allowing them to rule my life. I'm stopping while I'm still alive. I already cost one man his life. I won't be responsible for you dying too."

He laughed at that. "You think you're responsible? Freckles, you couldn't be more innocent if you were a baby. Nothing about tonight was your fault."

"Yeah? Then whose fault was it?"

He was silent as he sat there sipping his alcohol. I was guessing it was whiskey, but I couldn't be sure. I hadn't seen any alcohol in the house, so I wondered where he got it.

"I swore I would never touch alcohol again," he said, staring down into his glass. "I mean, I have a beer every now and then, but I never touch the hard stuff."

There was something in his voice that gave me pause. His voice was so different than what it usually was, commanding and strong. Now he was indifferent. His voice came out harsh and unfeeling. He seemed like he was just on the tipsy side of drunk, not quite there yet. I decided this was my opportunity to try and find out what was going on in his head. To see if he hated me as much as I hated myself.

"Why don't you drink the hard stuff?"

He finished his drink and poured two more fingers into the glass. "When I got back from basic, I found my old man face down in his own vomit. He suffocated himself because he drank himself into oblivion."

"Was he always a drunk?"

"Ever since my mom left him when I was fifteen."

"Why did she leave?"

He looked up at me with a glaze in his eyes and laughed. "Ran off with the milkman."

"Do they still have those?"

"Well, he wasn't technically the milkman. He was the local grocer that delivered her groceries every week. Fell in love with him and decided to make a new life for herself. Dad couldn't handle it and started drinking. By the time I was seventeen, I couldn't stand to be around his drunk ass anymore, so I signed up for basic and left. I should have stayed and tried to get him help, but all I could think about was how he was the adult and he was supposed to take care of me. I gave up on him."

And that right there was why he couldn't give up on Cal. He saw the good in him and didn't want Cal to be another casualty. Sebastian was a good man and he deserved someone that looked after others the way he did. I didn't look out for others. I put them in danger, because I only thought of myself.

"You didn't give up on Cal, though. You tried to help him."

"Fat lot of good that did. I ended up getting him killed."

"That wasn't your fault."

"Damn straight it was."

"No, it wasn't. It was my fault. I pushed to go along. I was the one that Cal jumped in front of to save. I was the one that just had to be a part of all the action! This was all my fault!" I yelled to keep from crying. My tears would not help anyone right now.

"It was his job. That's what he signed on for. Same as in the military."

"Then how could you say it was your fault?"

He turned away from me with a sneer, the first sign of his anger since I came downstairs. I knew I shouldn't push. He'd been drinking and wasn't in the right state of mind, but the investigator in me needed to know why he thought this was his fault.

"Tell me, Sebastian. You weren't the one that Cal jumped in front of. You killed the man that shot him. You tried to save his life. How can you say this is your fault?"

His head whipped toward me as he shouted, "Because I couldn't fucking see!"

CHAPTER 11

SEBASTIAN

"What do you mean, you couldn't see?"

Her voice was soft and comforting. I didn't deserve that right now. I had gotten my teammate killed. I should have been more aware. We cleared the warehouse, sure, but anyone could have been hiding. It was dark in there and we couldn't see every corner. I was so eager to find out what was being hidden that I wasn't being as watchful as I should have been.

"Sebastian."

I turned and looked into her eyes. Her sweet face was red and swollen from all the crying she'd done. It broke my heart when she cried over Cal. She was out of her mind when he died and I had to pry her away from his body. When she slumped in my arms, the only thought I had was getting her back here and protecting her from all she had seen tonight.

I knew Cal had come to mean something to her when I heard them talking at dinner. He had been telling her the story of how his wife and child died and she had comforted him. I didn't want to intrude on Cal finally talking to someone about it, so I went back to the bedroom to give them some time.

Cal hadn't received much sympathy after his family was killed. Everyone understood where his head was, but that didn't take away the sting of betrayal. It had taken me working with him again to truly understand how much his betrayal had hurt his soul. He had been an honorable man in an impossible situation, and I let him down.

"Sebastian."

I realized that Maggie had been saying my name for a good five minutes. I shook the alcohol from my brain and tried to clear the fog.

"Nothing. You should go back to sleep."

"Not until you tell me what you meant."

"Damn it, Freckles. Can you just listen to me?"

"No. You're blaming yourself and I want to know why."

"Aren't you doing the same thing?" I snapped.

"I have a good reason. I was the one he jumped in front of."

"And if you weren't there, it would have been one of us. Either way, he'd probably still be dead because Cal would have jumped in front of me, too."

"Then why do you feel guilty?" She pushed.

"Because I couldn't see the guy!"

"No one saw him," she shouted back at me.

"I should have seen him. This is why I'm not in the field anymore."

She looked confused. "Is this because of your eye?"

"Ding, ding, ding," I said mockingly. "I shouldn't have been in the field. I have poor vision out of my left eye. The way I was standing, I should have been able to see the front door, but I couldn't. Any other guy on my team would have seen it sooner."

"No. Cal was standing to the left of you. He had a better angle and he would have seen first. If he didn't see until the last minute, then you couldn't have seen either."

"It doesn't change the fact that I'm a liability out there."

"Let me ask you something. When we walk somewhere, why do you always take my left side?"

"Because I can't see out of my fucking eye. That's the only way I can protect you."

"So despite your vision problems, you still find a way to compensate and make sure I stay safe?"

"It's not the same. I do what I have to, but that doesn't mean that I'm the best person for the job. I should have assigned someone else."

"But Darren insisted it be you."

"And I should have fucking told him no."

"And I would have been dead that first day. Maybe you do have a slight disadvantage, but you've kept me alive despite my lack of rule following abilities. This was not on you."

"I'm the team leader. It will always be on me. If the guys can't trust me to have their backs, then I don't belong out there!" I roared.

"Cal trusted you! Didn't you hear those words he said to you? Do you think he would have said them if they weren't true? He was dying. Why would he lie?"

Anger coursed through me with every word she spoke. She kept getting closer to me, pushing me toward an explosion. I gripped the back of my neck and closed my eyes, willing myself to reel in my anger before I hurt her.

"Freckles, you need to get out my face, right now."

"No, I'm not backing down from you. You shouldn't be punishing yourself for something that you couldn't have avoided."

"Get out of my face, Maggie! I don't need your shit right now!"

I started pacing, trying to work down my anger so I didn't do something stupid.

"You're pissed because Cal died, and I get that, but I think what upsets you more is that you weren't able to save him."

"Well, no shit, Sherlock. He died and I didn't save him," I yelled as I pounded my chest.

"Not what I meant. He died before you had a chance to prove to him that he deserved a second chance. You're pissed because he died feeling like he let his whole team down and didn't deserve to be a part of anything. But guess what? Nothing you could have said would have fixed him. If he wasn't ready to accept what happened and accept that the team still wanted him, then nothing you said or did would have made him see it. In his eyes, it was worse that he let his family down than his team. They were waiting for him. That's what he told me. That's what was eating him up inside, because no matter what decision he made, they were going to die."

Bullshit. I grabbed her by the shoulders and shoved her up against the wall, pinning her hands above her head. I was so mad right now that I didn't trust myself not to hurt Maggie. Why did she have to keep pushing?

"Shut the fuck up. He didn't let them down. He tried everything he could to save them. Sometimes there just isn't anything you can do. Bad shit happens, and no matter how hard you try, people still die."

Her eyes turned sad and a single tear fell from her lash, rolling down her face. "Sometimes bad shit happens," she whispered. "We both feel guilty, but we both need to let it go. Cal's happy now. He's with his family." More tears fell over her beautiful cheeks. "Did you see him smile right before he died? He said Jenna's name. He was going home to her, to see his wife and kids again. He was at peace. Let him be at peace."

My anger deflated like a balloon and I pulled Maggie to me, wrapping her tightly in my arms. Her warm body soothed my aching soul. The tighter she held me, the more I needed her. I kissed her cheek over and over.

"I'm so fucking sorry," I murmured, still kissing her. "I shouldn't have yelled at you.

She clung to me, pulling me in tight. "It's okay."

"It's not okay. It'll never be okay. I shouldn't have taken it out on you."

She gripped both sides of my face, forcing me to look at her. "Hey..."

She pressed a soft kiss to my lips, her touch healing me. She was right about everything. I wanted to save Cal and I failed. Her kisses ignited something deep inside me. A charge shot through me as I kissed her harder and deeper. I couldn't get her close enough to me. I lifted her in my arms and carried her upstairs where I laid her down on the bed and lifted off her shirt as I kissed every inch of her perfect body. Her full breasts heaved with desire as I slowly released her bra and laved her rosy nipples with my tongue. Her moans urged me on as my erection grew painfully hard.

Kissing my way down her body, I slowly popped the button on her pants and lowered the zipper. As I pulled her jeans from her body, I kissed down each leg and back up until my mouth hovered over her panties.

"Please, Sebastian. Kiss me."

I ran my tongue over her panties where her clit was. Her liquid heat could be felt through the thin material of her silky panties. I couldn't get enough of her. I ripped the material from her body with a growl and dove back between her legs to taste her sweet honey. With every moan, I licked her and teased her with my tongue. It wasn't until her sweet taste filled my mouth that I finally gave in to my desire and pulled myself from her.

I quickly rid myself of my clothes before settling back between her legs. Her face was flush with desire, making me pause to really study the woman before me. She was everything I wanted and needed. She challenged me and drove me crazy, but she also calmed me. Her tenacity matched my own, leaving me feeling like I had found my perfect match. I wasn't sure if this was love, but I knew I didn't want to let her go any time soon.

I slowly pushed inside her, watching her beautiful, vibrant, green eyes as they slowly drifted closed in pleasure. I rocked in and out of her slowly, cataloguing every breath and emotion that crossed her face. I pushed slow and deep, listening for the little catch of her breath when I thrust in to the hilt.

I felt her delicate, little hand reach behind our joined bodies and gently pull my balls.

"Oh, God. Maggie..."

Her eyes popped open and she stared at me with a slight smile. "You called me Maggie," she said quietly. Then she smiled widely at me. "Don't make a habit out of it."

I bent down and kissed her long and deep, pouring all the love I was feeling into it. I wasn't sure I was ready to say it, but I could damn well show her how much I needed her.

A few more thrusts and I was pulling out just in the knick of time and spilling my seed on her beautiful skin.

"Damn, I forgot the condoms again."

I got up and grabbed a washcloth, wiping my cum from her stomach. She stretched contentedly as I climbed in behind her and pulled her against me. She felt right in my arms, better than anything I'd ever felt before.

"You know, you could take me back to my place to get my birth control."

I kissed her temple, shuddering at the thought of taking her back to her place and putting her in danger again. "I'm not sure that's a good idea."

"Well, it may not be, but it'll throw me off if I don't get back on soon."

"Alright. We'll go over there in the morning. How's your head?" I felt the small bump on her head, seeing her wince as I ran my fingers over it."

"Okay. Just a small headache."

"Let's get some sleep. It'll feel better in the morning."

I didn't like the idea of going to sleep right now, not when there was no one else here to keep watch, but I needed it. I had Rob staying at the office to watch the monitors since no one could get out here until tomorrow afternoon. My phone was next to me and he would alert me the moment anything seemed suspicious.

I felt Maggie drift off in my arms, and checked my phone one last time. I couldn't wait for this case to be over so we could both move on, hopefully together.

~

"So, let me get this straight. Your neighbor Aggie has a thing for your other neighbor Harry, but they're both in their seventies and neither is making a move?"

"Something like that. Neither will admit it, but every time Harry's around, Aggie starts fluffing her feathers."

I looked at her in confusion. "What does that even mean?"

"It means she's preening for him, you know, she's trying to make herself presentable for him. Then he gets all macho and starts puffing out his chest, which is pretty funny when you see a seventy year old do that. They should just get together already. It's disturbing to watch old people flirt."

"Why would that be disturbing? Are you going to stop having sex when you get old?"

"No, of course not, but I don't want to imagine all the wrinkles and things...drooping. It can't be very attractive."

Images of my grandma and grandpa floated through my mind and suddenly I was seeing my half naked grandparents kissing passionately. A shudder ran through me as I tried to wipe the image from my brain.

"Enough said. I think that's plenty for my imagination for one day."

She laughed at me and I glanced over to see her gorgeous green eyes light up. Damn, she took my breath away. Realizing that I was staring at her when I should be paying attention to the road, I cleared my throat and paid extra special attention to the yellow lines in front of me.

We pulled up in front of her house a few minutes later and I shut off the engine as I looked at her house. There was a board over her front window, but other than that, everything appeared fine.

The front door of the house to her right opened and a man dressed in trousers with suspenders and a white t-shirt stepped out holding a shotgun. From this distance, I was guessing a Remington 1100, a decent shotgun.

My eyes drifted to movement in the house to her left. The curtains moving gave way to the fact that she had some very nosy neighbors. I couldn't say that made me totally unhappy given her penchant for trouble.

"Looks like your neighbors are here to greet you."

"Yeah, they're quite nosy, but they mean well. Come on, I'll introduce you."

I put my hand on her arm, stalling her movement. "Wait. I'll take you to Harry's house and you can wait with him while I check out your house."

She rolled her eyes, but didn't argue. Finally. We walked over to where Harry was staring at me with murder in his eyes. He took in where my hand was holding Maggie's and narrowed his eyes.

"Boy, you want to tell me what you think you're doing on my property?"

"Just dropping Freckles off with you so I can check out her house."

"That true, girlie?"

"It's fine, Harry. Will you two put your guns away?"

Since I didn't have mine out, I could only assume that she was talking about a different weapon.

"Do you know how to use that thing?" I asked Harry.

"Of course I do, you shithead. You point it at the bad guy and pull the trigger."

Not quite that simple, but he was obviously busting my balls. Still I wanted to see just how protective he was of Maggie.

"It's a nice gun. I just wanted to make sure you actually knew how to use it and it wasn't just decoration."

"Boy, I served my country long before you even had hair on your ass."

"What branch?"

"Marines."

"Oohrah!"

"Served for nine years, mostly in Vietnam—lance corporal. You?"

"Ten years in Iraq and Afghanistan. Captain."

Harry stared me down for a minute before nodding. "Come inside, girlie." Maggie handed me her house keys and then walked toward the door. Harry stepped to the side so Maggie could pass, but turned back to me.

"Haven't seen anything since she's been gone, but then I ain't as quick as I used to be."

I nodded and walked over to Maggie's house, pulling my weapon as I approached her door. I quietly unlocked it and pushed the door in, scanning the house. There were still small specks of glass on the floor, but otherwise it looked pretty clean. If someone broke in here, they didn't leave any traces behind. I cleared each room, then holstered my weapon and grabbed Maggie's birth control pills that were laying on the bathroom counter before making my way back to Harry's.

Maggie was sitting at the kitchen table when I walked in, sipping coffee and looking through a photo album.

"It's all clear."

"Hello?" An older woman's sing song voice came from the front. "Harry, did I see Maggie come in here?"

The three of us made our way to the living room where an old lady stood running her little hands over her hair. She flushed when we walked in.

"Maggie, dear. It's good to see you doing well." She turned to Harry and gave a cute, little smile. "Harry, you look well today."

Harry seemed to grow three sizes bigger as he straightened his back. "Did three laps around the neighborhood this morning."

"I saw. You need to watch it or old Mrs. Craggle will pounce on you. She's had her eye on you ever since Mr. Sims broke his hip a few months ago."

He growled low in his throat. "That old hen is crazy if she thinks I'd ever fancy her. Who dyes their hair silver? It's just not normal. I prefer my ladies to have a natural look," he said as he raised an eyebrow at her.

"Well, I have a feeling that's not the only thing about her that's fake. Have you seen her t—"

"Aggie! Please. We do not need to hear the rest of that sentence," Maggie said desperately.

"Dear, you need to get your head out of the gutter. I was going to say her teeth. They're obviously false teeth." She turned with a smile to Harry. "I still have all mine."

"You know, I just saw the doc and got the all clear for more... strenuous exercise."

"Really? Maybe we'll have to go down to that new gym and try out those exercise balls. They're supposed to be great for stretching."

"And maybe relax a little in the hot tub when we're done. I hear it's a good way to wind down after exercise."

"As long as you promise to walk me home afterward. I would hate to be all alone, you know, in case I got a leg cramp and needed you to rub it out."

Good God, this was like watching old people's soft porn. The way they were looking at one another, we needed to leave before one of them broke a hip trying to mount the other. Luckily, my phone rang, interrupting the strange old people foreplay.

"Yeah."

"Boss, it's Becky. We have a lot of stuff to go over. Is this a good time?"

"Give me about a half hour. I'll call you back."

"Sure thing, boss."

I hung up with her and thanked my lucky stars that work was interfering.

"Becky's got something. We have to get back."

"Alright. Thanks for everything, Harry. I'll see you two later."

"You be safe, girlie. Sebastian, I'm trusting you to take care of our girl."

"Of course."

Aggie gave Maggie a big hug and then we walked out the door and headed to the SUV.

"Wait. I need to get my pills."

"Already grabbed them, Freckles. Was there something else you needed?"

"Well, it would be nice to have my own clothes."

I sighed heavily. "You have some at the safe house. If we go back to your house, I have to clear it again, which means you have to wait with the dirty grandparents."

She shuddered. "No, that's okay. I'll just wear what's in the closet."

WHEN WE GOT BACK to the safe house, I placed a call to the office. Either Sam or Derek would be running things, depending on who was taking on the night shift. Usually, I worked until about midnight and then monitored team activities from my house with the help of Rob. Usually Becky worked days and Rob worked nights, but I couldn't solely rely on them to monitor all situations with the teams.

"Reed Security. Derek Cortell speaking."

"It's Sebastian. How are things holding up?"

Derek blew out a harsh breath. "Well, all our cases are going fine. In fact, Ice's team just finished up last night. The rest of us are splitting duties where we can. We really need some more people here."

"I know. We need to start interviewing."

"Cazzo pulled some files and started weeding out the underqualified. He set up some interviews for tomorrow."

That was a relief. There had been so much going on that I really needed one of these guys to step up and help out, or I was going to drown. We were growing too fast and it was becoming too much. Most nights, I was lucky to get three hours of sleep before I had to be back in the office. Some nights I just slept there. I had gotten more sleep being here on duty than when I wasn't in the field.

"I appreciate that. After I talk to Becky I'll have a better idea of how much longer we need on this case. I think we might be getting close, but...damn, we took a hit with Cal. How is everyone taking it at the office?"

"Honestly, I think everyone's pretty upset. I don't think people were ready to work with him, but he was still one of us. I think...I think we all wish we would have talked to him, you know, tried to help him a little. Now it's too late."

"I talked to him. He wasn't ever going to be okay. I know Maggie talked to him quite a bit and I think that helped him a little, but honestly, I think he's better off now."

"What? How could you say that?"

"Derek, he was miserable. I'm not saying I'm glad he's dead, but you should have heard him. He wanted to be with his family and wished he had died along with them. He might have gotten over it eventually, but that guilt would always eat at him. He was never going to be comfortable being on our team again. He was doing it because he felt he owed us. At least now he's at peace."

Silence filled the line. I wondered if that was the wrong thing to say to a fellow teammate, but they had to understand what I now knew. Cal was a broken man that no one could have put back together.

"I get it. I just wish we could have done more," Derek finally said.

"Me too."

"So, do you want me to send Ice's team out to you?"

"Let's hear what Becky has to say first. Why don't you patch her through and stay on the line."

"Sounds good."

I heard a few clicks as he switched over and connected Becky to our call. I motioned Maggie over and put it on speaker.

"Boss, I'm so sorry about Cal. I always liked him." Her voice quivered as she spoke. I glanced at Maggie and saw tears filling her eyes.

"Me too, Becky. I'll talk with you when we're done and we'll make some funeral arrangements, okay?"

"Yeah. I'd like to do that."

"Okay, so you said you had a lot for me."

"Right. First, the tests came back from the gas chromatograph. There was an acid that couldn't be identified and organic matter. Unfortunately, it was basically sludge, so that's about all the test showed. The lab said the acid was most likely hydrofluoric acid because of the way the organic matter was broken down."

"Organic matter. What does that mean exactly?"

"Basically, it could be any living organism. They couldn't positively identify what it was. For all we know, it could have been a deer in there, but why would a deer be in a beer vat?"

"So, it looks like it could be human remains, but we have no proof that it was."

"Exactly. The second thing we need to discuss is the offshore accounts. It took a lot of work, but Rob and I were able to trace all the accounts."

"Good. Lay it on me."

"You're gonna love this boss. The offshore accounts were all listed in different names, but after much searching, I traced them all back to none other than Mayor Johnson."

Maggie's eyes lit up and she started writing down notes, officially in work mode.

"The money was all sent through several different banks, and every time the money was sent to a new bank, it was split up to go to several different accounts, so it was very difficult to match all the funds. Eventually, I traced all the money back to three companies: RND Construction, Gray Electric, and Hogan Concrete."

Maggie practically shoved me over to get in front of the phone. "Hi, Becky. It's Maggie. So, let me get this straight. The three companies filtered money through different banks that eventually ended up in offshore accounts that are all linked to the mayor?"

"That's correct."

"So, what am I missing? Why would they do that?"

"Here's the best part. I got all the financials from the city on the

projects you sent me. Then, I convinced some rather nice ladies at the three companies to send me the reports on those projects. The projects listed showed the cost of the materials and what the city was being charged for the project. The numbers don't match what the city paid, though. On all the projects, the city overpaid by about ten percent. I followed the money and guess how much was missing from what the city paid?"

"Ten percent?" Maggie theorized.

"Nope. Nine percent. And that matched perfectly with the amount of money that was deposited into the offshore accounts."

Maggie stood up and started pacing. "So, the mayor strikes a deal with these three companies. They overcharge the city by ten percent and keep ten percent of what was overcharged. The rest of the money is sent to offshore accounts for the mayor."

"Correct."

"So that's why the mayor always wanted to choose which companies the cities dealt with. He'd struck deals with them to skim off the city. Then, when he couldn't get city council members to go along with his plans, he blackmailed them and then paid them off. He kept records of who he paid off so that he had back up blackmail in case the members ever decided they'd had enough. With all of this information, a lot of people are going to jail."

She turned to me and gave me a big smile. "This is great. The mayor is going down big time. Becky, could you send me copies of all the information you found? I'm going to need all of it to reference, and then I'll need copies also for the police."

"Boss?"

"Yeah, go ahead and put a packet together. Freckles, I think you should come back to the office with me while you write your story. We have great protection there and you'll have all the documents faster."

"I can do that. Wait. I need figure out a different paper to send this to. There's no way Darren will print this if he's involved like we suspect."

"Derek, did you get any leads on Keith Breckenridge?"

"Lola and Hunter are picking him up as we speak. They should be back within the hour."

"Good. I want him to stay at the office until we get back and get a plan in place. We need to convince him to stay with us so he doesn't get himself killed before he can talk to the police. He's going to need a security detail, or stay in a safe house until everyone's in jail. Tell Cazzo we need to start interviews today. We need more people ASAP."

"Will do, Cap."

"Alright. Freckles and I should be back at the office in a few hours. We just have a few things to wrap up here."

"Ten-four."

I hung up and looked at Maggie who was already writing down notes and thoroughly engaged in her story. We needed to clear a few things up about us before we headed back to Reed Security.

"Freckles, I think we should talk before we head out."

"Sure, just let me finish this thought."

I waited patiently as she wrote for another five minutes, but she was totally lost in her thoughts. I got up from my seat and walked over to her, ripping the notebook from her grasp.

"Hey! I was working on something."

"I know and I've been waiting for five minutes for you to finish your thought. We need to talk."

"Okay, what do you want to talk about?"

"Us."

"Us. What's there to talk about?"

"I hate to sound like the girl in this relationship, but where is this going?"

"Um. Well, I'm not sure. Call me old fashioned, but I kinda expect the guy to take the lead."

"And normally I would, but seeing as how you're about to break a major story and will probably be following up on it, that doesn't exactly let me know where your head's at. We live an hour apart and we're both very busy, so I need to know what you want out of this. Do you want to try to make this work?"

"Of course I do. I mean, obviously it's not going to be easy, but we can at least see each other on weekends or one of us can drive to the other during the week. I'm sure we'll work it out."

She grabbed her notebook from my hand and then gave a quick smile before going back to her writing. It didn't give me very much hope this would all work out. Maybe I should have told her exactly how much I wanted her, and that I wanted to make this work so badly that my gut hurt. I thought when we made love last night that it meant something more. I could swear that she felt what I felt, but maybe that was just because of everything that had happened yesterday. Maybe she didn't really feel as strongly as I had.

"I'm going to pack up our stuff and get it in the SUV. We'll leave in fifteen minutes."

"I thought we were going to be here at least an hour?"

I had planned on taking her upstairs and having my way with her one more time, but her mind was somewhere else. Better to just get back to Reed Security. I had a business to run and it was time I got back to that.

"I have to get back and get some work done."

"Okay. I'll just get my stuff together."

Fifteen minutes later, the safe house was locked up and we were back on the road. Maggie worked on her story the whole way back to Reed Security, so I focused on the drive and tried not to think about our relationship, or lack thereof. By the time we made it back, I was fuming over her lack of interest in exploring our relationship. She couldn't even be bothered to talk to me about it. *I'm sure we'll work it out.* Yeah, that didn't make me feel like she was taking this seriously.

We made our way upstairs and into the conference room where Becky informed me Keith was waiting.

"Keith, it's good to see you alive and in one piece." I held out my hand and shook his.

"I gotta say, I was scared when I showed up to The Downtowner and saw the flash drive was missing. Then I went home and my place was ransacked. I took off and hid out at an old friend's house. Your people scared the shit out of me when they showed up there."

"Keith, we think that Darren is involved in this. I didn't see anything on your flash drive that would implicate him, but I called him and asked about Mark's disappearance, then Sebastian was being shot at when we went to retrieve the information. It's just awfully suspicious."

"Are you sure about this? There's no one else that could have followed you? I mean I suspected him being involved with the mayor, but...shit."

"The first day that Sebastian was protecting me, I told Darren about the list of properties I found and which one I was going to check out first. Some guys showed up when we were there and tried to kill us. At first, I just thought it was bad timing, but then Sebastian was telling me how much he was being paid and it turns out the paper isn't paying for my protection. Darren is."

He looked at us in confusion. "I don't follow. What does that mean? You know he thinks of you as a daughter."

"Darren doesn't have that kind of money, unless he's getting it from somewhere else. We think he was using Sebastian to try to keep tabs on me, so that he could stay a step ahead of us. Only Sebastian didn't do regular check-ins like Darren wanted."

"Look, Keith. Obviously we don't have any proof yet, but until we can clear Darren of any involvement with the mayor, I think it's best that he doesn't know anything."

"Alright. Whatever you say. So, how does this work?"

"We'll put you in a safe house with some guards until we can get the information to the police and everyone's arrested and in jail. It may end up taking until you testify. We don't want anyone coming after you to silence you. Is that something you can deal with?"

"Yeah, but how do I even pay for that?"

"Don't worry about it. We'll talk to the police chief and work it all out. Maggie will be with you, so—"

"What? I thought I was going to be with you?"

I'm not sure when I decided that she wouldn't be staying with me, but it seemed like a really good idea. She had a story to write and I had a business to run, something that I wouldn't do a very good job of if I was distracted by her.

"Maggie, I have a business to run. There's a lot of work that still needs to be done as far as gathering information the police can use. On top of that, it will take less people on guard duty if you two are in the same place."

Maggie looked slightly hurt by that, the first sign that she wanted to be close to me. I had to take a step back, though. If we tried to be together after the case, that was a different story, but for now, this was best.

"Keith, why don't you go see Becky. She's down the hall, second door on your right. She'll want to go over all the particulars of what you know and see if she can come up with anything further."

"Sure."

He turned to leave and Maggie waited until he had shut the door before whirling on me. "What the hell? What was all that about wanting to work things out? Now you're sending me off to a safe house where other people can keep an eye on me?"

"You didn't seem all that worried about it when we talked. I seem to recall you saying *I'm sure we'll figure it out.*"

"So this is payback because I didn't have all the answers?"

"No, this is me taking a step back. I've been playing bodyguard for the past week and I have to get back to running my business. You'll be fine with another team, and frankly, if you had really wanted to work it out, you would have said so earlier."

"I was distracted. We'd just gotten all that information from Becky and I wanted to get started on it. I wanted to write down my thoughts before I forgot."

"Look, I understand that, but I think that's why we need to just step back. Let's just get through this and then we can see where we stand. I can still come see you, but I have a shit ton of work to catch up on and people that I need to hire. You have work you need to do. This way, neither of us will feel bad if we let the other down."

"Fine. If that's what you want. Where will I be going?"

"I'll talk that over with the team and we'll make a decision, but you won't know until you get there."

She nodded and then turned on her heel and headed out the door. It was for the best. I could see I was already way too enamored with Maggie and I couldn't afford that right now. At least, not if she didn't feel the same way. It was time I got my shit together and got back to work.

CHAPTER 12

MAGGIE

"Hey, Freckles. Sebastian's on the phone."

It had been two days since I came to stay at the safe house again. Luckily, I was in the same one as before, so I still had clothes that fit me. I got up from my bed and made my way downstairs to the phone.

"Hello?"

"Freckles." His deep voice rumbled through the phone, sending chills down my body. I may be pissed at him, but that didn't mean I didn't still crave him.

"I wanted to let you know that Cal's funeral is tomorrow. We're just having a small ceremony since—well, since he didn't have anyone else left. Do you want to go?"

"Yes, but I'll have to see if there's anything to wear. I don't think I saw anything in the closet upstairs that would be appropriate for a funeral."

"I'll have something sent over for you. The funeral will be at one and Derek's team will take you to the cemetery. I'll meet you there."

"Okay."

"I'll see you tomorrow."

"Wait! Is that it?"

"Is what it?"

"I mean..." I stammered for a moment trying to come up with exactly what I wanted to say to him. "I guess I was wondering if you'd be coming here any time soon?"

There was a pause on the line that pretty much told me all I needed to know. He had no plans of coming to see me.

"Look, Freckles, I need some time to wrap up some business over here. Being away for almost a week has really set me back."

"Oh. Right. I'm sorry. I didn't—"

"I'll see you tomorrow."

The line clicked and I stood there feeling totally dejected. Damn it. Why didn't I say something when I had the chance earlier? All this confusion could have been avoided if I'd just told him that I wanted him too. Just a few days ago, we'd stood here and he asked me to talk about our future, and for some reason, I couldn't do it. I was such a coward.

THE DRESS SEBASTIAN sent to me was absolutely beautiful. It was a form-fitting, sleeveless, black dress that hit just below the knees with a cowl scoop neck. He also sent me a simple pair of black heels and a black jacket since it was turning cooler. Even more surprising was the second box I opened that had black, lacy lingerie with garters and silk stockings. He definitely had good taste, and based on the brand, it came with a hefty price tag, too.

What did this mean? Was he sending me this because he was thinking of me, or did he just ask someone to pick something out for me? I didn't really have time to sit and think about what had run through Sebastian's mind. We had to leave for the funeral in a little under two hours and I hadn't yet showered.

However, once I got in the shower, all I could do was think about him running his hands up my silk stockings and taking off the garters.

That thought alone had me pulling out my razor and doing a very thorough job shaving.

After my hair was dried, I pulled it back in a twist and made sure it looked nice. I lathered myself in lotion, then went to the bedroom to slip into the lingerie. I looked at myself in the mirror when I was dressed and decided I looked quite nice, but then felt bad when I remembered why I was wearing this.

The hour drive back to Reed Security left me too much time to think about all that had happened over the past week. It made me sad to think of the friendship I had started to build with Cal that was cruelly torn away, and the relationship I had with Sebastian that seemed to fizzle. Perhaps I was doomed to be alone in life. At least I still had Harry and Aggie, for now.

"So, why aren't we going right to the cemetery, Derek?"

"Security reasons."

"Is there a threat I don't know about? I thought the funeral was private."

"We're just taking precautions."

It didn't seem like I was going to get any more answers out of Derek, so I let it drop. We pulled into the garage several minutes later where all the members of Reed Security stood waiting. I hoped that Sebastian would get in the SUV with me, but he just signaled to Derek and then got in another vehicle.

We arrived at the cemetery about fifteen minutes later where the hearse was pulling in with the casket. Derek got out first and opened the back door for me to step out. I grabbed the roses off the seat that I had asked Derek to pick up for me and stepped out into the bright sun. Lola, who had been sitting in front, came around and took up my other side. The other members of Reed Security got out of their vehicles and some of the men approached the back of the hearse.

Sebastian, Sam, Hunter, John, Chris, Blake, Julius, and Mark all took up positions around the casket. There was no doubt in my mind that it didn't actually take that many men to carry the casket, but it seemed they all wanted to do their part in laying their friend to rest.

Derek and Lola guided me behind the casket as we walked over to the gravesite. There were some men already standing by the grave I didn't recognize.

"Derek, who are all those men?"

"Those are men Cal served with in the Army."

"I thought this was going to be a private funeral?"

"Those are his brothers, also. Sebastian thought they should be here."

"Like his real brothers?" I didn't think that was possible. There were ten men standing over there.

"No, but when you serve with someone and put your life in their hands, ask them to do the same, it forms a bond that can't be broken. That's why this has all been so difficult on all of us. No matter what he's done, he's still our brother."

I didn't want to think about what Cal had done. Not today. Today was for remembering the man I knew, that gave his life to save mine. He was a good man, and I would be damn sure he got the respect he deserved today. I had prepared a speech for the ceremony, though I hadn't yet told anyone. If they didn't like it, they could stuff it.

The minister stood in front of the casket and spoke of Cal's life of service and about the family he'd lost. A few of his brothers from the Army stepped forward and spoke about their time together serving. I found myself laughing at some of the stories they told, realizing Cal had once been a happy man, full of life and energy. It made me sad that the last year of his life had been so different.

When the minister asked if anyone else would like to say anything, I stepped forward only to feel Derek wrap his hand around my arm.

"What do you think you're doing?"

"I'm paying my respects."

"Now's not the time."

"Now is the only time I have."

I ripped my arm from his grip and stepped forward. When I

turned to face everyone, I saw Sebastian's stony face glaring at me. Obviously he wasn't too happy with me either.

"I only knew Cal for a few days, but in that time I saw a tortured man that had lost his way in life. He felt he had nothing left to give, but I saw something different. I saw a man that would have given anything to go back in time and make one different choice. A choice that would have changed the course of his life and that of his family's. You don't always get a second chance in life. Sometimes the decisions you make are final and there's no going back.

"The day Cal died, he made the decision to step in front of a bullet to save me. That was the man I knew. He was a protector at heart and didn't think twice about jumping in front of me when he saw the shooter. It cost him his life, but I like to think he's happy now and at peace with his family."

I looked up and saw a look of panic on Sebastian's face as he started a flat out run toward me. Several of the other members of the team were running to me also, while others had their guns raised and were looking around.

Everything seemed to be happening in slow motion. I watched as Sebastian's feet slowly propelled toward me and his arms slowly reached out for me. His mouth was moving as he yelled something, but I couldn't understand him. My eyelids slowly drifted closed as I turned my head and opened them once again to see guns raised toward an unknown target.

Then suddenly everything sped up and happened all at once. I felt his body crash into mine and then we toppled over the casket and fell roughly to the ground before sliding into the hole that had been dug for the casket. Sebastian landed on top of me, covering my whole body. He was so heavy that I couldn't breathe.

"Sebastian," I croaked.

"Shh."

He put a hand to his ear as if listening and lifted himself slightly from my body. I had no idea what was going on and wanted to ask questions, but I knew better than to bother him while he was working. If this were the first day we met, I would have yelled at him for tackling me like he had, but after what happened with Cal, I understood the importance of shutting up and following his orders. I heard movement up above, but it was only the sounds of feet shuffling along the grass.

Lying down here in a grave with no idea what was going on was not my idea of how a funeral was supposed to go, nor how I wanted to spend my day. Since I couldn't ask Sebastian what was going on, I decided that I needed a distraction. I thought about the last time that Sebastian had been on top of me, and how close we would be to screwing if only we weren't fully clothed.

And in a grave.

With all his men around.

Okay, there were a few things that I would change that could make this situation a little more ideal, but we *were* pretty deep in the ground. Perhaps no one would see us. I was very aware of how well our body parts were lining up right now and shifted slightly feeling the bulge that was currently inflating beneath his pants.

"Would you stop moving?" he bit out through clenched teeth. I loved growly Sebastian. There was something about his commanding presence that turned me on. Yes, it could be annoying, but I found I liked to push his buttons. Best not to push them right now, though.

After what seemed like an hour, Sebastian lifted himself from my body and pulled me to a standing position. His gun was raised as he scanned the area, but he dropped his arm when his team converged on the grave. He grabbed me around the waist and hauled me up into the arms of Sam, who was flanked by Lola and Hunter. Once I was steady on my feet, I looked around and saw the rest of the guys from the teams were standing facing outward in a circle around us. Even Cal's old Army brothers were holding weapons and scanning for potential danger.

I was so confused. What had caused Sebastian to tackle me to the ground? Was someone here? Sebastian took up my left side and grabbed my arm, dragging me to the waiting SUV, while Lola was on my right and Hunter behind me. Sam was leading us at a quick pace.

Sebastian practically shoved me inside and only stopped when I grabbed onto his jacket.

"Sebastian, wait. Tell me what's going on."

"I'll fill you in back at the safe house."

"No!" I had to be forceful. I needed to know what the hell was going on and why no one would talk to me. This may seem like a bad time to have this discussion, but damn it, this was my life and I deserved to know what was happening.

"I'm not waiting until we get back. You can ride with me and explain on the way or I'm getting out and I'll find my own way back to Pittsburgh."

I knew I had him because his jaw clenched and he turned to Sam, murmuring something to him before climbing into the SUV with me.

"Are you happy now?" The SUV took off, but I barely noticed as I waited for Sebastian to finish laying into me. "I have a business to run and I don't have time for a client to throw a temper tantrum when I'm trying to provide protection."

"A client? Is that all I am to you?"

It wasn't hurt in my voice, just pure bitch. I knew that I was something more to him, but for some reason, he felt compelled to push me away.

"That's not what I meant. Freckles, you don't know how close that was."

"No shit, because you won't tell me anything. I waited while we were in that grave, because I knew you were trying to concentrate on your job, but now you need to tell me what's going on."

He looked out the window for a moment, then turned to me and his gaze dropped to my chest. I looked down wondering what he was looking at. Surely he wasn't checking me out. There wasn't much to see with my jacket covering my chest.

"Someone was there to kill you."

"What? How do you know?"

"There were wind markers in the trees."

"What does that mean?"

"When a sniper is preparing for long range shooting, he needs the wind speed and direction to have a precise shot. There were wind markers positioned in the trees and on sticks near the graves."

The blood drained from my face. "Someone was going to shoot me?"

"And they would have if I hadn't seen the markers. Even if I had seen the red dot from the laser sight, there's no way I would have gotten to you in time."

I took a big gulp, trying to get some moisture back in my throat.

"The team searched the area and came up with a few footprints, but that doesn't mean a whole lot in the middle of a cemetery. As soon as he saw us run to you, he was gone. Considering that the cemetery is surrounded by woods, he could have easily blended into the trees and we would never find him."

A chill ran over me and the goosebumps were almost painful. I felt a little dizzy at this new revelation, but I willed myself to hold it together. I had put myself in more dangerous situations already and now was not the time to get cold feet.

"Okay. So what do we do now?" I asked with more confidence than I really had.

"Now we get you back to the safe house and have you finish your story and gather all the evidence for the police. The sooner the mayor is behind bars, the sooner we can breathe easier."

"Will you be coming with me?"

"No. I have work to do. Why? Did you need something?"

I blushed as I remembered that I was wearing the lingerie he'd bought me. I couldn't help that my libido had chosen now to show itself.

"I thought maybe you could come stay with me for a few hours or even the night."

He narrowed his eyes at me and lowered his voice so that hopefully only I could hear. "You want to fuck? Now? After you were almost killed?"

"Technically, I wasn't almost killed. You said yourself that you saw the flag things, and as soon as he saw you move, he took off. Besides, you were laying on top of me for a really long time. I had to distract myself from what was going on, and you seemed like an awfully good distraction."

His eyes grew dark as he stared at me. Not looking at the front seat, he spoke to Derek, who was driving. "Derek, we're heading back to the safe house."

"Sure thing, Cap."

Sebastian whipped out his phone and dialed Sam, relaying that he would be at the safe house for at least a few hours and that Sam was to take over back at the office.

"I have a few calls to make before we get to the safe house."

He placed his calls while I pretended not to care or think about what was going to happen when we got to the safe house. I clenched my legs together several times when he glanced my way and his eyes strayed down to my legs. I decided to put on a little show for him as he talked on the phone.

I bent my right leg a little more, pushing it higher than the other leg and pulling my dress up my thigh. I ran my hand along the outside of my thigh and pulled my dress up just a little more so he could get a good look at the garters that were holding up my stockings. The stockings were a little torn from our tumble, but I figured it would just mean he wouldn't have to be as gentle when we got to the bedroom.

I spread my legs slightly and ran my hand along my inner thigh, moving it back to my knee and again down a little further. I heard him fumble several times on the phone and gave a little chuckle. It wasn't until I glanced up and saw Lola smirking at me that I slammed my knees together and adjusted my dress. I had almost forgotten that there were other people in the SUV with us.

~

Sebastian stalked me up the stairs after he barked out a few orders. By the time I reached the bedroom, he was on my heels and spinning me into the bedroom door. My back hit the door as he shoved me against it and pulled my leg up. His hands ran up my thigh, his fingers finding the small clasp that held the stockings to the garters. His low growl sent shivers down my spine. His lips crashed into mine and he kissed me with an intensity that left me weak in the knees.

"Bed, now."

I nodded against his lips as my fingers fumbled with the door knob. I finally got the door open and was about to turn, but he pushed himself into my body and wrapped his arms around me, lifting me up. My legs automatically wrapped around his waist and I felt his hard length pushing against my hot core. I barely heard the door slam shut over the pounding of my heart.

"Sebastian, I need you."

"I've got you, Freckles."

We flopped down on the bed and his hands once again drifted up my leg. His fingers brushed along the top of the stockings before sliding up to the lace panties he bought for me. I could almost feel his thick fingers on my pussy when he suddenly pulled back.

"What are you doing?"

"Unwrapping my gift."

He slid my jacket off and then pulled me up to stand in front of him. He grabbed the hem of my dress and slowly pulled it up, his eyes blazing a trail over my body. My arms lifted as he pulled the dress over my head. His eyes were roaming over my body, taking in the lingerie he had purchased.

"Beautiful. Absolutely fucking gorgeous."

I blushed slightly at his compliment. I knew I was a pretty woman, but I had never thought of myself as gorgeous. Then again, the way Sebastian looked at me, I couldn't possibly feel anything but gorgeous.

He leaned in and brushed his lips along my neck and across my collarbone, then down to my breasts. My eyes drifted shut as I took in the feel of his lips on my heated skin. His teeth nipped at my breasts through the bra and then his tongue ran down my stomach. I ached to feel his mouth on me, licking and sucking and driving me wild.

The heat of his tongue trailed over my panties, making me whimper when his tongue swiped across my inner thigh instead of my pussy. I felt dizzy as he worked his way down my body to my heels and then moved to the other leg. His hands caressed me and made me feel like the most cherished woman in the world.

He pulled my heel up onto his thigh as he knelt in front of me. "These are come fuck me shoes." He placed a few wet kisses on my inner thigh. "I want to feel these heels digging into my back as I bury my cock in your sweet pussy."

His lips landed hot and wet on my mound. His hands ran up the back of my legs until each one was cupping my ass. His fingers ran along the edges of the panties and then inside over my cheeks.

"God, I love your ass. Your ass was made for fucking. One of these days, I'm going to fuck you there." I started panting as his fingers slipped into my wet folds, teasing me and rubbing up to my clit. My breath caught when he started rubbing slow circles with one finger and the other hand pulled the front of the panties to the side. I felt his hot breath moments before I felt the first swipe of his tongue.

"Ahh!" The sensations were overwhelming as he assaulted my aching pussy with his tongue and fingers. It took only a few minutes before I was clenching around his fingers and screaming his name. My legs trembled and threatened to collapse, but Sebastian wrapped his arm around me, holding me close.

Before I knew what was happening, I was flat on my back and Sebastian had torn my panties from my body. His pants were down around his ankles and his hard length bobbed in front of me. I reached out to touch him, but Sebastian took a step back.

"Not now. I need your pussy squeezing my cock."

He stepped between my thighs and thrust all the way inside me. It was almost painful how far inside me he was.

"Fuck. I'll never get enough of you." He thrust hard again. "Your pussy was made for me." Slam. "That's right, baby." Two hard thrusts. "Squeeze me tight." Every thrust was harder, more powerful than the last. "Milk my cock."

My body shuddered as another orgasm washed over me, and I did as he asked. I squeezed his cock. His pace quickened, pushing through my clenching pussy with such force I thought I would split in two.

He stilled moments later as his cock jerked inside me. He laid down on top of me and pressed kisses over my cheeks and lips. "Damn, woman. You're going to be the death of me."

He rolled off of me and pulled me into his arms. When my breathing finally returned to normal, I found the courage to tell him what had been weighing on my mind.

"I'm sorry I ignored you the other day. I think I was just scared. I haven't really been with anyone for more than a few dates in a long time."

He kissed my temple, but didn't say anything.

"Am I too late?"

"No, we just have so much to get through first. Things are crazy at work right now and you have a story to write. We have to get all the evidence over to the police and you have to give your statement. There's a psycho trying to take you out. It's just a lot to deal with."

"On top of figuring out what's going on with us," I finished.

"Yeah. Let's just get through the next couple of weeks. I'll see you when I can, but I can't make any guarantees that I'll be around."

I understood what he was saying, but the disappointment I felt had me stiffening slightly. I always knew it would be difficult for us to work this out, but now it seemed more like reality. Was it weird that I was more concerned about finding a way to work this out with Sebastian than whether or not I would be taken out by a sniper?

~

I HAD BEEN in this safe house going on a week now and I was pissed. Sebastian had been out here one time, and he only stopped by for a few hours before he left. About a half hour of that time was spent with me. He fucked me and then made some excuse about having to get back to work. I hadn't felt that cheap in a long time.

Honestly, I could have told Sebastian exactly what I wanted that night we were alone at the safe house, but I was scared that he wanted something different than I did. I wanted him so much and I thought maybe we could build something together, but instead of telling him that, I pretended to be more interested in my story. No wonder he couldn't wait to get away from me.

Then, when we talked about it again, he seemed to have already made up his mind about what he wanted, and I didn't see the point in telling him I had been wrong. When I finally admitted to him that I was scared, he seemed hesitant to make a decision either way. Maybe he was right, we just needed to get through this story and then we could see where things went.

I'd gathered all the information I could on the case and went over it with Derek yesterday. Sebastian had sent Derek, along with Hunter and Lola, to keep an eye on Keith and me. Keith mostly kept to himself and spent most days in his room or in the living room catching up on the news. He also spent some time talking with Derek and going over questions the police would have.

My story was written, and Keith went over it with me and did fact checking since that was his job at the paper. After getting his approval, I decided that I would offer my story to the largest paper in Pittsburgh, *The Pittsburgh Post-Gazette*. I was going to them with my story after I spoke with the police and turned over all the evidence. I was pretty sure the cops would tell me when the story could break, so I would have to make that known to the editor over there.

Becky did some more digging over the past week and found the account that the payments to Reed Security were coming from only had cash deposits. There was nothing to track. That didn't explain how Darren had that kind of money, and the only thing I could come up with was that both the mayor and Darren both felt like they each had something significant on the other.

A knock at my bedroom door startled me from my thoughts. "Yes?"

The door opened and there stood the man that I had been fantasizing over one minute and vowing to kill the next. I wasn't sure how to react to seeing him, though a large part of me wanted to run over and kiss him. Instead, I sat there and stared at him.

"Can I talk to you for a minute?"

"Of course." I gathered my papers and stacked them neatly, making space for him on the bed. He didn't sit down. He just stood by the door after he closed it. That didn't seem good.

"We need to get the evidence over to the police. Is your story ready?"

"Yes. I finished it and I want to schedule a meeting with the editor at The Pittsburgh Post-Gazette."

"Okay. Don't schedule the meeting. I think it's best if we just walk in there. I don't know if the mayor has any other contacts we aren't aware of. We need a good read on the editor."

"Alright."

"If you're ready, I think we should head over to the police station now."

"I'll grab my things."

I didn't think now was the time to bring up everything that was bothering me at the moment. We were finally on our way to being done with this whole thing.

CHAPTER 13

SEBASTIAN

It had been a few days since Maggie, Keith, and I went to the police station to hand in our evidence on the mayor. My buddy in the police, Sergeant Andrews, made sure the case was taken up by the right detectives that would be sure to investigate the matter thoroughly. They were men he completely trusted and knew they weren't in the mayor's pocket.

Becky walked in as I watched the news in my office. "They're arresting the mayor."

I nodded to the TV. "I'm watching it right now."

"It's a shame you couldn't get anything on her boss. Do you think he's a threat?"

I shook my head. "It's hard to say. I'm sure he suspects Maggie, since she ran the story with a different paper. Who knows, maybe he was under the mayor's thumb just like the council members."

"But then there would have been blackmail evidence on the drive," she said thoughtfully.

"I have someone watching him. If he decides to make a move, we'll know."

"Yeah, but how long can you watch him?"

That was a good question. I wasn't sure I could keep anyone on his tail for that long. Resources were stretched thin as it was.

"The police have search warrants for all of the mayor's properties. After what they found at Beltzhoover, I'm guessing they'll find more at the other properties. Sergeant Andrews told me they already found similar concrete slabs missing at another property. And they're going to drag the river for bodies. Maybe once the investigation is over, they'll have something to connect to Darren."

"Maggie went home then?"

"Yeah, with a bodyguard."

"Why didn't you take over her detail? I mean, it would have been easier."

"Yes, but I have too much work to do."

She was quiet for a moment as we both watched the footage from the mayor's arrest. "You know, she's pretty smart."

I assumed she was talking about Maggie, which meant she wanted to gossip.

"I mean, to run with that story from the start and never give up? Now the mayor and his corrupt number two are being marched down to the police station...She's kind of the perfect fit for you."

I rolled my eyes, not wanting to continue with this whole back and forth she started. "How do you figure?"

"Well, she's just like you. Just as tenacious and strong-willed—"

"But I don't run off without telling anyone where I'm going."

"Well, sure if you want to really break it down," Becky grumbled.

"And I know how to use a gun. I don't just run into danger without being prepared. I don't purposely knock anyone unconscious just so I can run off and do my own thing. I know what I want out of life and I'm not afraid to go for it."

"Except with Maggie," she said quickly.

"Hey, she's the one that couldn't decide whether or not she wanted a relationship."

"And then you backed off so you didn't get hurt."

She laid a folder on my desk and smiled at me. "Yeah, it sounds like you really go after what you want, bossman."

As she walked out of my office, I turned off the TV and looked at the stack of recruit files with a sigh. We went through several days of interviews and only found two candidates that fit the bill. I had a few more interviews today and I was really hoping I could find two more recruits. I wanted to go see Maggie. I hadn't been able to see her for a few days and our phone calls were short. I knew she was going crazy back in Pittsburgh. I had Lola stick with her and Hunter stay with Keith. For the time being, everyone seemed safe. There had been no threats on their lives, and the reports were all good at the end of the day.

I dug into my work and only stopped to meet with the scheduled recruits for the day. As luck would have it, three of the candidates were more than qualified and I had a great feeling about all of them. If all five recruits accepted positions here, Sam and Derek could possibly pick up more of the slack, which I desperately needed.

It was a little after five when I finished with my work for the day. I still had a ton of work for tomorrow, but I needed a break. I needed to see Maggie. I walked out of my office and headed down the hall to Sam's office.

"Sam, I need a favor."

"Shoot."

"I need you to take over tomorrow."

"Shit. You know I don't like the shit you do," he groaned.

"Tough shit. You and Derek bought into this company. Now I need the two of you to step up and take on some of the load. I can't keep working eighteen hour days."

He sighed, but nodded. "Yeah, I know. I got a good look at what your days are like while you were watching Maggie and I was sharing the load with Derek. Don't worry. We'll get on board."

"Good. We'll have a meeting next week and decide which tasks you two can start taking on." Again, he nodded. "I'm out for tomorrow. I'll check in with you sometime during the day."

"See ya, Cap."

I went down to my SUV and called Lola, letting her know that I was on my way and she could have tomorrow off. She was happy to get a day off, but offered to go help Hunter out for the day. She said she was taking Maggie out to dinner in celebration of her front page story on *The Pittsburgh Post-Gazette.*

An hour later, I was pulling up to the restaurant, parking just a block down from the entrance. I was lucky to get parking this close tonight. I was just stepping out of my SUV when I saw Maggie and Lola about to cross the street. A man ran into Maggie hard and grabbed her purse, shoving her to the ground. Lola yelled at her to get back to the sidewalk and took off after the man with Maggie's purse.

I was already running toward Maggie when I heard the rev of an engine. Maggie looked up just as headlights barreled down on her. She ran for the sidewalk, but wasn't quick enough and was clipped by the car that roared off. Pulling my gun, I aimed at the windshield and emptied my clip into the driver. The car swerved before crashing into a light post. The driver was slumped over the wheel and I could hear people on the phone with the police already, so I took off to go check on Maggie. There was a crowd gathered around her, so I pushed my way through, only to stop when I saw her.

She was lying on the ground, not moving. My heart was beating out of my chest as I crossed the last few feet to her broken body. Her body was contorted with one leg twisted across her body, while her torso was going the other way. Blood was pouring from her head, which was really scary, but then head wounds tended to bleed profusely. I knelt down next to her and after a moment of trepidation, I brushed my fingers along her neck feeling for a pulse.

Relief poured through me when I felt the steady beat beneath my fingers. In the distance I heard sirens getting closer. I knew better than to move her, so I grabbed her hand that felt so small and frail in mine and whispered in her ear.

"Hang on, Freckles. You're going to be okay."

"Cap, I'm so sorry. I shouldn't have left her."

I turned around to see Lola standing behind me with Maggie's attacker in handcuffs. Fury ignited my blood as I leapt up and grabbed the fucker by the neck, squeezing until he couldn't breathe.

"Cap, don't! Cap!"

My hand was wrenched from his neck and he dropped to the ground coughing and sputtering. One swift kick to the stomach later, the fucker was down for the count. I turned to Lola and saw her eyeing me like I might explode again. I gave her a slight nod to know that I was in control again and went back to Maggie.

The next half hour was a flurry of questions from the police. I wanted to ride with Maggie in the ambulance, but since I had discharged my weapon, there was no getting out of this. Lola promised not to leave her side, which was the only reason I didn't tell the cops to fuck off.

After giving my statement, I headed to the hospital and waited for someone to tell me something about Maggie. I told the nurse she was my fiancé and she gave me a look of sympathy, promising to tell me as soon as she knew something.

After about an hour of waiting, the nurse came out with an older male doctor. She directed him over to me before stepping back behind the nurse's station.

"Mr. Reed?"

"Yes. How's Maggie?"

"She's stable. She has a concussion and a pelvic fracture, but we won't know more until she wakes up. I believe she'll be just fine after some rest and therapy, but we'll know for sure when she wakes up. Other than that, just bumps and bruises. She got pretty lucky."

"When can I see her?"

"The nurse will take you back there in a few minutes. We're just getting her settled in her room."

"Thank you, Doctor."

I shook his hand and then slumped in the chair behind me. That could have been a lot worse. Still, she was going to have a lot to recover from and it was my fault. I was in charge of the team and her bodyguard took off. The ringing of my phone drew me out of my depressing thoughts.

"Reed."

"Mr. Reed, this is Detective Barnes. I'm working the case where Ms. Curtis was struck by a car earlier this evening."

"Yes, what can I do for you?"

"I understand that Ms. Curtis was working with police on a matter concerning the mayor and city council members."

"Yes, she was."

"We have reason to believe that this attempted hit and run was related to that."

"I figured they were. What did you find out?"

"The driver of the vehicle survived and he told us that he was hired to do a job. He wouldn't give up his employer. Yet. I think after a deal is put before him, he'll give him up. As of right now, it appears the mugger was sent to distract her security so the driver could take her out. She got lucky, from what I understand."

"Yes. What do you need from me?"

"Keep us up to date on her condition. When she's up for talking, we need a statement from her. We also need to ask you a few questions."

"What do you need to know?"

"Have there been any threats against her? Any attempts on her life that we should know about?"

"Besides the one at the cemetery and the flash-bang through her front window?" He laughed slightly. "We did suspect that her editor was also involved with the mayor. He had some large cash deposits, but nothing we could track."

"We'll look into him also. Thank you for your time. Let me know when she's ready."

"Will do."

I hung up and leaned back in the uncomfortable waiting room chairs. This was not how I had planned on spending my night. Maggie was supposed to be in my arms, not lying in a hospital bed. I wondered why Lola had run after the mugger instead of staying with Maggie. That was not protocol and it had almost cost Maggie her life. I hadn't had a chance to talk with Lola since everything happened. It probably should have been my first priority, but my worry for Maggie was clouding my judgement.

"Mr. Reed, I can take you back to see Ms. Curtis."

I jumped to my feet and followed her down the hall, wishing she'd walk faster so I could see Maggie. When we got to her room, I stood in the doorway looking at her lying in the bed. She looked broken. She had bruises all over her body and scrapes from where her body was flung across the pavement.

Slowly, I stepped into her room and took a seat beside her bed. Her skin looked pale and when I touched her hand, it felt cold. Looking around, I didn't see any other blankets nearby.

"Excuse me," I said to the nurse. "Can you please bring in some more blankets? She's freezing."

"Of course, sir."

The nurse left and I stared at her, willing her to open her eyes. When the nurse returned, she started to unfold the blankets, but I took over, needing to do something. After she was all tucked in, I held her hand under the blanket, squeezing it every so often, hoping she would squeeze it back.

Light was creeping in from outside when I finally felt a little twinge from Maggie's hand. I had been resting my head on her bed, grabbing little cat naps here and there, but never really sleeping. I woke every time the nurses came in and checked her vitals, so I hadn't really gotten any sleep.

When I felt her hand move slightly, I bolted upright to see Maggie trying to open her eyes. She was squinting from the light, so I moved over to the windows and pulled the shade. I rushed back over to her side and saw her eyes were coming into focus.

"Freckles, you scared the shit out of me. I swear I lost ten years off my life last night."

"Lola and I had it covered." Her lips turned up at the corners slightly. Her throat was dry and scratchy, so most of what she said came out in a croak. I reached over and poured her a cup of water, then raised it to her lips. She drank greedily and I had to pull back so she didn't drink too fast.

"What do you mean?"

"She was supposed to catch the thief and I was supposed to stop the car." A smile appeared again. "Did you see how I used my body to stop the car? I'm like Superman."

"Except the car ran you over and I stopped it with bullets."

"Well, sure. If you want to take all the credit."

I smiled down at her, brushing my thumb across her cheek lightly. God, this woman was insane and infuriating, but I only wanted her.

"I'm gonna get the nurse in here to check you out."

She nodded and closed her eyes again, wincing slightly when she tried to adjust how she was lying. I helped her move, then went to the nurse's station.

"Maggie's awake. Can someone come check on her?"

"I'll call Sandy and let her know," the nurse behind the desk said.

Five minutes later, Maggie was being checked over by the nurse and ten minutes after that, the doctor. She had a concussion and the doctor said she may experience some dizziness and headaches over the next few days, but she was looking a lot better. Her pelvic fracture was minor, so thankfully she would only need some physical therapy and bed rest. She would be walking with crutches for a while, but her recovery time was eight to twelve weeks. It could have been so much worse.

When the room cleared out and it was once again just Maggie and me, I sat down on the bed beside her and held her hand.

"Would you like to tell me what you meant earlier about the plan that you and Lola had?"

"Someone was following us. We were trying to see if he was after me or if he thought I had something. So, Lola pretended to slip me something and I pretended to put it in my purse. The guy was watching us the whole time and when we got up to leave, he followed us. Lola figured if he just followed us, then he was after me, but if he tried to take my purse, then he wanted whatever I had."

"He was a diversion."

"What?"

"He was supposed to take your purse to draw Lola away from you. The car was meant to kill you. You got lucky."

She sighed and laid back on her pillow, staring up at the ceiling. I wished that I could find a way to comfort her. It had to be difficult to know that someone was after her and they weren't going to stop.

"I'm so sorry, Maggie. Maybe we should consider some other options."

"Such as what?"

"There's always going back into hiding until you testify."

"No. What I need is to find a way to get dirt on Darren. He's behind this. Or at least the mayor is using him to get shit done. He's the only one left that could possibly be doing anything."

"Freckles, you don't need to be worrying about this stuff right now. You just need to focus on getting better."

"Maybe if I contacted Keith. He has better contacts at the paper and knows who we can trust."

"You're supposed to be on bedrest for the next week."

"Although, now that I handed over the biggest story of the year to *The Pittsburgh Post-Gazette*, I bet I could get someone to help me out over there. Did I tell you they offered me a job?"

"Freckles, maybe you need to—"

"Of course, now that the police are starting their investigation, I really need to be doing follow up stories. This isn't over by a long shot."

"Freckles—"

"I really need to give the paper an answer so that I can get started on their payroll."

"Freckles, stop!"

Finally, she turned and looked at me with a confused expression.

"Freckles, you need to rest and recuperate. I get that you want to get out there and get your story, but you need to focus on getting better."

"I can do both."

"If anyone can, it's you, but I want you to come home with me where I can help you. You heard the doctor. You need to take it easy and start physical therapy. He said it will take at least six weeks to recover. How are you going to chase down stories on crutches?"

"I—I can't go home with you. The story is here. I need to be here where I can follow it. This is my story."

"I understand that, but this is your life and you almost died several times because of this story."

"I can't just walk away. I have to finish the story. I'll just have to have someone come stay with me at my house."

"At your house? You do realize that would make you a very easy target, right?"

"Then you tell me how I'm supposed to stay in the middle of the story if I'm not here."

Frustration built inside me as she kept coming up with excuses not to come home. She didn't get how close she came to dying. I didn't know how to get through to her. I needed her to be safe, and just for a while, I needed her with me where I could see at all times that she was alive and in one piece.

"Maggie, I need you to really hear me, okay?"

She nodded. I took her hand in mine and squeezed gently, hoping she would understand what I was saying.

"What happened last night was too much. When I saw you lying on the ground, I thought you were dead. It almost killed me to think of you being killed because I hadn't protected you. I need you to come home with me. Let me take care of you and help you heal. I promise, as soon as the physical therapist says that you can start doing more, I'll take you back to your house and have a security detail set up, or you can stay at the safe house again. Just, please, give me just a little time to make sure you're okay before you run off after your next story."

She was quiet for a moment and then nodded her agreement. "I can give you that."

I smiled, my whole body relaxing just knowing that I would get this chance with her. It was the best release of endorphins anyone could ask for. "Good."

"Now, come up here and lay with me. I need some sleep."

"I can't fit on the bed with you."

"Sure you can." She attempted to move only to gasp in pain.

"That's why I'm not lying down with you. I promise, when we get back to my house, we'll sleep in a giant bed where I can hold you all night."

"When are you breaking me out?"

"I think the doctor said later today. Why don't you get some sleep and I'll see if I can find out?"

Her eyes had already started drooping by the time I made it to the door. As I hoped, Lola had taken up a post outside the room without me asking. She nodded as I walked out and continued to stand at attention. I would have to talk with her later, but for now, I needed to find out when Maggie would be released.

"No! I am not going to be pushed around in a goddamned wheelchair while I'm here. They gave me crutches and I'll use those."

I shook my head in frustration and bit back the growl that was threatening to break free. We had been home five minutes and she was already bitching about me trying to help her. I had carried Maggie inside and set her on the couch. That's when she saw the wheelchair I had delivered this morning sitting across the living room.

"Maggie, you're supposed to be resting this week. You can't put pressure on your pelvis."

"Look, I am not a seventy-year-old woman that broke her hip. I can get around fine. Just give me my crutches and I promise I will follow the rest of the instructions."

Lola walked past her with the suitcase we packed when we stopped at Maggie's house on the way home. "Where's she staying?"

"Last room on the left."

Maggie turned to me with a glare. "If you keep ordering me around, I'll sleep in the guest room."

"Woman, I'm trying to help you. Would you just let me?"

She huffed and crossed her arms over her chest. It was getting to be dinner time, so I left Maggie on the couch to pout while I went to see what I could make for dinner. Unfortunately, I had zero food in the house, so I called for Chinese food.

"Why don't I take you to lie down for a little bit? When the Chinese is here, we can veg out in bed and watch a movie."

"Alright."

That was too easy, but then I saw her discreetly rubbing her eyes. The doctors had released her with the stipulation that she not be left alone, and that I check her throughout the night to be sure her concussion didn't show signs of a more severe injury.

I carried her back to the bedroom, and thankfully, she didn't protest when I helped her into more comfortable clothes and tucked her in. She was asleep in five minutes, so I went into the living room where Lola was waiting.

"Cap, about the accident—"

"Maggie already told me what happened."

"I'm so sorry. I should have stayed with Maggie, but I thought it would be useful to find out what the guy wanted."

"I understand that, but you should have called in someone else. Doing that alone breaks protocol. Our priority is always the safety of our clients."

"I know, but she was so convincing. I had a hard time saying no to her."

"Well, I can definitely understand that. Look, I get that Maggie can twist anything to sound like a good idea, but if you want to continue working at this company, I need to know that you will follow protocol at all times. There's no room for mistakes or going your own way. Remember what happened the last time someone took matters into their own hands."

I looked at her forehead where the still visible scar ran across her forehead. She ran her fingers over it and looked down.

"I know. It won't happen again."

"Good. Now, why don't you get some rest. I'll take first shift. There's a guest bedroom and bath down the hall on the right. Unless you want to wait. I ordered some food."

"I think I'll take a nap first. I'm pretty beat."

"Alright. I'll wake you for second shift."

Lola went down the hall and I stood there for a few minutes just thinking about how this whole situation could have turned out so differently. I could have lost Maggie, maybe Lola too. Whoever was pulling the strings on this was not going to stop until they got rid of Maggie.

I needed more information on what was happening, and the only way that was going to happen was to get back to work. I paid the delivery man when he arrived, then pulled out my phone and called Detective Barnes.

"Detective, this is Sebastian Reed."

"Mr. Reed, it's good to hear from you. How is Ms. Curtis?"

"She's doing well, resting right now. We're back at my house, about an hour outside the city. Would you be able to meet us here tomorrow morning?"

"Of course, but why didn't you just call us when you were in the hospital?"

"Let's just say Maggie wasn't the most cooperative. She wanted to get out of there and I didn't think it would be a very productive visit."

"I see. Well, we can be out there, say ten o'clock?"

"That works for us. Have you found out any more from the driver or mugger?"

"Neither of them know who hired them. They were both sent letters with instructions. We're checking for prints and they should be back tomorrow some time. We ran both men through the database, but so far, we aren't finding any links to the mayor or Mr. Webb, his right hand."

"Would you be willing to give me the names of the men? I could have my IT staff run it and see if we come up with something."

"We don't usually do that." There was silence and I got the feeling he was trying to decide if he should break that protocol. "Their names aren't being kept secret, so there's no harm in telling you who her attackers were. However, as a member of the law enforcement community, I can't *give* you authorization to do background checks and gather information on suspects that could be obtained illegally."

"I would never ask you to."

"Good. I'll send you the names and see you tomorrow."

I got to work on sending the information to Becky and then caught up on office work. I was going to have to be at the office most days because there was only so much I could do from home. After a few hours of working, I saw Maggie out of the corner of my eye. She was walking down the hall, leaning against the wall and not using her crutches. Damn.

"What the hell are you doing? You're supposed to be using your crutches. Didn't we just have a big talk about this?"

"I'm hungry. Now stop your bitching and bring me some food."

"You are the most frustrating woman I've ever met. Go back in the room. I'll bring the food to you."

A few minutes later, I had a tray full of food for us to eat. We spent the afternoon lying in bed and watching movies. Maggie was still wiped out from not only the medicine, but also what her body had been through. I wouldn't be able to stay with her all the time and take care of her, but I would do whatever I could to make her comfortable.

CHAPTER 14

MAGGIE

I was going batshit crazy. The man wouldn't leave me alone for even five minutes. For three days, he stayed home with me, tending to my every need. I wanted to say it was a blessing, but I wasn't used to a man taking care of me. And when I saw that damn wheelchair, that had been the moment I knew this wouldn't work between us, not if he was going to behave like this. I didn't like to be coddled, and I couldn't stand the constant looks of concern.

I should be happy right now. The man I fell for was at my beck and call, but it was because I was injured, not because he wanted to be here. I could see how he constantly checked his phone, even while trying to look after me. His business was suffering because he was here with me. And while I appreciated his efforts, the insanity had to stop. He couldn't work like this, and I wouldn't survive his constant watching.

He walked in with a tray of food and arranged it just so over my legs. "Is that comfortable?"

"I can eat at the table."

"You shouldn't be up walking around."

"I have to at some point," I snapped, feeling like I was on the edge of a cliff, ready to fall over. I didn't want to be a bitch, but I woke up this way every morning since the accident. I was in such a grouchy mood, and nothing could make me feel better. I just needed to get back into my routine.

His phone buzzed and he quickly checked it, shoving it back in his pocket.

"Why don't you just go into work?"

"Because I need to stay here with you."

"Sebastian, it's obviously important. Your phone has been going off every five minutes since this morning."

"I'm dealing with it."

"Obviously not," I snapped. Feeling like a total asshole, I sighed, shutting my eyes. "Sit down," I said, patting the bed.

He did, making sure he sat far enough away that he didn't hurt me. "Look, this isn't going to work if you don't leave me alone."

"Excuse me?"

"You need to go to work, and I need space. We're both driven people. We need space to do our work."

"You're not supposed to be working."

"But I could be researching. I could be following the story and chasing down leads from here. You need to let me do that so I don't kill you. And you need to go into work so your employees don't kill you."

He sighed heavily. "I just don't know how to let go. Seeing you on the ground really fucked with my head. I didn't protect you."

"It's not your job to protect everyone."

"It literally was," he said, practically growling at me. "You are still under my protection."

"I'm not even paying you," I said, throwing up my hands.

"You're my girlfriend. Doesn't that give me the right to protect you?"

"Yes, but could you do it from a distance? Seriously, I don't blame you for what happened. Lola and I had a plan and we went with it."

"Yeah, don't think I've forgotten how you manipulated my employee."

I blushed and ducked my head. "So, she told you."

"Of course she did."

"She's not in trouble, is she?"

He picked up my hand, rubbing circles over the back of it. "If I didn't know how manipulative you could be, she would be fired."

I slapped him, knowing it wasn't true. "Don't be a jerk. It was a good plan."

"Yeah, right up until the point where you got run over."

I waved him off, tired of hearing about my accident. "Look, I'm not the type of person to dwell on the past. We need to both put this past us."

He nodded, looking down at our joined hands. "Somehow, I'm not sure that's true. I think you cling to the past because of what happened to your parents. It's what makes you such a good reporter. But at some point, you have to let go."

"Fine, I'll work on that, but you need to return the favor."

"What do you want?" he asked warily.

I did my best to look innocent. "Nothing much. I just want you to promise me that you'll start going into work again."

"And in return, you'll promise to be good."

"Hey, I already said I would work on the whole letting go thing," I grinned. "Don't try to trick me. It won't work."

He laughed and leaned forward to kiss me. "I'll go into the office tomorrow."

"Good.

"Just do me a favor, don't try to sneak out. I'm having Lola come over here. She's above your trickery now."

"You make me sound like some kind of witch."

Still standing over me, he grinned wickedly. "You must be, because you've bewitched me."

I rolled my eyes at him. "You're so cheesy."

CHAPTER 15

SEBASTIAN

"How's her therapy going?" I asked Lola over the phone. I had a mountain of work to get through, but with Derek's help, I was making progress.

"Um...do you want the truth or a lie?"

Sighing, I rubbed my head. "Lie to me."

"She's doing great. She's doing exactly what the therapist is instructing, she's not wearing herself out, and she's not pushing herself too hard."

"That was a terrible lie," I grumbled, irritated that I had to find this out through Lola.

"It's better than the next lie I'll tell you."

"Fucking perfect. What is it?"

"She's been an angel at home, resting and not doing any work."

I snorted lightly. "Right, like I'd ever buy that."

"She pretty much works nonstop. I'm surprised she's kept it from you this long."

She hadn't. Every night I walked into the house, she was finishing up a phone call. She always told me she was checking in with Harry and Aggie, who were watching her house. Like I'd ever believe that.

"Alright, I should be home at the regular time tonight. Just try to…just make sure she doesn't break anything else."

Lola's laughter filtered through the phone. "I'll do my best, Cap."

I worked for another couple of hours before finally heading home. With Derek's help, I actually got to go home at a reasonable hour. It was strange, but very satisfying when I walked through the door and saw Maggie, even if she was working and pretending not to.

Tonight was no different. I walked inside and pretended not to notice Maggie working. It didn't bother me for some reason. This was who she was, so as much as I wanted her to take it easy, at least she was just working on her laptop. At least, that's what I thought. She apparently hadn't heard me come in, because she hung up the phone and got up from the couch, walking without her crutches.

"What the hell are you doing?" I barked out, terrified she was going to hurt herself.

She gasped, clutching a hand to her chest. "Jesus, Sebastian. You scared the crap out of me."

"Likewise. Where the fuck are your crutches?"

"Um…" She glanced around the room frantically, meaning she hadn't been using them all day. Fuck, she was going to hurt herself even more.

"Christ, the doctor told you to stay on the crutches until your therapist gave you the all clear."

"Maybe he did."

I laughed outright. "You know I check in with your therapist, right?"

She fumed, that beautiful face turning flaming red. "Those are my medical records. It's none of your business."

"It is my business, because you're mine."

"Right, we can't even figure out how to make this work after I leave, but you have every right to all of my personal information."

"It's like you don't want this to work," I grumbled to myself.

"It's not that I don't want it to work. I just need to figure out how it works. And when are you going to take Lola off my protection detail? You practically live in Fort Knox."

"Are you forgetting that people want you dead?"

"You don't live that far from work. It's not like you couldn't get here fast if I hit the panic button. And before you say anything, you also have a panic room."

"Maybe I should just lock you in the panic room everyday," I muttered under my breath.

"Like I would let you do that."

"Is that a challenge?"

She stared at me for a moment, uncertainty flickering across her face. In a flash, I was in front of her, hauling her up into my arms, being careful of her injury. I walked down the hall with her screaming and hitting my back. After getting the panic room open, I placed her on the bed inside and quickly walked to the door, locking her inside.

I pulled out my phone as I walked away, opening the app to see in the panic room. She was at the door, pounding on it and scream-ing, not that I could hear out here. The room was soundproof. Grin-ning, I got started on dinner, wondering why I hadn't thought to do this sooner.

Maggie was slightly upset with me after locking her in the panic room for a couple of hours. But the sex afterwards was hot as hell. Rage could be a very good way to get your frustrations out. And since I took Lola off her detail, she easily forgave me, though I was still waiting for the payback.

Things were getting worse and worse, though. She was constantly on the phone day and night in her attempt to find a way to take Darren down, and follow up on the first story she'd written. Then she begged me to take her to Pittsburgh in the middle of the night to follow up on a lead. The only reason I agreed was because I knew I couldn't fall asleep or she'd rush out the door and steal my truck. I started setting the alarm to notify me the minute she opened any door or window.

On top of all that, I was terrified every day that she would do something to notify Darren of her location. I didn't think she would do it on purpose, but Maggie didn't always think things through. What if she lead him straight to her?

I unlocked the door, instantly on alert when I didn't hear my alarm go off. I pulled out my phone and checked for notifications, but there weren't any. As far as my system was concerned, she was still here. I gently closed the door and pulled out my gun, checking the living room and kitchen for her. I didn't say her name, because I wasn't sure she was still here.

My heart thundered in my chest as I checked each room off, but when I got to the bedroom, it felt like my heart dropped to my stomach. Her laptop was thrown across the bed on the screen. The rest of the room was an absolute disaster, as if there had been a fight in here. I searched for any signs of blood, but didn't see any. Either she went willingly to avoid a fight, or she was dragged out of here safely. Neither way was good.

I pulled out my phone and called Sam. As the phone rang, I checked the panic room, hoping she was hiding in there. After entering the code and scanning my hand, the door popped open, but it was clear.

"Cap, what's up?"

"Maggie's missing."

"What do you mean?"

"She's not fucking here," I said, barely controlling my anger. "There are signs of a struggle in the bedroom, but the alarm never went off."

"I'm getting a team together now. Who has the power to do this?"

"Fuck if I know. The mayor? He could still be working with Darren. They both have a lot to lose."

"I'll get Becky to start checking for any hits."

"Thanks," I said, even though that left a sour taste in my mouth. I knew someone was after her, but hearing the word hit just made it all too real. I searched the house again, looking for anything I might have missed. But as I thought, there was nothing. The door had been locked when I got home. I stomped to the back door and looked it over again. It was locked also. I went around and checked every window. All of them were locked, except for one. In the bedroom, one of the windows was open slightly. Fuck, they crawled right through the damn window. How the fuck had they done this and the alarm didn't go off?

Trucks pulled up in the driveway and practically everyone from Reed Security stepped out. "Cap," Sam ran up to me. "Anything?"

"They went in through the window, but they somehow bypassed the alarm system."

"Seriously? How did they do that?"

"I have no fucking clue. Have Becky pull up the system and find out how someone broke into my fucking house."

"On it."

"I'll check for prints," Sinner said, getting right to work. His stern face told me that he was still kicking himself over what happened in the parking garage.

"Burg, get on the phone with P.P.D. and find out if anything's going on we need to know about. I don't care how fucking small it is. If even—"

I stared at a cab pulling up to the house, anger surging through as Maggie got out and stopped on the sidewalk. Her mouth dropped open as she saw everyone gathered around, checking out the house and waiting for my orders.

"Maggie, what the fuck happened?"

"Um..."

Stalking toward her, I got right in her face. "Did you sneak out?"

She looked around at everyone else, before her eyes came back to mine. "Technically, I didn't sneak out. I walked out the front door."

"It was locked."

"Because I locked it behind me," she said slowly. "It's not like I was going to leave your house unprotected."

I clenched my jaw in irritation. "How did you get out without the system sending a notification to my phone?"

She flushed bright red and looked at the ground. "Okay, I may be responsible for that. I sort of...disabled your notifications."

"And how did you figure out how to do that?"

"Um..."

"For Christ's sake, just spit it out."

"I may have picked Becky's brain about how to slip out undetected."

"Is that so?"

"Well, she didn't exactly know what I was up to."

"I bet she didn't. I know how you operate."

She sighed, "You have to understand, I needed to get out and investigate a few things, and you're not going to believe—"

"Don't," I held up my hand.

Turning to the guys, I motioned for them all to go. They did without another word, all of them loading up and driving off before they became part of this conversation.

"Did you ever think to at least leave a note?"

"I was hoping to be back before you found out."

I nodded. "And how many times have you done this?"

"A few," she admitted, biting her lip.

"And you didn't stop to consider how this would affect me?"

"How about how this hostage situation is affecting me?" she snapped. "It's been weeks. My hip is healed, yet you still keep me locked up all the time."

"I'm keeping you safe," I snapped.

"Did you ever think that maybe I don't want to be kept safe?" She sighed heavily. "Sebastian, you can't just lock me away forever. I need to be able to get out and live my life. And before you start, yes, I know about the threat against me, but I've been out several times and nothing has happened. Let's face it, the mayor has been subdued. The threat is gone. I've been working on this story for weeks, following what's going on with him. His assets are frozen. He has no power anymore."

"That makes him even more dangerous. When you have nothing, you have nothing left to lose."

"And what about after his trial? After he's convicted, will he be even more dangerous then? Will you lock me away until he's been imprisoned for five years?"

"You haven't testified yet. I'm trying to keep you alive long enough to do that, and then you can go live your life."

"And what about us?" she asked. "What will happen to us?"

I wish I could say that Maggie and I got closer with her living with me, but that wouldn't be true. I thought living together would be an opportunity for both of us to put the other first, but instead, we barely spoke to each other, and when we did it always ended in a fight.

"Freckles, what would you think about finding a job around here and sticking around?"

"And what? Live with you?"

"Well, yeah."

"I know we talked about seeing where this goes, but honestly, how can I? I live in Pittsburgh. That's where my life is. That's where the stories are. You live here. Unless you could move to the city?" she said hopefully.

"I can't just move the business. I have the space I need here and it would be extremely expensive to move the entire business. Besides, most of my employees live close by. If they got called in for an emergency, it would take too long to get everyone gathered."

"What would I do in this town? There's nothing going on here. I mean, I heard a story the other day that could go somewhere, but I doubt a town this size has stories that would grab my attention."

"So that's what it comes down to— our jobs."

"I'm sorry, Sebastian. I wanted this to work, too. I just don't see how it will."

I took her hand in mine, surprised at how sad it made me that this wouldn't last. I still had a little bit of time left with her. She couldn't just leave yet. She still had a week of therapy before she could be on her own. I just had to grab every moment I could with her.

CHAPTER 16

SEBASTIAN

It had been a week since Maggie and I had our little heart to heart, and our time together hadn't gotten any better. I started working longer hours and Maggie started venturing out more and more, looking for something to fill her time. Working from here was not easy for her, so I didn't imagine she would stick around too much longer.

I was on my way back to the house after a long day of work when I saw Maggie hanging around the police station. She didn't look like she was going inside, more like waiting for something to happen. I parked across the street and let the SUV idle while I watched her. I waited for fifteen minutes before I saw her approach a detective that had just stepped out.

My buddy Sean walked away from her after she started talking, but Maggie hobbled along behind him and seemed to be shouting questions at him. I rolled down my window, hoping to hear some of what was said.

"What do you say about the allegations that you've been taking drugs from crime scenes?"

He didn't answer.

"If you haven't been taking the drugs, where do you think they're disappearing to? It seems awfully convenient that it's only drugs from your busts. Do you have any comment?"

Sean spun around so fast I thought Maggie would topple over. "Listen, lady. I don't know who you are. I've never seen you before, and I would appreciate it if you would get your nosy ass out of my face."

"I'm a reporter from Pittsburgh."

"Let me guess? You weren't that good at your job, so you came sniffing around our little town to try to find some big story to impress your boss with."

"I'm a freelance reporter at the moment."

"Even better. No one will hire you."

I got out of my truck intending to put an end to this. I was almost across the street when Maggie spotted me.

"Sebastian, you can't follow me around town. I'm not getting into any trouble, and I'm perfectly capable of getting around on my own."

"Freckles, why are you harassing Sean?"

Her lips pursed and her eyes flared. "I'm questioning Detective Donnelly because drugs have mysteriously gone missing from almost all of his cases. It would seem to me that he's the common denominator."

"Detective Donnelly is one of my closest friends and there's no way in hell that he's stealing drugs. Maybe you should have talked to me about this first. This isn't Pittsburgh, you know."

Her cheeks flamed at my tone, but I couldn't give a shit. Sean was a friend of mine and I wasn't about to let her itch for getting back to work let a good man's reputation get destroyed.

"Is this the woman you were telling me about?"

"Yeah, this is her."

Sean chuckled. "Yeah, she seems just as you described her."

"And how exactly did you describe me?"

"Feisty, a troublemaker, doesn't know when to quit."

"Excuse me, but that's called having ambition."

My body stilled at her words. I was going to have to make one thing very clear to her before she got herself in a world of trouble. I stalked up to her and got in her face, being sure she knew how pissed I was.

"Let's get one thing straight. Your ambition is fine and all in Pittsburgh, but here, most people are hard working folks that are just trying to make a living. If you start shit like you did in Pittsburgh, all you're going to do is ruin a lot of good lives. If you can't deal with that, then you need to go back to the city."

She stepped back in shock. I wasn't sure if it was because I sided with Sean or because I told her she might want to go back to the city.

"Maybe we should talk about this back at your place."

"Fine."

I turned to Sean, dismissing her. "Sorry about that, Sean. Don't worry. You won't find anything bad in any papers tomorrow."

Maggie had started down the sidewalk, hobbling away from me as fast as she could. I was half tempted to let her walk home, as pissed as I was.

"Are you sure about that? She doesn't seem to get that a small town like this doesn't have the hardened criminals that Pittsburgh does, and there's not a conspiracy behind every story."

"She's adjusting. I'm not sure if she's going to stay here or not yet. She really wants to get back to work, but if she goes back to Pittsburgh, that'll be the end of us."

"Well, despite her wanting to make a story out of me, I can see why you like her. She's beautiful and she's not one to sit back and take shit."

"That's just the problem. I don't know how to make a relationship work with a woman that always wants to get her way. She's so stubborn."

"Have you met Harper? Do you think it's easy for Jack? That woman has him so tied up in knots, it's a constant battle, but that's a good thing. Can you imagine how life would be with a boring one?"

That definitely gave me pause. It would be horrible to be without

Maggie at my side, and I couldn't even imagine if she wasn't the spit-fire I knew her to be. I didn't think I'd be able to stand it if that fire inside her died, and that's what would happen if she stayed here with me. There would be no major stories to break, nothing to drive Maggie to dig deeper until she learned the truth. We'd had a serial killer on the loose in the surrounding counties and even here, but that was a once in a lifetime story. It wasn't likely to happen again. Would she really be happy here?

I PICKED up Maggie on the way home. I let her get about a mile down the road before I took pity on her and forced her into the truck. She didn't speak to me the whole way home and I couldn't say I blamed her. I had been harsh with her, but I needed her to under-stand things were different here.

When we pulled in the driveway, she hopped out without waiting for me to help her like I usually did. I walked behind her in case she lost her balance, but every time I got too close, she would turn and glare at me. When we got inside, I put my stuff down by the door as I usually did and took my extra gun off, putting it in the gun safe. When I came back to the living room, Maggie was sitting on the couch with her arms crossed over her chest.

"Freckles, we need to get some shit straight."

"You bet your ass we do. Don't you ever talk to me like that again, especially in front of your friends. I was working, not on a witch hunt."

"Sure didn't look that way to me. Sean is a good friend of mine and there is no way he would ever do anything you're suggesting. Maybe you need to do a little more research into the people you're investigating before you ruin someone's life."

"I would never ruin someone's life."

"Sure, you wouldn't intentionally, but did you ever stop to think about what people in this town would think if they knew you were investigating him for missing drugs? Investigations would be started in the department. He could be put on probation pending an investigation. His reputation would be shot. He could even lose his job. He's a good cop and he doesn't deserve that. Maybe to you, everyone is guilty until proven innocent, but this isn't the city. We're not a bunch of scummy politicians."

"I never said you were and I would never do anything to put his job in jeopardy. I just wanted some answers on the missing drugs. The people of this town have a right to know."

"Of course they do, but the police department probably has an active investigation going and they can't comment on it. If they did, they could tip off whoever's behind it if they let the wrong information slip."

"So you want me to just stop doing my job? This is who I am. I'm a reporter. I find the truth. I have to. There are too many people that get hurt because nobody looks for the truth."

"Maggie, I understand why you need this, but you have to realize you're not going to find it here. I really like you, but if that's what you need, then maybe you need to consider if this is what you really want."

She looked down for a minute and I swore I saw a little shake to her shoulders, but when she looked at me again, her armor was up and her eyes were clear.

"You're right. I won't find what I need here. I need to go where I can be useful and I don't think that's here. I wish I could stay for you, but I would be unhappy and that would make you unhappy."

I was sad to hear that, but I had already figured that's what she would say. We had great chemistry while we were working on her story together, but we just couldn't seem to find our footing. We had gone back to the way it was when we first met, angry indifference. There was really no hope for us now. We were just too different, or at least our perspectives were too different.

I loved the fire in Maggie and the drive to find the story, but she needed the investigations and all the crap that came with it. She would never be happy here with me, without that aspect of her life. It seemed that our short-lived romance was coming to an end.

"I'd like you to stay until the trial is over. I need to know that you're safe."

"The trial could go on for months. I can't stay here that long. I'm still waiting to hear back from the editor at the Post-Gazette. I think it's best if I head home. I can ask the police department for protection until the trial is over."

"It won't be enough. I can't keep one man pulled off a team for you. I wish I could, but the teams don't work efficiently that way."

"Don't worry. I'll be fine."

"I could still try to make it to the city on the weekends. We can still see each other and—"

"Sure. We'll work it out," she said, smiling slightly. It was strained at best.

She'd told me we'd work it out once before, but I didn't believe her then and I didn't believe her this time. She might try to get together, but work would always come first for both of us.

Lola took Maggie home the next day. They stopped by the police station and had a patrol set up to check on her every hour, but that didn't make me feel any better about the situation. It had been six weeks since she was attacked and there were still plenty of people that wanted her dead. I wanted to follow her. I wanted to go stay with her and keep her safe, but I had a company to run, with no one willing or capable to step into my shoes at the moment. Sam and Derek were stepping up, but they were nowhere near ready to take on day to day operations as a full time job. I had to let Maggie go.

WITH MAGGIE no longer around to take up all my time, I dove back into work and spent more hours at the office than was necessary. Now that Sam and Derek were on board with helping out more, I didn't really need to spend all my time at the office, but going home was too depressing.

Sam had taken over the strategic part of the security company. Derek had taken over training. Both of them seemed to slide right into their positions, and after the first two days, I didn't hear any grumbling. It took a lot of pressure off of me and left me more time to stare at the wall, which I was doing a lot of lately. I found myself constantly wondering what Maggie was up to, only to realize I hadn't accomplished a single thing for an hour. That was probably why I was always at the office so late. I was no longer working efficiently.

It was two weeks after Maggie left and I was still having regrets about how that whole situation turned out. Part of me wanted to go to Pittsburgh and beg her to come back to me, but the other part of me knew there was no point. She was where she needed and wanted to be.

My cell rang, bringing me out of my depressing thoughts. It was Drew, a friend of mine, calling. He was engaged to Sarah and I had high hopes that Drew would be the man that she deserved.

"Yo. What's up?"

"I'm on my way to see you. Are you at the office or home?"

"Office. What's going on?"

"I'll see you in twenty."

He hung up before I had a chance to say anything else, but his voice had tension that made my spine stiffen. Whatever he wanted didn't sound good. I placed a call to the receptionist to let her know to allow Drew access and then cleaned up my desk. Drew stormed into my office fifteen minutes later looking like a pissed off bear.

"You tell me that she's safe. Tell me that no one's coming for her."

"Drew, you know I can't talk to you about—"

"I know! I saw her without her contacts this morning, and she's always dying her hair brown, but she has blonde hair. I ran her through facial recognition software. I know who she is! So you tell me right now if someone is after her!"

I took a step back and moved back around my desk. "Sit down so we can talk about this."

He did as I asked, taking a deep breath and calming down slightly. Shit. I wasn't prepared to bring Drew into all of this. The whole point of WitSec was to keep the witnesses completely hidden, and I wasn't even sure if new spouses were allowed to know any details. I wondered what was going on in Sarah's head right now. I hoped to God she didn't run.

"She's safe, for now. There's a hit out on her, but she's being protected by WitSec. They can't know that anyone knows who she is. They'll pull her out of here so fast, you won't have a chance to say goodbye."

"What if we're married?"

"I don't know. The rules of WitSec are not widely known. That's how people stay safe. This is such a clusterfuck. Three people now know who she is. That's not safe for her."

"I would never say or do anything to put her in danger." Drew spat at me.

"I know that. Calm down. Sean and I would never say anything either, but it's more dangerous for anyone to know. I've been keeping an eye on the situation from here. No one here knows about her or even suspects there's anything different about her. As far as people around here are concerned, she's just a friend of mine."

"Okay, so where do we go from here?"

"You go on with your life as if nothing has changed. You and Sarah should have an honest discussion about what happens if someone does find out about her. You should have a plan in place, map out some areas you might go, but don't keep any records of anything. No paper trails. I can handle vehicles for you, if you need to leave in a hurry. I'll keep watching on my end, and I'll give you a heads up if I hear anything and so will Sean. As soon as I call you, I'll have vehicles ready for you and I can put together some IDs for you. They won't pass all inspections, but they'll work until you settle somewhere else. You should also have some bags packed for all of you to keep in your closet. Not too much stuff, but enough to get by. Let me get some stuff together for you all over the next few days. Then let's meet up again."

He nodded, taking in all I was telling him. He seemed a little unsure, or maybe it was just a lot to deal with all at once, but I needed to be sure. My trust issues were still front and center. "What would you do for the love of a good woman, Drew?"

His face morphed into anger and his nostrils flared. "Don't ever doubt me. I won't ever let anything happen to her or the kids and I would do anything for them. If we need to run, I'll be ready."

His answer was exactly what I needed to hear. If I hadn't thought Drew would step up to the plate, I would have moved her myself and kept her hidden.

"I have no doubt in my mind. She's a good woman. I'll call you in a few days."

"Thanks, Sebastian. I appreciate you looking out for her."

After he left, I made all the necessary arrangements and got Sam to put together all the necessary paperwork they would need. Later that afternoon, I got a call from Drew saying they needed to add Cara to the list of people that would need new IDs. Cara was Sean's sister and if she planned to run, Sean would be pissed, and I would probably be the one that had to tell him if they ran. What a clusterfuck.

Drew and Sarah got married the following weekend and I made sure to clear my schedule so that I could attend the wedding. It was fucking cold out and a snowstorm had just blown in. They were having an outdoor wedding, which of course meant that I was going to freeze my ass off.

The whole time I stood at their wedding, though, I kept thinking about how I wanted more with Maggie and had hoped that what we had would go somewhere. I was in a place in my life that I wanted a wife and someday kids.

So after the ceremony ended, I congratulated the happy couple and then said I had an emergency at work to take care of. I couldn't stand to be around all that happy shit anymore. If I stayed, I'd have to have some whiskey to get through it and I really tried to avoid the hard stuff.

A WEEK PASSED and luckily the weather warmed up, which improved my mood slightly. All the teams were busy with different assignments and Becky and Rob were efficiently running the communications side of the business. Everything was going as it should. Even the new recruits were adjusting well to their new teams.

"Boss, do you have a minute?"

"Sure, Becky. What's up."

"I just got a message from an old friend of mine. She's a jeweler and she's transporting a very rare gem to a gallery in Philadelphia and needs a little extra protection. I know the other teams aren't available, but would you be able to do it?"

"Is there any threat against her or anything that would lead her to believe that someone plans to steal it?"

"No. She said that she just wants to be on the safe side because it's very valuable."

I nodded. "Get me the information and I'll look it over. When is she arriving?"

"Tomorrow."

"Why did she wait so long to ask for help?"

"I don't know. Honestly, I haven't seen her in a long time."

"Alright. Let me look at everything you have and I'll make a decision."

"Thanks, boss."

THE NEXT DAY, I was on my way to the airport to pick up Angela Martins and take her to Philadelphia. Everything in the packet said that this was an easy case. No one knew about the gem, and therefore, wouldn't know about the plans to transport it. This should be a fairly easy job.

I pulled into the small airport and went to check out the few small buildings. The airfield was basically dead because it wasn't really used any more now that a nicer airfield had been built outside of Pittsburgh.

After assuring myself that the airfield was as secure as I could make it, I waited for the small plane to land. Twenty minutes later, I was walking up the steps to the plane to greet Angela.

"You must be Sebastian. Becky told me great things about you."

I shook her hand while checking the rest of the plane. "It's nice to meet you. Do you have everything you need?"

"Yes. I only brought a small bag and this."

She held up a small courier bag that I assumed held the gem. "May I see?"

She looked at me questioningly, like she wasn't sure if she could trust me.

"Ma'am, you called me. I don't transport anything without seeing it first. For all I know, you could have a bomb in that pouch."

Her eyes widened and she quickly unzipped the bag and pulled out a small box. She glanced up at me before handing it over hesitantly. I opened it and was satisfied to see a gem sitting inside. I quickly checked the lining, making sure there was nothing hidden, before replacing the box and handing it back to her.

"Becky said you were very good."

"Yes, you said that already. Let's head out and get you to Philadelphia."

"Of course."

I was just approaching the doors when I saw two black sedans pull up to the hanger. I put a hand out to stop Angela from moving forward further. Several men got out of the cars and headed toward the plane. All of them were armed, though they hadn't pulled their weapons yet.

"Shit." I pushed her further back into the plane. "I thought you said no one knew about the gem?"

Her face turned red and she looked down at her feet.

"Well, I...I didn't tell anyone, but it is possible that someone found out."

"How?"

"My brother was there when I received the package."

"And your brother would betray you?"

"Let's just say he doesn't always run in the best crowds."

"You didn't think this was important information for me to have? We're in a plane with men approaching us with guns. How did you think we were going to get out of this?"

"I'm sorry. I didn't know this would happen."

"Play along."

I peered around the side of the door and saw the men were now a few feet from the steps. They hadn't yet pulled their weapons which meant that I could still get us out of this. I stepped into view and thanked my lucky stars they didn't grab their guns and start shooting. I was highly outnumbered.

"Can I help you gentlemen?"

"We're just waiting for the woman on board."

"My wife? What could you possibly want with her?"

"We know she's not your wife. Angie's not married. Her brother gave us all her flight information and I want what she has."

"I suggest you gentlemen head back to your vehicles. This isn't a fight you want."

The man standing furthest from me pulled his weapons and took a shot. I was faster though and dove back toward Angela, pulling her to the ground.

"Stay down and don't fucking move."

I took a deep breath before peering around the edge of the door and firing a few shots. Luckily, I had several guns on me and many more magazines, so I could hold them off for a little bit, but eventually they would get the upper hand. I pulled my phone out of my pocket and handed it to Angela.

"Speed dial one. Tell Becky I need back up now!"

She fumbled with the phone so many times that I finally grabbed it from her hands and dialed myself.

"Becky, I need back up now! Your friend left out a few details that would have been useful."

"No one is here, boss."

"Then get on the phone and get someone, or we'll be dead."

"I'll get someone to you right away. Give me two minutes."

"I can't hold them off long."

"I know, I'm on it."

I continued to fire sporadically, trying to save as much ammo as possible. The men were now back further in the hangar so they had cover. I sent up a prayer that I wouldn't die here today in a plane with a woman that was practically hyperventilating. Damn, I missed Maggie.

CHAPTER 17

MAGGIE

Since I refused to stay with Sebastian, I was now back in Pittsburgh alone and without protection. The way his protective details were set up, he couldn't continue to have one person on me. He hadn't wanted me to come to the city alone, but I couldn't stay with him and miss all that was happening with my story.

There had been a ton of follow up stories for me to do once the mayor's case went to trial. The investigation into the mayor's less than savory dealings with the city council, the different construction companies, and even the gangs they had used to get rid of people led to many stories that I was aching to sink my teeth into.

The police searched all the properties that belonged to the mayor. They found eighteen bodies so far. Some were gang members that no doubt gotten on the mayor's bad side. Cheryl Haynes, the office worker from RND Construction, had been found in Wilkinsburg. That had been the first site we suspected any foul play.

Mark Beane, the reporter that had disappeared, was found at the bottom of the river by the shipping company. He'd been rolled in a chain link fence, and it was said he drowned. I couldn't imagine what it would be like to be trapped and not able to escape. Knowing every second you lost oxygen you were going to die. I also heard there were several other victims at the bottom of the river that had yet to be identified.

I never found out what happened with Danielle. No one ever found her body and I felt horrible that I couldn't give Tom, the bartender, more answers. I did stop by, however, and discuss the case with him, letting him know the police hadn't finished investigating yet.

I'd been back in Pittsburgh for a little over a month now and had been busy almost every day and night. When I wasn't chasing down a story, I was being interviewed about how I managed to blow this story wide open and the subsequent threats on my life. I'd even been approached by a publishing company about writing a book about all the characters and how they all worked together to make this master plan work.

I considered it and even started calling people, asking if they would give interviews. Most of the council members, while ashamed, wanted to get their stories out about how they hadn't wanted to go along with the mayor's plans, but needed to because he was black-mailing them. It looked like if I got enough people, I could start on my book very soon.

I accepted the job at *The Pittsburgh Post-Gazette*, because I didn't trust Darren and didn't want to ever work with him again if I didn't have to. Though I didn't have proof, there was no way I would ever trust him. Still, I hoped I would someday find evidence to get his ass thrown in jail also. There had to be something that I was missing. Though, now that his extra source of income was gone, I didn't see him being much of a threat anymore.

Still, my time with Sebastian left me craving the excitement I had with him. Lucky for me, Sinner felt I shouldn't be left unprotected. The first time I met up with him, it was because he came looking for me.

. . .

I OPENED my door to see Sinner standing there, looking at me curiously.

"Are you here to spy on me?"

"Not for Cap."

"Then for who?"

"Me?"

"You're not sure?"

"I feel bad that I let Cap down when you beat me up with the door. I should have seen that one coming."

I snorted in amusement. "You didn't know me."

"I knew enough about you. Anyway, I came to make sure you're okay. I can't have Cap riding my ass because you get hurt."

"Well, I'm fine." An idea came to me though. "Although, I feel so vulnerable out here all alone. With no protection, I'm constantly worried about my safety."

He frowned, biting his lip in thought. "Have you taken any self-defense courses?"

I shook my head. "I can't. Not yet, with my body still recovering," I lied.

"Right. Have you ever thought about carrying a gun?"

I held my hand to my chest in shock. "You think I should carry a gun?"

"Well, for safety reasons. Without anyone here to protect you, it wouldn't be a bad idea."

"If you think it's really necessary..."

"I wouldn't have suggested it if it wasn't."

"So, when should we do this?"

"Well, Cap can't know about it. He would kick my ass if he knew I was taking you to a gun range."

"He won't hear it from me."

He nodded. "Do you have time today? The sooner we teach you, the sooner we can get you a permit."

I nodded excitedly. "I can make time."

"*Good.*" *He turned to walk down the sidewalk and then paused, turning back to me. "You just played me, didn't you.*"

I grinned and shrugged. "I wanted to learn."

"*Now I understand what Cap felt like when the two of you were dating,*" *he grumbled under his breath.*

UNDER THE SUPERVISION OF SINNER, I had been going to the firing range to practice shooting. Last week I got my first gun, which I was quite proud of. He said that a woman that got into so much trouble needed a weapon to defend herself. Sebastian knew nothing about Sinner and I getting together and I wanted to keep it that way. Sinner understood my need to get back to my job and knew that it would be more difficult if Sebastian knew we were getting together.

I met Sinner about a half hour from Pittsburgh three times a week and he showed me the finer points of firing a weapon. Afterward, we got lunch or dinner and caught up. We never talked about Sebastian or how I was doing being away from him. It had been my choice to go after all.

Things were not at all how I had imagined they would be. I thought I would be happy once I got back to my house and my things. Even my lovey-dovey neighbors weren't enough to bring me out of my funk. I missed Sebastian more than I cared to admit. My job had always meant so much to me, but now every time I left the house to go after a story, I thought back to my time with Sebastian, when he was helping me with my story.

I knew deep down I couldn't go back to that time. It was a special circumstance and I had to treasure what we had. Still, I couldn't help but wonder what could have been if I'd had the courage to see where things went.

I was heading into the paper one morning, taking shortcuts through side streets and alleys. My car was on the fritz this morning and I was ahead of schedule, so I decided to walk into work. The extra exercise helped my pelvic muscles regain the strength they'd lost after I was run down.

I just turned from an alley onto the sidewalk in front of some old shops when I heard my name being called. Hope sprung that it was Sebastian and he'd come to declare his undying love to me and ask me to come back to him. I turned around to find my old boss Darren standing on the sidewalk. He was disheveled and smelled like alcohol. I wasn't even standing that close, but I could smell it coming off him in waves.

"Darren."

"You just thought you could get away with it, didn't you?"

"Get away with what?"

"You screwed up everything. When you told the investors what you suspected, they started looking into my work and decided to pull out. I have no investors. I'm finished!"

"Darren, we both know that you were working for the mayor. I may not have proof, but there was no other way to explain some rather large coincidences."

I glanced at my watch and saw that I was going to be late.

"Look, if you want, I'm doing a book on the people that were caught up in the scandal. They all get a chance to tell their side. If you want, I can include you in the book."

"What? You think I'll sit down with you and give you an interview after you destroyed my life?"

Flashbacks of Sebastian telling me that I could very well destroy someone's life by accusing someone of wrongdoing without evidence came roaring back to me. I actually felt bad for Darren. He was right. I didn't have proof that he had done anything wrong. My actions led to his downfall, and while I truly felt that he was guilty, I wasn't the one that should have decided his fate for him. I should have left it to the police.

"Darren, I'm sorry. You're right. As much as I feel that you're guilty, I shouldn't have said anything without proof. I should have left it to the police."

"You're sorry? You little bitch. I have spent my entire career dealing with you reporters that feel you know everything. I watch you pull your strings and do anything you need to for a story. Well guess what? I was always the one pulling the strings. You're right. I did work for the mayor. I decided which stories went in the paper, and I gave him a heads up when someone was hot on his tail. Do you know how many times you almost died and I protected you? You were my most valuable reporter, and I thought that if I could just stay one step ahead of you, I could scare you away. When that didn't work, the mayor wanted you gone and still I tried to help you. You had a body-guard. Why couldn't you just go into hiding and wait for the story to die?"

I wished more than anything that I had my recorder on me right now. This would be perfect for the police and great for my book. I was just about to walk away when he pulled a gun from his waist. Shit. My gun was at the small of my back. I carried it with me when-ever I could now. I wasn't fast enough to just pull it and shoot without him shooting me first, even if he was drunk.

"I built that paper. I made it what it is today and you took that from me. I guess you'll get something really big for your book."

"What's that?"

"Someone else can write about your death."

Sure he was going to pull the trigger at any moment, I looked quickly to his right as if someone was there. His head snapped left and I took my chance, pulling my gun from my waist and aiming it at his chest. I didn't hesitate to pull the trigger. If I did, he would no doubt shoot me. My aim was true and I hit him square in the center of the chest. Of course, I was only standing about ten feet from him, so that would be pretty sad if I missed him. Sinner would have given me grief to no end.

The next thing I thought of was how much I wished Sebastian was here to give me a hard time about getting into trouble. He would have scolded me for walking instead of driving or taking a cab. He would have yelled at me for walking through an alley and not paying attention to my surroundings. Then he would have asked where the fuck I got a gun and who taught me how to use it.

I laughed to myself, which seemed highly inappropriate at the moment, but I couldn't help it. An ache settled in my chest the longer I stood there. I knew now what I really wanted.

Surprisingly, the police showed rather quickly and took down my statement. They didn't give me too much trouble seeing as how Darren was holding his gun and had already been questioned in relation to the mayor's scandal.

When I got to work, I sat at my desk and thought for all of five seconds what my next step would be. I couldn't just go off half cocked. I needed advice. I told my editor about what happened and promised a great piece by tomorrow, but told him that I needed to go home for the day. He was totally fine with it and even called me a cab. I didn't argue.

When the cab pulled up outside my house, I quickly paid and ran over to Aggie's door. I pounded and yelled for her, but when she didn't answer fast enough, I opened the door and stormed in.

"Aggie, I need some—Ahh! What the hell?"

Two wrinkly, naked figures hustled as fast as they could off the ground and started pulling blankets off the couch to cover all their parts. I covered my eyes with my hands as fabric rustled in the air.

"Oh, dear. Maggie, if you had waited a few minutes, you wouldn't have walked in on Harry giving me the old one, two punch."

"Ewww. I don't ever want to hear you say that again."

"It's just sex, Maggie. I'm sure you get plenty of it with that young fella of yours."

"No, no, no. I am not discussing sex with you two. Alright, I'm going to wait outside while you two put some clothes on and then we need to talk."

"Girlie, I think we're old enough to know what we're doing. Besides, I really doubt we need to worry about me putting a bun in Aggie's oven."

"Stop. Please, for the love of God, stop. I'll be back in five minutes, and you better have all your clothes on."

I stepped outside and waited on Aggie's front stoop, giving them an extra few minutes just to be sure. I knocked extra loud and waited for one of them to answer. When I stepped inside, they were both clothed, and you would never have guessed that the living room was just a breeding ground for old people's bodily fluids. Glancing at the couch, I pointed to the kitchen.

"How about we talk in there. That's safe territory."

"Well, I suppose, but then you should know that Harry gave me a little afternoon delight on the table the other day."

"What? How? How does that even work at your age?"

"Well, with my bad hip and Harry's—"

"Never mind! Forget I asked."

I sighed and ran a hand down my face, then scrubbed both hands over my ears, hoping to erase the last fifteen minutes of my life.

"Alright, let's just get this over with. I need to know how to get Sebastian back."

"What happened? What did that little cock sucker do? I'll tear him limb from limb," Harry said as menacingly as possible. Though it wasn't nearly as effective as he hoped because he started coughing at the end and asked Aggie for his inhaler.

"He didn't do anything. I left him. I thought we couldn't make things work because of our jobs and how far apart we live, but then I realized today that I just wanted him in my life for him to yell at me."

"You want him to yell at you? Oh, dear. Harry, I've heard about these women today that like that kind of stuff. Do you think we should try it? Maybe it'll spice things up."

"Aggie! It's not like that. I just meant that he yells at me when I do the wrong thing and he keeps me in check. I miss him telling me what to do and being a little too protective."

"Sounds to me like you want a babysitter," Harry muttered.

"Or a Sugar Daddy. You know I used to work at this club and

232 of GIULIA LAGOMARSINO

these ladies would give themselves to one man and do anything they asked for. It's like they couldn't think for themselves."

"Aggie—"

"You never struck me as that type of woman, but I guess appearances aren't everything."

"I don't need a Sugar Daddy."

"Just a babysitter. Girlie, when I was your age, women were off working in the Red Cross and fighting wars!"

"Harry, I didn't say that I need a babysitter. I was saying—"

"Of course, I wouldn't mind having a Sugar Daddy if it was you, Harry. It could be fun."

"Sugar Daddies have multiple women. Is that what you want? You want to share me?"

"Of course not."

"Good, because I don't think my knee could handle it. You always know how to take care of me afterward. I'm not sure I want to take a chance with another woman. Have you seen Mrs. Craggle go after the mailman? She tackled him to the ground the other day. Pretended she tripped. If she did that to me, I'm not sure I'd be getting back up."

Rubbing my temples, I willed away the headache that was forming. "Can you two please concentrate for a minute? I need to get Sebastian back. How do I do it?"

"Let him come to you, dear. Don't go chasing down a man. It's always better to find a way to get him to come to you. Besides, dear. Do you really want a man that let you go so easily?"

"He didn't let me go easily. I didn't really give him a choice."

"You need to go to him, Girlie. Show him you want him more than you want your job and he'll worship you forever."

"How do I do that?"

"Well, that's something you'll have to figure out, but make it good."

"You're sure it'll work?"

"Honey, there's nothing a man won't do for the love of a good woman."

~

I WENT HOME and quickly typed up my article on the events of this morning and sent it off to my editor. There was no time to stop and pack, though I intended on staying with Sebastian once I got to Reed Security. I quickly got in my car after grabbing my backup weapon. The police had kept my gun until they finished investigating Darren's death. He hadn't made it and I couldn't say I was too upset about that. I drove faster than I ever had in my life, making it to Reed Security in just under fifty minutes.

I hadn't counted on not having the passwords this time around, so I had to wait for someone to let me in. So much for my grand entrance. When I made it up to the offices, I was met by a receptionist that hadn't been there when I was last here. I guess someone had to replace Cal, even though that had never truly been his job.

The offices seemed empty, but I knew that Becky or Rob would be here, so I headed to the computer room. Becky came running out of the office in a frenzy, barely missing me while yelling into her com set.

"No one is here, boss. I'll get someone to you right away. Give me two minutes. I know, I'm on it."

The elevators had opened at some point and Sinner had walked in.

"Mark! Sebastian needs you ASAP. He's under fire. I'll send you the coordinates."

Sinner quickly turned on his heel and over to the elevator. I didn't think, I just followed.

"Where do you think you're going, Freckles?"

"With you."

"Yeah, I don't think so. Cap would have my ass if I brought you to a gunfight."

"Let me deal with him. You don't have any backup and you taught me how to shoot."

"This isn't the same thing. Shooting at targets is nothing like shooting at people."

"I shot someone just this morning," I said as we ran out of the elevator and over to an SUV. We got in and Sinner cranked the engine, taking off moments later, yet still arguing with me.

"You shot someone?"

"Yeah, my boss. Well, my old boss."

"Christ, Freckles. I didn't teach you to shoot so you could go commit murder."

He took a corner way too fast and I was flung into the door. I quickly pulled on my seatbelt so I didn't end up through the windshield.

"I didn't commit murder. He pulled a gun on me, so I distracted him and shot him."

"And you killed him? Not just scared him or grazed him?"

"Nope. Dead center in the middle of the chest, just like you taught me," I said proudly.

"Why do I not believe you?"

"Okay, well he was only standing ten feet from me, but still, I nailed him. Dead as a doornail."

"Yeah, let's hold off on telling Cap any of that information until absolutely necessary."

We swung into a small airport and sped over to an aircraft. I could see Sebastian peeking out of the door of the plane, firing at the small hangar. Sinner pulled up to the plane, parking in front of the stairs and blocking the shooters momentarily.

I hopped into the backseat to get the door for Sebastian and the young woman that was running down the stairs with him.

"Your chariot awaits, Cap." Sinner had rolled down the window to yell to Sebastian. When I opened the door and Sebastian saw me, he stalled momentarily, but the return gun fire got him moving.

"You brought my girlfriend? What the fuck were you thinking? Were you hoping to attract trouble?"

"She's my back up."

"Your what?"

Gunshots pinged off the SUV and I waited for them to stop before flinging open the door facing the hanger and taking a few shots. When I saw a man drop to the ground, I squealed, raising my gun in the air and doing a happy dance. Sebastian reached around me and pulled the door closed.

"Get the fuck out of here!"

"I shot him! Did you see that, Sinner? He went down."

"Why are you holding a gun and when did you learn to shoot?"

"Sinner's been teaching me."

"Freckles, I thought we agreed to save that information for when it was absolutely necessary."

The tires squealed as we took another corner and headed out of the airport. I looked out the back window and saw two cars following us.

"There are two following us," I shouted to Sinner.

"Two on our six," he corrected. "Don't say ten words when four will do."

"I didn't say ten words."

"He's trying to teach you about shorthand. The longer you speak, the less time you have to shoot," Sebastian said before turning to Sinner. "Why are you teaching her shorthand? And why are you teaching her to shoot?"

"For protection. Someone just up and left her unprotected, so someone had to make sure she could take care of herself."

"I didn't leave her unprotected. She left me, remember?"

"They're gaining on us," I said as I watched the boys have their little argument. I started digging through the supplies in the trunk, looking for something that could slow down the cars behind us. I seriously doubted I could shoot anything while in a moving car.

One of the cars pulled up fast alongside the SUV and rammed

into our side. Sebastian shoved the trembling woman, who I just noticed, down onto the floor and rolled down the window. He fired off shot after shot until the car swerved and went off the road into the ditch on the other side. We still had one car behind us.

I continued going through the trunk, finding some kind of awesome looking gun. It was huge and looked like a mini cannon. I lifted the heavy thing up, but Sinner nixed me from the front seat.

"Don't even think about using a launcher. It's too heavy for you and you'll get us killed."

I set it back down and dug some more.

"I still don't understand why you brought Freckles. You do remember all the trouble she attracted before, right? Did you hope that bringing her would get more action for you?"

"She's fun to keep around, see?"

He nodded in the mirror toward me. I was holding up two grenades like they were gold. This was going to be fun.

"Just pull the pin and throw?" I asked.

"Yep. Let 'er rip."

"Awesome."

The trembling woman on the floor covered her head and whimpered. "Oh my God. I'm gonna die."

"No you won't, sweetie. Sebastian's really good at his job."

"Hey! What about me?" Sinner asked in indignation.

"You're good too, sweetie. Alright. Here goes nothing."

I moved to roll down the window, but Sebastian stopped me.

"You seriously think that I'm going to let you use that thing?"

"Oh! I totally forgot to tell you the reason I'm here."

"And you need to do that now?"

"Yes. I'm here to get a job with you."

"As what?"

"A field agent. See, this way we can be together."

"What makes you qualified to be a field agent?"

He leaned out the window and took a few shots at the car that was trying to gain on us, then reloaded his gun with a new magazine.

"I have mad shooting skills."

"It's true. She shot and killed someone this morning," Sinner said with pride from the driver's seat. I beamed at his compliment.

"You what?"

"Yep. Totally true. So, here I am. Ready to go into training. I figure this is a pretty good interview."

"You're insane. There is no way I'm hiring you to go into the field with any of my men."

"Why not?" I asked like I was confused.

"Because shooting one man does not make you qualified. Sinner, get us away from this asshole."

"Trying, Cap, but you're distracting me with this indecision. Just hire her so that we can get on with it."

"Why don't you hire me to do research then? I can help Becky out."

"Why do you want to come work with me?"

"So I can be close to you. Duh."

"Why now? Why not a month ago?"

"Do you think we could get someplace safe before you two go into counseling? You're supposed to be keeping me safe!" the woman on the floor screamed with a shrill to her voice.

"Relax, sweetheart. With Annie Oakley back there, you're perfectly safe," Sinner said. I noticed that we were now far from Reed Security and in the middle of nowhere. I wondered briefly where Sinner was taking us, but was snapped out of my thoughts by Sebastian.

"Why now, Freckles?"

"When I shot Darren this morning, the first thing that popped in my head was that I wished you were there to tell me I should have had my gun ready or I shouldn't have been walking in an alley—"

"You were walking in an alley? Jesus, Freckles. It's like you didn't learn a damn thing."

"See? You understand what I mean, right? This is good between us. Then I walked in on Aggie and Harry doing the horizontal mambo and we talked—"

"While they were having sex?" Sinner asked in disgust.

"No. That image is seared into my brain, though. Anyway, Harry told me that if I wanted you, I had to come show you that you were all I wanted."

"That's so fucking wonderful, but can we please discuss this when I'm not curled up on the floor of a fucking SUV!"

I leaned down to speak with the woman. "Sweetie, do you need something for anxiety? I think Sebastian keeps something in here in case the guys get shot."

"Will you move that fucking gun out of my face?" she screeched.

"Oops." I pulled the gun away from her and faced Sebastian once more.

"So, you want me now? Now that you had a life altering experience? That's not good enough, Maggie."

"Ouch. Using my name? That's harsh. No. I realized that I love you, and as much as I love my job, it just isn't worth it without you."

Sebastian stared at me for a minute. "I'm not letting you go into the field."

"How about this? You let me throw the grenade and I'll do only research with Becky. Maybe a little field investigation?"

"I'll think about it."

"Okay, so I pull the pin and throw?"

"Yeah, don't hesitate or we'll all end up in pieces on the side of the road."

"Oh, God. I don't want to die!" the woman yelled.

"Don't worry, honey. I'm a quick learner."

I rolled down the window and gave a loud yee-ha before pulling the pin and launching the grenade, left handed I might add. The grenade came up short, but then the car drove over it and was right on top of it when it exploded. The car lifted off the ground and burst into flames.

"Whoo! Splash four!" I turned to Sebastian who was grinning at me. "I always wanted to say that."

Sebastian moved across the seat to me, pulling me into his arms. "That was so sexy."

"Does that mean you'll teach me how to use the launcher?"

"Not a chance in hell."

He kissed me fiercely, possessing me mind, body, and soul. "I love you, Freckles."

"I love you, too, Cap."

ALSO BY GIULIA LAGOMARSINO

Thank you for reading Sebastian and Maggie's story, but it's not over! Catch more of your favorite characters in upcoming books! And don't miss the next in series *Sean* !

Join my newsletter to get the most up-to-date information, along with new content in the Reed Security series.

https://giulialagomarsinoauthor.com/connect/

Join my Facebook reader group to find out more about my obsession with Dwayne Johnson!

https://www.facebook.com/groups/GiuliaLagomarsinobooks

Reading Order:

https://giulialagomarsinoauthor.com/reading-order/

To find the individual series, follow the links below:

For The Love Of A Good Woman series

Reed Security series

The Cortell Brothers

A Good Run Of Bad Luck

The Shifting Sands Beneath Us- Standalone

Owens Protective Services